M000201939

ALSO BY CRAIG A. ROBERTSON

BOOKS IN THE RYANVERSE:

THE FOREVER SERIES:

THE FOREVER LIFE, BOOK 1
THE FOREVER ENEMY, BOOK 2
THE FOREVER FIGHT, BOOK 3
THE FOREVER QUEST, BOOK 4
THE FOREVER ALLIANCE, BOOK 5
THE FOREVER PEACE, BOOK 6

THE GALAXY ON FIRE SERIES:

EMBERS, BOOK 1
FLAMES, BOOK 2
FIRESTORM, BOOK 3
FIRES OF HELL, BOOK 4
DRAGON FIRE, BOOK 5
ASHES, BOOK 6

THE FOREVER QUEST

BOOK FOUR OF THE *FOREVER SERIES*

by Craig Robertson

LIFE IS THE CURE FOR HAPPINESS.

Imagine-It Publishing
El Dorado Hills, CA

Copyright 2017 Craig Robertson

All rights reserved. No part of this book may be reproduced or utilized in any form or by any means, electronic or mechanical, including photocopying, recording, or by any information storage or retrieval system, without the written permission from the author.

ISBN: 978-0-9973073-5-1 (Paperback)
978-0-9973073-6-8 (E-Book)

Cover art work and design by Starla Huchton
Available at http://www.designedbystarla.com

Editing and Formatting by Polgarus Studio
Available at http://www.polgarusstudio.com

Additional editorial assistance by Michael Blanche

First Edition 2016
Second Edition 2018
Third Edition 2019

Imagine-It Publishing

I wish to dedicate this novel to all the great authors who proceeded me. Orwell, Bradbury, Shakespeare, Keats, Milton, and Tolkien, for certain. To all those masters not mentioned, my hat's is off to you too. Your inspiration made my humble efforts worth the time and effort. Thanks!

Note: Glossary of Terms is Located at the End of the Book.

PROLOGUE

In a dimly lit, smoky cantina, a tall, thin figure sat cradling his drink. His shoulders slumped forward, and his hood was pulled so far over his head that his face was invisible. Sitting beside him sat a woman of such radiant, luminescent beauty that their tiny corner glowed warmly. It seemed to struggle to hold back the darkness that surrounded them. She also had the pretense of a drink on the table, though it was untouched and forgotten. They'd not spoken in several minutes, but there was no tension in the air between them, only understanding.

Finally the man spoke. "So, Elaina, *are* you the mother of us all?"

She returned a smile of such coyness, such joy, that it would melt the heart of the devil himself. "My but that's the *oddest* question anyone has ever asked me."

The man's head notched up slightly to stare into her endless eyes. "I doubt that very much."

"Do you suppose," she responded with flowing grace, "that I entertain questions of such a nature as a matter of routine?"

"No," he replied in his low, dry tone. "But I suspect you've been asked that question before."

She placed the tips of her fingers over her ruby-red lips and angled her head ever so slightly. "Why, you make me sound like the oldest hag in the universe. How am I to respond to such an inferred insult?"

"Honestly, and maybe without fishing for compliments."

Before she could voice her next evasion a huge, mean-spirited Bralk rattled their table with his thigh. He stood looming over them, breathing like a bull halfway through a good goring. In the harsh rasping echo only a Bralk's throat could produce, he said loudly, "How much for your whore, little pimp?"

The slight figure of a Nalt accompanied the Bralk. He reacted to his friend's vulgar witticism with a sickly giggle and tumbled his hands to look like a rolling ball. As he possessed twelve hands in all, the motion was impressive.

The man sat like a statue determined not to engage the Bralk, as unlikely as that was to happen.

Elaina looked through the massive man-beast. In her eyes there was only calm—and a trace of pity.

"I *asked,* how much to use your bitch for three minutes," the Bralk roared. "Assuming, of course, she lasts that long."

The Nalt couldn't help himself. "Asss … ssuming she lastsss that lo … ong, he sss … sayss"

The Bralk grunted a laugh.

The man remained unmoved. The Bralk grabbed the side of the table and tossed it against the wall like it was made of paper. It shattered to splinters. "I said—"

And then the Bralk was gone.

The now unaccompanied Nalt sniffed the air and whined pitifully, as if he'd just fallen off his mother's teat. "Wh … where's Korge? What ha … have you d … done with him?"

"I'm sorry," the man said directing his eyes halfway up to the Nalt. "To who are you referring?"

Elaina smiled and spoke. "To *whom,* my dear, not to *who.*"

The man nodded his head. "Yes." He turned to look straight at her. "Right you are as usual." Without moving his head, the man asked of the Nalt, "To *whom* are you referring, little worm?"

"K … Korge. He was just h … here." He aimed six index fingers toward the floor, "sss … tanding next to m … me."

"There's no one standing next to you," the man replied. "Leave, now."

"B … but where's Korge? You … you made him dis … disappear like magic."

The man turned his hooded face toward the frightened Nalt. "Magic?" The word rolled around in his mouth. "Yes it's all a kind of magic. Yes." His eyes glowed through the darkness his hood created. "Leave or join him."

The Nalt scurried away, like the vermin he was.

Bralk Korge hit the icy water spread-eagle and supine. He crashed through the mammoth waves and sank like the proverbial rock. Bralks couldn't swim. What with their armor-plated hide and massively thick skulls, water was their natural enemy. Korge made matters worse, because he wore boots stuffed with guns, knives, and clubs that added thirty kilograms to each side.

As he rotated to a feet-first descent and accelerated into the bitterly cold darkness, he became angry. Not that he wasn't in a huff before, and for most of his rapidly expiring life. Just then, plummeting downward, he was even angrier than his norm. As the frigid salt water exploded in his chest like a million shards of hot metal, he was infuriated that his death would go without retribution. His klan would never know what became of him or who to hold responsible. To die unavenged made his death rather pointless. That really pissed the bugger off.

ONE

I was nursing a drink in Peg's Bar Nobody in the far-left corner under the broken Coors Light sign. Peg's was a dump on the outskirts of one of the three towns established on the farmship, *Granger*. Those were the cored-out asteroids dedicated exclusively to food production. Each worldship in the fleet was designed to be completely self-sufficient, including food production. The farmships were intended as backup food producers. They also afforded us the opportunities to have some excess for reserve, and a few luxuries.

Farmships were big, smelly, sparsely populated, and most of all, isolated. They were how I pictured Old West towns. Tough, coarse, and populated with hard-working folks who kept to themselves and were leery of strangers. Perfect by me. I had discretely arranged for a sequestered landing spot on *Granger*, so I could come and go with complete anonymity. No panicky, needy politicians dogging my every step. No gaggle of sycophants, male and female, eager to garner favor with the one guy who owned an intergalactic cube. I needed none of that.

I became chummy with Peg pretty quickly. She was my kind of gal. Four feet eleven in shoes, two hundred fifty pounds, and a vocabulary that would make a Marine Corp master sergeant blush. She was barkeep, cook, and bouncer all rolled up into one big old bowling ball of spit and vinegar. When I say cook, I mean the bar served food that was above room temperature. You had to be a special kind of hungry to dine at Peg's. Most people in the fleet tried to take soy protein and make it taste like meat. She took meat and managed to make it taste like bad soy protein.

She was loyal, she hated small talk, and she guarded the privacy of her limited patronage more fiercely than a Scotsman did his wallet. There was a movie made a long time ago that some people still idolize. It had a character named Jabba the Hutt. If Jabba took a mistress, it would have been Peg. Not that she'd have him, mind you. No, she made it clear to all who cared, and all who didn't care, that she was done with men permanently.

Over the last—oh, I don't know—year or so, when I wasn't somewhere else, I was at Peg's. She even tried to stay open longer to accommodate this sleepless android, bless her heart. Many a night, I found her sleeping face down on the bar, the rag she used to circulate the dirt converted into a wet pillow. I'd shoo out any stragglers, carry her to her bed—a cot in the storeroom—and lock up for her. And she never once asked what happened the night before, or said thanks. Nope, not her style. She'd just greet me with a deep grunt when I came in early the next morning and slam a beer and a shot in front of me, without me needing to ask.

Was I in a rut? Sapale would have said, yes, a very deep one. But she wasn't around to kick my ass out of it. No one on *Granger* was about to try to whip me into shape. Most were just as much a loner as me. Even the ones who weren't didn't care what I did. I could tell Peg thought I was a jerk for pissing my time away in her dive, but she liked me too much to say anything. Plus, she'd worked laboriously to create her hard-ass persona. She'd never risk being perceived as a do-gooder. So languish I did. The fact that I couldn't technically become an alcoholic didn't alter the fact that anyone who followed my presence at Peg's sure as hell thought I was one.

I liked the downtime. I had a lot to think about. I had a lot of decisions to make. War hero celebrities weren't allowed to sit alone most places. A dive bar in a smelly farmship was as close to anonymity as I could get. No one tried to buy me a drink, so they could have a selfie taken with me, and no news crew showed up to shove a microphone in my face. I was a sideshow and wouldn't be alone if I went anywhere near a populated area. Toño told me I was acting like a jackass of the first magnitude. He'd said, *forget about what Sapale might say,* I'm *ashamed of you.* Yeah? Well, he wasn't me, so screw him and the high horse he rode in on.

5

His attitude toward me had a lot to do with me not hanging around Azsuram much. No. It didn't. Who was I kidding? He was just trying to help. It wasn't my family, either. They asked nothing of me and gave me oodles of love in return. If I wanted to drink myself into an early retrofit, they'd let me. They were happy just to have me around. Was it the memory of Sapale that made me feel this way? Her gruesome death? Nah. I wasn't the first, middle, or last person to lose a loved one in a pointless war. Yes, I loved her mightily. Yes, I was entitled to a massive amount of grief. But no, I wasn't entitled to wallowing in a mire of self-pity and uselessness for all eternity. I guess that's what bothered me. I didn't know exactly *why* I was at Peg's drinking moonshine intended to clean the underside of a tractor, and eating food that paired well with the solvent Peg passed off as booze.

I had a cube. I could go anywhere. I had friends all over the place and projects up the wazoo. But there I sat, festering. I had uncharacteristically taken the advice of wiser people and didn't set out on a vengeful mission to kill all Berrillians. But boy, howdy, they deserved it. My only consolation was that they'd be back in my lifetime, and in greater numbers. I could do some major avenging then. I most surely would.

As I stared into my fifth mug of whiskey that morning, I felt someone who wasn't Peg stop at my table. When Peg stood nearby, there was no mistaking her, the fat little Tasmanian devil. Without bothering to look up I grunted, "Go away."

"Aren't you even going to find out who you're blowing off before you act like a complete buffoon?"

That voice. I turned to look. There stood Amanda Walker, President of the New United States. She had on boots and blue jeans, and her hands were stuffed into a worn sweatshirt that read, *Farm Girls Ain't Afraid to Get Dirty*, with a picture of a beat-up Ford truck on it. She was alone. No men in black wearing sunglasses indoors with wires coming out of their ears.

"And before you ask, no. They're not outside scaring the locals either. I came alone. You're the only person who knows I'm here. Everyone else thinks I'm doing my annual girl checkup. *No one* wants to cover that story."

"You drove here," I said perking up, "all by your lonesome? I'm impressed."

"No," she said slipping into the seat opposite mine, "you're a hot mess. You're a complete load of bollocks and a disgrace to the uniform you're not wearing. *That's* what you are."

"Yeah." I smiled despite my otherwise dour mood, "but how do you really feel about my condition?"

She glared at me. "I feel like coming around to your side of the table and openin' up a big old can of whoop ass on you."

"Madame President, wherever did you learn to speak so foully?"

"I'm complex."

"I'm beginning to think that's the case." I pointed to my mug. "May I buy you some refreshment?"

"I can smell that from here. It's about as refreshing as battery acid." She waved to Peg, who was watching us like a hawk to begin with. "Bartender. A sarsaparilla when you're done staring at us. No rush. You got time to take a picture. It lasts longer than a memory."

I throated a chuckled. "You know she's going to spit in your glass for that, right?"

"I hope that's all she does," she replied with a smirk. "Couldn't help myself. It was worth the added saliva."

"So," I began gesturing around the room with my mug, "you come here often, little lady?"

"Never before and never again."

"You can't say that until you've had the hash. *Then* you can say you'll never come back, with real conviction."

She leaned back, met eyes with Peg again, and raised her finger. "Two hashes, sweetheart." She pointed the same finger toward me. "His bill."

"You must really hate me."

Mandy knitted her fingers together on the table. "I don't have to. You're doing a bang-up job all by yourself."

"Ouch. And you got elected to public office with that attitude toward those who are suffering?"

"Suckers are born every minute of every day." She smiled widely.

"So, Mandy, what brings you this far from pleasant to see me?"

She looked at me, then her joined hands. "I heard how you were doing." She scanned the room. "And where you were doing it. I came to give you some neighborly advice and a gentle push."

"My, but that sounds unwelcome. Seriously, I'm okay. If I still had to bathe, I would be." I pointed to my scalp. "Hair is both clean and combed. Score two for team Ryan."

She crossed her arms but said nothing. Her jaw was set like steel and her eyes weren't laughing at my jocularity.

"You're just another person wants a piece of me. Everybody wants something. A lot of them want everything I got. You lining up, too, doesn't make me want to change my ways."

Damn. She just sat like a statue. I was throwing my best stuff at her, too. She was good.

"Sorry. I run my mouth off a lot, nowadays."

Peg came over and dropped two plates of corned-something hash on the table so hard chunks flew to the floor. She slid Mandy a soda so roughly that a third of it spilled.

"Some people," she said, glaring at Mandy, "have the common decency to leave a man be when he ain't lookin' for company." She spat. She actually spat on her own floor. "Some, I guess, don't." With that she blobbed away.

"You like my new girlfriend?" I asked thumbing in the direction of Peg. "She's the reason I'm here all the time. Can't get enough of my little dumpling."

"There's nothing *little* about that woman," snipped Mandy. "Plus she's more *my* type than *yours*, sweetie. Hate to be the one to break the news and burst your love bubble."

"Look, I appreciate you coming. I do. I'm working through some stuff, that's all. I'm not going to hunker down here for good." I poked at my hash with a fork. I wanted to make sure nothing moved before I put any near my lips.

"I'm here because we're friends. I wanted to see for myself how you were. You look like shit, and you're acting like a pathetic wuss."

"Gee, thanks. I'm looking forward to your next visit already."

"There won't be a next visit. The next time we meet, if we ever do, it won't be on *Granger*. *Enterprise* maybe. Your cube possibly. But here, I only come once."

"No future state visits? The locals will be crushed to learn."

"Please be serious for the next five minutes." She took a bite of hash. "This isn't so bad."

"Mine is. Yours has extra ingredients. Maybe that's what put it into the edible category."

"Pass the ketchup, and tell me when you're leaving this dump for good."

I slid the plastic bottle over along with the hot sauce. "Soon, maybe. I don't rightly know."

"What about your quest to find the other you, the one you mentioned back in my office?"

I scratched the back of my head. "That one. Yeah, sort of put it on hold. Everybody told me I was nuts, suicidal, or both, to try and find someone very dangerous who didn't want to be found."

"They're all wrong. They're forgetting one thing. You."

"You're as unclear as a fortune cookie. What's that mean?"

"They're all forgetting just how low you can sink, and how impossible it is for you to ever kick your legs to try and reach the surface."

"Okay now you're up to two fortune cookies worth of *huh*."

She set her fork down, set her elbows on the table, and clasped her hands. "Look, Jon. Literally look at yourself. Take a moment." She checked her watch. "I have time. I'll need to be back in a couple hours. But come to think of it, I'll need time to stop by a hospital and have my stomach pumped, so do speed it up."

"I'm done. I took a long, hard, informed, and critical look—"

"I said take five minutes. I expect you to *take* five minutes. I deserve five minutes' worth of your otherwise pointless day."

"You got four left. Sorry."

"Here's the short and sweet of it. You, Jon Ryan, lost a loved one, a handful acquaintances, and a bunch of buildings. That put you in an epic tailspin, the likes of which I've never *personally* witnessed. I don't see you

9

pulling out of this dive, seriously. Short of having you committed to a psych hospital in perpetuity, I don't know what to do. But," she stabbed her fork at me angrily, "I'll remind you of this. That other Jon Ryan, if he's really out there, lost a hell of a lot more than you did. He lost *everything*. He lost his *people*, *planet*, his *roots*, and any sense of purpose he could ever have. He probably watched as nine *billion* lives were blown to pieces, and he couldn't do anything to save them. Ever think about that, *Jon Ryan*? Hmm?" She slammed her fork to the table and it skidded off onto the floor. "If your sad, pint-sized loss did this to you," she pointed at me with four fingers, "just try and imagine through your fog of self-pity and self-loathing what that would do to *him*."

She pulled in a few ragged breaths and pushed back from the table. "There. I said what I came to say. I'm outta here. You're free to be flippant, funny, or drop deader than the Christmas goose. Thanks for the indigestion and the lousy conversation." She stormed out so fast I swear I saw a smoke trail behind her.

Peg came over uninvited. "I think I misjudged that gal. I kind of like her." She slapped a mighty hip against my shoulder nearly pushing me out of my chair. "I think she kind of likes you, too. Oh, and she's right. You *do* look like shit, and you *are* acting like a pathetic wuss."

"It's not polite to eavesdrop on private conversations."

"I don't have a polite bone in my body." As she walked away Peg turned and asked, "And if you're not going to call her, give *me* her number."

"Do you even *know* who that was?"

"Yeah. The girl one of us should be sleeping with tonight."

TWO

I walked slowly into Kymee's cluttered work area. Over the last few years, the two of us had become the unlikeliest of friends. But we were good friends. Kymee's multi-million-year life dwarfed my two-century lifespan. Heck, I actually still thought of myself as human. Kymee was Deavoriath, an ancient and mysterious race that I wanted to learn more about. Kymee and his people wanted to be left alone. They felt they were too violent and destructive to be amongst others and decided long ago to avoid outside contact. But kindred spirits tended to find one another, and we two certainly had.

"Jon," Kymee said as he rose to greet me, "I'm surprised to see you again so soon." In place of the human tradition of shaking hands, we exchanged the Deavoriath version. We grabbed the each other's right elbow and bumped shoulders. "But it's always nice to see you. Please," he gestured to a chair, "sit."

"So soon?" I responded. "It's been, what, almost six months?"

"For you, six months means little." He slapped his chest. "For me, it means considerably less than nothing. The space between heartbeats."

"What you guys have hearts? Huh. Never would have thought it."

"That's because you know Yibitriander. Even his own people think he's a sourpuss."

We shared a cordial laugh.

"So, my young friend. What brings you to this stale, old planet?"

What did? Why had I come? It took a second, but I realized why. "Because I missed you, y'old curmudgeon."

Kymee reflected a moment. "Curmudgeon? I'm accessing the files I downloaded from you when you first arrived. I see the word, but I don't think we have that concept. Curious. A crusty, ill-tempered old man. Me? I think I've just been insulted by an inferior species."

"Species, nothing. I'm a robot remember? We don't get a biologic classification."

He aimed a bony finger at me. "You're as human as they come, boy. You can't hide it."

"Wait, now *I'm* insulted."

"It's good to see you, too," Kymee said with genuine warmth. "I'd forgotten how good it is to see an old friend." He shook his head so his long white hair whipped against his cheeks. "We've been isolated for so long, externally and internally."

"Then come with me," I said. "I could use a good mechanic on a long voyage. You might actually become useful in your retirement."

"Me, join your adventure? *Hardly.*" He sat back down and fumbled with the items on the bench. "I'm well past the age and inclination of *vacationing,* let alone questing."

"Oh, so now my mercy mission is a quest? Maybe I should change my uniform, add some armor and wear a funny-looking hat?"

"Call it what you will. A crusade, a pilgrimage, or a night on the town. I see it for what it is."

"I know what you advised. Let's not go there again."

"Then why, I press, have you come?"

I remained silent a long spell.

"And please, sit down. At least provide me the illusion that I'm not passing the day talking to some oversized children's toy."

I sat, folded my hands, and proceeded to twiddle my thumbs. Finally I spoke. "I don't have too many people I can talk to, Kymee. Not anymore. Sapale's dead, the kids are, well, they're my kids. Aside from Toño, I'm not that close to any other androids around. I guess I need another immortal with a kind ear to bounce my sorry excuses for ideas off of."

"Thank you. That's the best compliment I believe I've ever been paid."

Shifting his tone Kymee asked, "That brings up a point I'm curious about. It's about the android program you mentioned. Many civilizations have developed similar technology, us included. Some used androids extensively, while others stopped producing them almost as soon as they were invented. You humans invented them out of necessity. I get that. But it seems to me the human fleet is not making much use of them lately. Why is that? Androids are phenomenal tools."

"I've been called that by the ladies on more than one occasion."

"I'm asking *seriously,* which is always risky business with you."

"Sorry," I said almost meaning it. "Reflexes are hard to tame. You're right. Uploads to androids seem to be a thing of the past. After the initial astronauts were produced and shipped out, the US was the only one to make many more. Stuart Marshall mostly did the creating. He wanted them as part of his plan to rule forever, the sick SOB. Maybe that's what did the program in? He acted about as badly as a person could. People probably figured one group of deluded self-serving robots was enough.

"Plus the worldfleet is doing very well. I keep half an eye on them and I'm impressed. There's a school of thought that androids would be needed to keep key skills alive; doctors, scientists, those sorts of occupations. But kids are learning the old ways and educational systems are booming, so no one thinks androids will be needed to fill in gaps. They even found people to do the dirty work—sewers and that kind of stuff. Can you imagine being immortal and cleaning out waste-water systems?"

"I'd switch myself off," replied Kymee. He then looked at me sternly. "So are you here to tell me you're going on your ill-advised quest, or are you here to try and trick me into helping you again?"

I winked at him. "Maybe both."

He rolled his eyes.

"As to my quest, I have to go. A good friend convinced me of that. I know your helping me is a touchy subject, but I would like to pick your brain a little before I set out."

"What a ghastly idiom."

I guess it was kind of gross. Never thought about it. Yuck. "You've traveled the stars. I don't know what I'm even looking for. I was hoping you could at least tell me where *not* to look."

"In what sense?"

"Places a human android wouldn't go. Areas void of life, too hostile, that sort of thing. Maybe give me a few insights as to where he might have gone, if you have any."

"Fair enough. I'll send *Wrath* such a file. I'm not sure it'll be of much help, but I see no problem providing you that type of information."

"I guess that's it." It wasn't. "I do wonder about *Wrath*."

"He can *be* a challenge."

"He's *nuts*. He has his own agenda that he's very sneaky about, and all he really wants to do is kill, kill, kill."

"That would be *Wrath*."

"Is that how you programmed him?"

Kymee was quiet again for a spell. "I don't think you can understand what *Wrath* is. I don't mean that as an insult. I think it's simply the truth. Yes, I oversaw his … fabrication. But he is not a machine. No one *programmed* him. He did what you and I did, what everybody does. He developed into who he was by the same mysterious process that forms us all."

"You telling me he's alive? A sentient being?"

"No, but, yes. Suffice it to say he's complicated. He can be reasoned with and, believe it or not, he wants to be led."

"I still say he's loco."

"Yibitriander used to tell me the same thing all the time."

"And is he like you guys? Will he live forever?"

Kymee twisted his lips thinking. "Possibly. He may just outlive us all."

"That brings up another thing I'm curious about. How long do the Deavoriath live? Have any of you died?"

"As far as I can tell, and I'm the most likely one to know, we'll stumble along next to forever." He thought a moment. "Only *one* man has died since we returned to Oowaoa, and that was a very long time ago."

"What happened to him? An accident?"

He took a while to respond. "It was no accident. His death was intentional

14

and it was at my hand." He was clearly disturbed to recall the event.

"Was he, what, a criminal?" Didn't seem likely.

"No, Farthdoran was the very opposite of a criminal."

What was the opposite of a criminal? A police officer? I hadn't seen signs of a constabulary on any of my visits. "Should I drop it?" I asked.

He sat mute a second, then snapped back to reality. "No. I'm just being a silly old man and losing myself in the past. Farthdoran was what you might call a priest, a religious thinker. We were never big on religion, as you might imagine. It would have interfered with all our killing, enslaving, and debauching. Couldn't have *that*."

He was quiet again. "Farthdoran returned with us and lived among us here at Oowaoa for a long time, but he was never happy. The longer we all contemplated our collective navels, the sadder he became. He maintained we served no useful, let alone greater, purpose. We were becoming, he was overly fond of saying, fungus on the bark of a dead tree."

"So he was sentenced to *death* for possessing an unflattering opinion? You guys *are* tough."

"No," he said sadly, "the sentence was *his*. His alone." Kymee was still for a while again. "He came to me and asked me to terminate his life. I laughed at him. Can you imagine that? I *laughed* at a man who begged me to end his suffering. *That's* the kind of tough we were, Jon Ryan. The worst kind I can conceive."

"What suffering? Was he, like, terminally ill?"

"By then such a thing was no longer even possible. No, he couldn't take what he felt was a futile existence any longer. He lost his interest and will to live."

"So—"

"So we did the Deavoriath thing. We conferred amongst ourselves, agreed upon his murder, and then patted ourselves on the collective backs for all of our new kindness and wisdom." He shook his head slowly. "What a sorry lot we are, Jon. What a terrible sorry bunch of outmoded irrelevant beings."

"It's not like you need me to help you out morally, but *dude*, the man wanted to die. Helping him actually might have been a kindness. If you hadn't helped him, what were his options? Lighting himself on fire? Putting a laser hole in his head? Not tidy, and definitely not without suffering."

"We could have *listened* to him. We could have tried to *understand* him and his position. But, no. The most enlightened race in the universe smugly euthanized him and promptly forgot all about his inconvenient proposition and opinions."

"Sorry," was all I could think to say.

"You asked. I told you."

"Kymee, you guys have spent a million years trying to reinvent yourselves as better people."

He shrugged. "And?"

"And how are you going to get anywhere if you don't stop hating yourselves? You guys need to move on."

I could see I'd hit him hard with that one, maybe below the belt. He started to tear up. Yeah, turned out lots of species cried. It's some kind of universal habit.

"How can one so young be so wise?" he asked, as he lost it.

I let him be until he was done. It took him a while. I got the impression he hadn't allowed himself direct contact with his feelings for a very long time.

"You okay?" I finally asked patting the back of his hand.

"No, far from it. But I am *better*. Thank you." After a while he said, "I'm going to take your advice about trying not to hate ourselves to the One That Is All next time we're all gathered. Maybe we can make some progress. Probably not, but who knows?"

"I'll send y'all a bill. Heads up. Counseling immortals ain't cheap. Be generous when the hat's passed."

"How does your species put up with you, Jon Ryan?"

"They loaded me into a tin can and blasted me into endless space, that's how."

"A judicious and wise species, it would seem."

THREE

So where does one look for someone who doesn't want to be found? I had very few clues. I knew Uto had been on Proxima Centauri two hundred years before, and maybe above Azsuram more recently. Two points define a straight line. Not much help. I'd been a few places on my Ark voyage. I wasn't looking for him then, but I'd seen and heard nothing to suggest he was anywhere I'd been. Kaljax was off the list. I knew just about all there was to know about that planet. No ancient, surly androids who looked just like me hid there. But crossing off a few worlds wasn't very useful. The list Kymee sent me contained thousands of civilized planets.

From what I'd observed, Uto wasn't able to fold space. That meant he wasn't anywhere extremely far away. Even with the FTL speeds possible with warp drives, he'd still be more or less local. He could, unfortunately, be sailing to somewhere a thousand parsecs away. He, like me, had all the time in the world. I pulled up Kymee's list and filtered it for planets within ten light-years. There were a few hits, but not many. I tried twenty-five light-years. Hmm. Dalque. It orbited Xi Boötis, around twenty light-years away. I had to chuckle at Kymee's footnote concerning the planet. *Good place for the damned.* Well, in the mood I was in and the mood Uto probably was always, too, that sounded like as good a place as any to start. I made my request to *Wrath*. No reason to rekindle our old squabble over the concept of me being his boss.

From a hundred kilometers up, Dalque looked okay enough. The oceans were kind of small, it had no polar ice caps, and the air wasn't exactly crystal clear. But hey, I didn't need to breath the crap so what did I care? I'd managed to attach *Shearwater*, my bitchin' old conventional ship, to *Wrath*. I used it to descend to the surface. The less I was associated with the Deavoriath, the easier life was likely to be. Appearing out of nowhere in a cube was pretty much a guaranteed way to instantly become public enemy number one.

There were several continents and multiple cities much like old Earth. Having no way to decide which place might be better than the next, I elected to land in a city right below *Wrath's* orbit. The closer I was, the more I got the *damned* aspect Kymee mentioned. Smoke billowed up everywhere. Some came from totally inefficient factories horrifically polluting the air, but most came from randomly scattered fires. Buildings, open fields, you name it, it was smoldering. Al was with me on *Shearwater*. He was trustworthy if not sociable. I asked him to find the least-wrecked place. We landed in a flat part of a city called Grelf, in sort of a downtown-appearing section.

Up close, the best part of Grelf was pretty bad. The streets were pockmarked with holes that looked like explosive craters. Many windows were broken, and the ever-present smoke wafted out of many openings. Cross this hellhole off your bucket list if it's there, trust me. I walked down the sidewalk, or what was left of it, debris and rubble crunching under my boots. I entered the most logical place. A bar. They're kind of a universal first stop in Crap City. In two hundred years, I'd been in some really nasty dives. This one, named the I You Dare, was far and away the worst. Litter on the floors, on the bar, and on the tables. It reeked of old smoke, cheap booze, and filthy patrons. I turned down my olfactory sensors to twenty percent and was still nauseated.

I stepped up to the bar and waved a finger at the barkeep. It, because I had no idea if its species had sexes, rotated its head toward me but defiantly didn't budge. I came to learn it was a Landaquin. The name rolls off the tongue real nice, but that's the only non-revolting thing about the beasties. They were squat and furry with a bunch of arms and legs. Think cube-shaped spiders with fuzz and bad breath. Finally, I decided to go to it since it wasn't coming to me.

"Do you have beer here?" I asked.

"Where here?" it replied and then it clicked like it'd cracked the funniest joke in the galaxy. A couple of mangy regulars coughed and chuckled, too. What a dump.

"Look," I said with my best hard-ass intonation, "are you going to get me a beer, or do I have to take my business elsewhere?"

It took a moment to decide, but finally it wriggled over to a cooler and grabbed a can. It slammed it down unopened and said, "Four fifty. Pay up now."

"I slid a bill across the bar and said, "Change now." It clanked a few coins down, which I scooped into a pocket. No tip for the mean spider.

The drunk sitting next to me did what drunks in swill-halls everywhere do. He began working me for a free drink. "You're new around here. I can tell."

"Why? Because I don't smell like rotten vomit?" I replied.

He pretended to laugh. "Nah," he said, "but, come to mention it you are pretty clean, ain't you?"

"That a problem, old timer?"

He leaned back a bit. "No, just saying. Making small talk, that's all. I'm Haslet, by the way. Nice to meet you. Say, I left my wallet at home." He lifted his empty glass toward me. "Can you buy me one till I can pay you back."

"Sure," I said to his great surprise. "I'll buy you a drink, if you answer me a question."

Haslet angled his head. "That'll probably depend on the question, but shoot."

"I'm looking for a man—my twin brother. You ever see anyone around here that looks like me?"

The man to next to Haslet spoke in a slow-slurred voice. "I did." He pointed to one side. "It was in a place about twenty paces from here on the wall. Place called Mirror Town. You go there, mister, and you'll see your identical face."

The fool nearly doubled over snickering, snot dripping from his nose. He was way too pathetic to punch out, so I just ignored him.

"How 'bout it, Haslet?"

"Naw, can't say I has. Wish I could help. You seem like a nice fella and all. Hey, how about that drink?" He held his glass up again.

WTF. It was my first foray as a private dick. Why not? I pointed to Haslet's glass. "One more for the man."

After that, I wandered the streets of Grelf a while wondering what the hell I was doing. There was no way I would find Uto this way. I decided a hundred times to pack it in and head home to Azsuram. I decided a hundred and one times to keep on looking. I owed it to Uto. As nice as it would have been, there really was no way I was going to find him the first place I looked.

On the other side of Dalque, I landed near the center of a city named Zorn. My immediate impression was that it wasn't nearly as nice as Grelf. Yeah. The sidewalks weren't battered and dirty. There were no sidewalks, just hard-baked dirt. The air looked like what came directly out of a bus's tailpipe when it started up. The smell was oh-so-much worse. Picture a sewage plant next to a massive stockyard on a hot day with mountains of tires burning all around. Not sure how any life form could live here, but that did make it a good place to hide. No one in their right mind would find you, even if you wore a sign. When I got back to *Shearwater,* I was going to burn my clothes.

Instead of a bar I entered a store this time. It looked like it sold mostly intoxicants. Big surprise. Grelf was a crossroads planet, so a handful of species visited it with some frequency. As a result, a liquor store had to carry several different kinds of mind-altering chemicals. What got one species high might kill another. Because of that fact, the store was colorful. Bottles and cans, flasks and clear bags of powders in a rainbow of colors were arranged for easy inspection. It was the only thing I saw on the entire planet that wasn't totally ugly. The shop sold some food stuff, again for a range of species. Back on Earth, I'd been to markets in several Asian countries. I thought what they offered for sale was bizarre. This store put them all to shame. There were crawly things in cages, howling insect-like creatures with over-sized eyes, and swimming things that looked more likely to eat the customer than vice versa.

I browsed the store casually. I didn't need anything, but I was in no hurry. Immortal here. After a few minutes, I must have exceeded the patience of the woman behind the counter. She was an odd specimen. How unusual, right? Probably Kaljaxian, but maybe a hybrid with one local parent. Wholly unrelated species couldn't interbreed naturally, but genetic tampering made outbreeding possible in some cases. Why anyone would want to have babies with incompatible genomes was beyond me, but it was technically doable.

Anyway, she barked out loudly, "Hey, you. Tall man. You here to buy, steal, or keep warm? If you're here to buy, buy now. I'm tired of your hideous face. If you're here to steal, come closer so I hit you with my first shot. If you're here to just to stay warm, same thing applies. Come closer." What a lovely ambassador of planetary goodwill.

"I need a class-10 signal amplifier for my ship. You got any?" I yelled back. I had zero need for one, but I had to want something.

"What," she said with a Kaljaxian growl, "you think this looks like a garage, rocket boy? You want booze, food, or company you're in the right place. Otherwise scram. I'm too busy to deal with a freeloader."

I looked at her, then around the store. It was empty but for us two. "Really," I said in the Kaljaxian dialect of Hird, "you don't look too busy."

She replied in Hirn, Sapale's dialect. "Smart-eyes, eh? The same thing that applies to thieves applies to them. Step even closer. My right eyes aren't what they used to be."

"What were they? *Tondre*?" Tondre were the droppings of a pest animal, equivalent to a rat. I was taking a chance insulting a stranger, but hello, we're talking Jon Ryan here.

She stared at me a few heartbeats, then burst out laughing. The woman half-collapsed on the floor she was so energetic about it. Finally, she waved me over. I was hoping it wasn't to shoot me.

She held out a fist, which was the Kaljaxian equivalent of an informal handshake. We banged hands. "You're all right, strange man. You speak Hirn like you were born to it."

"My brood's-mate was."

"Was? That doesn't sound good. My name's Valmar." She held out her fist again.

"Jon Ryan," I said as I hit hers with mine.

"Good to meet you, Jon Ryan. Hey, you want a sip of *glaxäl*?" That was a strong alcoholic beverage from Kaljax. Made moonshine seem like fruit punch. Also, the intoxicating agent was propanol, as in rubbing alcohol. Toxic to humans. Fortunately, not to robots.

"I thought you'd never ask."

She reached under the counter and pulled out a bottle and two shot glasses. The glasses were well-worn, but not well-washed. She poured two shots as sloppily as I'd anticipated, picked one up, and slid the other to me with the same hand. "May Davdiad kiss your children." That was a classic Hirn toast. Made me miss my sweet Sapale a little more. Damn it.

I returned a typical response toast. "And may the falzorn kiss my enemies."

We threw back the shots. Man, was her glaxäl rough. I hoped I didn't light my breath on fire with a short circuit.

"Ah," she said, "that hit the spot."

"Well," I gave the corresponding response, "then let's hit it again and make sure the spot stays down."

We slammed back a second round. Glad I was an android. The glaxäl didn't burn though the back of my neck.

"You're all right," Valmar repeated.

"I know. You already said that."

"Not too many all right folks come in here. Not too many all right folks live on this trash heap of a planet."

"I know. But it's a good place for the damned." I ripped off Kymee. It was a great line.

That time she did collapse to the floor laughing. Valmar kicked the base of the counter so hard I thought she'd break it and make me to pay for the damages. High-spirited lass.

"You need any help?" I called down to her as I leaned over the counter. "Maybe a doctor?"

"No doctor," she responded. "My heart's still beating. Any local quack would likely kill me before he did me any good." She climbed off the floor. "So, my tall friend, what're you really here for?" She poked me in the ribs. "Maybe you miss your brood's-mate and only a Kaljax girl's good enough anymore? Maybe I can help you there. I may not look pretty as her, but I know a few things. Things the good girls don't know about." She was a laugher and went at it again. I liked her already.

"Who said Sapale was a good girl?" I winked at her.

She shut up like the librarian just hissed at her. I've never seen anyone go from drunken mirth to deadly serious so fast or so completely.

In a calm quiet tone she asked, "Sapale Nervaltp-Ser was your brood's-mate?"

"That would be her," I said equally serious. "Did you know her?" I started to wonder if she might reach for the gun she mentioned before.

"You might say so. Yes. I knew her well a *long* time ago."

"I'm hoping you liked her. I'd hate to have to defend her honor with a new friend." What I said was semi-coded Hirn. It meant I didn't want to kill her if she had a problem with Sapale. I would have to. Always stand up for family. Always.

"She was my best friend when I was little. I loved her like a sister. Always will."

I tapped the glaxäl bottle. "I always will, too."

She poured two shots and we drank them slowly, silently.

"You noticed I'm kind of funny looking."

I started to say something tactful, but she put a finger to my lips.

"Don't bother. I *am* funny looking. You saying I ain't won't change the fact or make me think you're screaming *yes* inside your head. Anyway, I grew up near Sapale. We went to the same schools, at least for a while. Kids like me, we don't get much time for school.

"I'm sure you know people on Kaljax can be mean. Their kids are meaner. Parents actually encourage them to pick on other kids and beat them up." She took a deep breath. "I got a lot of both from them kids. More than my share, by a factor of three. But you know what?"

I shook my head.

"Sapale *defended* me. Yeah. When a bigger kid or a bunch of kids were hurting me, she knocked them silly. She also sat by me at mealtime." She sniffed loudly. "I don't know how it is where you come from, but eating alone for a kid where I did is worse than death. Death only happens once. Isolation happens every day. Your brood's-mate, she made my life better, almost tolerable." She turned to face me squarely. "I know you're not shopping for snacks or engine parts, tall man. You smell like someone who wants information or trouble. Maybe both. Whatever you want, if I can give it to you, I will."

"Can you start with a hug?" Kaljaxians aren't huggers by nature, but Valmar was, at least when it came to my Sapale.

"Now what else can I do for you?" She was a serious as a heart attack. If I'd asked she'd have chewed off her arm.

"I'm looking for a man."

"Figures," she said with a nod. "What's his name?"

"I don't know. Sometimes he goes by Uto. Mostly, I'm betting it's something else. He looks just like me. Exactly"

"Your brother?"

"I'd rather not lie to you."

"Then don't. What business is it of mine?" She made a quiet growl. It was the "sorry" growl. "No, friend, you're the first man I've seen that looks like you. If anyone on this planet did, I'd know about it. You kind of stand out, you know."

I smiled. "Because my face is so hideous?"

She patted both my cheeks. "Your face isn't that hideous. Ain't pretty, but it ain't too scary, neither. I guess I get a little cranky when I'm bored."

"I'd hate to be around when you're really bored."

Valmar made a giggle-growl, kind of like a purr. "No, you wouldn't. You're too nice a fella. Sapale, she'd have had the best there was, or she'd have had none."

I left shortly after that compliment. Valmar never asked what happened to Sapale. I was glad for that. I'd have come apart at the seams if I had to tell the story again.

FOUR

With Dalque being a write-off, I returned to *Shearwater* and headed back into space. And yes, I did burn the clothes I'd worn. Modern science provided no cleaning methods powerful enough to salvage them. One planet down, and only an infinite number to go. My odds of success were improving by leaps and bounds. As to where to waste my time next, I had no proper idea. I scanned Kymee's list. A star system we called Ross 128 caught my eye. He listed three civilized planets, all maybe a couple of hundred years ahead of the current human technological level. Three planets close together. Maybe they'd have shared knowledge. Maybe that improved my chances. Maybe, maybe, right?

So—eeny, meeny, miney, moe—I picked the outermost planet, Meiffol, to try first. Kymee's cheat sheet said it was a rowdy, rough place, but not uncivilized. Cool. I could turn the visit into a vacation. I selected one of the larger cities, Drantac, as a starting point. Al alerted me that I'd need to file a flight plan and ask permission to land. I left the vortex in a very remote orbit and flew *Shearwater* down like last time.

The planet was, at least, more civilized than my first stop. After I parked my ride, I saw that Drantac was much nicer than anything on Dalque. The air was hazy, but it didn't break off in pieces when touched. Spaceports were what they were and never representative of the local city or culture. So, I located public transportation and headed toward the center of town to get a taste of the local color.

Eventually, I entered a section that had a local feel to it. I set off on foot looking for, you guessed it, a dive bar. Best place to start, plus I could sample the local offerings. Hey, I was, by training and inclination, an interstellar explorer. That's what we do, push back the frontiers of knowledge for the betterment of humankind. Since nothing could poison me, the worst that could happen was that I'd put something nasty tasting in my mouth. Al had pre-downloaded several translation algorithms for Meiffol into my head. That made identifying the bar I selected easy. The sign read *Take A Chance*. Why, thank you very much, I believe I will.

As with any acceptable drinking establishment, the doors were propped wide open. The decor was … well, it was tacky. Sort of cheap industrial meets poorly done tropical. Whoever thought of the design should have been shot— several times, in fact. But, I wasn't buying the dump, just passing through, so what the hell?

The bartender was humanoid, but only just. He was maybe seven feet tall, thin as a fence post, with four arms equivalently thinner than his trunk. His head was attached to his stick frame like someone crushed it on too hard. I guessed he was male, but honestly, how would I know? Plus, it didn't matter too much either way, because *if* that thing was a female, I wasn't going be be dating her anytime soon.

I sat at one end of the polished-steel bar. Some stools were loosely configured for a species like mine, some distinctly were not. There were a couple of guys at the bar and a scattering of people sitting at tables. The voices were low and the smoke level was high. The bartender eased over and asked in the local tongue what I'd like. I asked if he had beer. That drew a blank stare. Plan B. I asked for what the guy sitting nearest to me was drinking. When he returned with a large glass of a bubbling, clear liquid, I asked his name. In retrospect, probably a mistake. For one thing, when someone asks for a name, it's suspicious. Made it clear I was an outsider looking for something. Second, his name sounded like the sound tires made just before a car accident, with an element of fingernails on chalkboard as an undercurrent. As an android, I could repeat it, but as a guy with ears, I never would.

Without bothering to ask my name, he lumbered away to check on another customer. I tasted my beverage. Hmm. Bitter soda water, with some taste I couldn't place. No obvious alcohol. I placed my left hand on the bar and said in my head, *One filament only. What are you?*

An almost invisible thread shot from one finger and dove into the fluid. Water, carbon dioxide, nitrogen gas, low concentrations of herbal extracts, trace manganese, trace potassium nitrate, and ... *no*. Crap, and it was too late to spit it out. Oh, well. The amniotic fluid I'd just swallowed would be incinerated in my gut almost immediately. Note to self. Never, repeat *never*, order what some alien in a dive bar was drinking. Ask, maybe, what it was, but don't just order it.

I waved the barkeeper over. "I don't like this as much as I used to. How about something with alcohol, lots of alcohol?"

He shrugged. "What form of alcohol?"

"The cheapest you got that's close to one hundred percent."

That brought a sound from him that might have been a chuckle. He came back quickly with a shot glass of deep blue liquid.

"Thanks, pal," I said. "Hey, I got a problem."

Man, was he good at blank stares.

I plowed ahead. "I sort of got this drinking problem." I lifted my glass and downed it in one splash. Hayah. It was strong. "Another, please," I wiggled the glass in the air, "and make it a double."

When he set a larger glass down I spoke again. "So, like I was saying, sometimes I drink a little too much." I harrumphed. "Most of the time I drink *way* too much. Anyway, I sort of lost something and can't remember where it is. So, maybe you can help me out. Have I ever been in here before?" The plan to pump him for information came out sounding way more lame than it had in my head. Crap on that.

Screeching tires stared blankly, then turned and walked away.

"Wait," I called to his back. "How much do I owe you?" Might as well cut my losses and make an ass out of myself to a new audience.

His head rotated one hundred eighty degrees without flinching. "Nothing, if you leave now and never come back."

Ouch. But on the up side I didn't have to pay for the grossest thing I'd ever put in my mouth. Or the amniotic fluid, either.

I slummed around Drantac a couple of days. I got thrown out of six more bars, two cafes, and a casino, but learned nothing other than that I was a bad undercover agent. On to planet two in the system. Kymee listed it as Balmorulam. *Sophisticated, political, and boring.* Okay, it'd be a quick visit. I decided on a different approach, since my other tactics were so incredibly bad. I left the vortex in very high orbit and flew to Balmorulam on *Shearwater*. I docked her on an orbiting space station and shuttled down to the surface via local transport. I put on clothes that suggested I was an itinerate sailor, and even slung a duffle over one shoulder to amplify that point.

I hit a working man's bar in the spaceport and asked where I might locate cheap lodging. They'd heard that question before. They directed me to a hotel a few blocks away. I guess he bought my cover, because the hotel was so sleazy I almost took a pass. But then again, I figured, why break my cover? It wasn't like their fleas could bite me. I walked to the desk and asked about a room. Weekly rates, pay in advance, no fighting, sheets and towels were extra, and no more than two whores at a time. I could live with that. I plopped some bills down and told him to keep the change. He called me a bad word in colorful vernacular and threw a handful of coins on the floor at my feet. Nice place. Maybe I could rent to own.

Over a few weeks, I hung around spaceport bars and asked about work. I got a lot of offers. I became quite the expert at saying *no*. That destination was too far, that planet smelled funny, I was wanted in that system, or my favorite, all the girls there are ugly. I always thanked them for their offers and said I'd think about them. They always asked me not to do them any favors. The job was take it or leave it. So I left it. One thing I mentioned in every conversation was my twin brother. Oh, boy, did I miss him and was he ever a bastard for sleeping with my wife and the jerk owed me a fortune in gambling debts. I always pretended to be drunk when going on about that darn twin of mine, so I don't think anyone ever got suspicious. No one said they'd seen my twin, but no one got hostile either.

I had just paid for my third week at the marvelous Hotel Deluxe—no comment—when I got a nibble of a lead. I was spouting off to some drunk about my saint of a twin brother, how I wanted to find him so I could tell him our mom had died. The bartender inched in closer while pretending to clean the counter. That caught my attention, because the bar was sticky and littered with crumbs. He wasn't routinely much of a clean freak. I gradually included him in our drunken conversation. I told him if my brother was there right then, I'd kiss him on the lips, I'd be so happy to see him. I also recounted what a star athlete he was in school. He played all the sports and got all the girls, the lucky so-and-so.

The bartender said my twin sounded like a real nice fellow. I confirmed he was. The barkeep said he just might have seen him, unless it had been me he saw a couple days ago, instead. I said it probably was, but asked where'd he seen me anyway. He reported it was down on Lectur Street by one of the warehouses. I opened my eyes like I'd seen a ghost. I said I had no idea where that was and hadn't ever been there. I pressed him to recall details. I slipped him a few bills to jog his memory. He said it was in front of a bar. Yeah, now that he thought about it, it was a bar named Conyers.

I tried to appear like I was going to jump out of my skin. There was obviously little chance his story was legit. But I wanted to stay in character and, most of all, since it was my very first lead. I needed one. I figured he had some agenda. Maybe he owned the place and wanted a regular like me to do my drinking there. I looked up the directions while he was saying he'd be such a proud man to have reunited two loving brothers. What a con.

I took my time making it over to Conyers. I didn't want to seem too motivated. Drunks were never motivated. If someone was trailing me, I'd blow my cover if I seemed motivated. I had Al see if he could find out anything about the place. He did some checking and reported back that it seemed like a run of the mill gin joint. He said I'd probably like it, because Conyers had twenty-four seven strippers. I asked what species the performers were. He said he was surprised that mattered to me. Ah, my dearest Al.

It was getting late by the time I walked into the club. It was loud—sounded like boulders falling off a cliff. And though there was, technically, a stripper pole-dancing, I was betting she was just as ugly to whatever species she belonged to as she was to mine.

I forced my way to the bar and ordered what had become my usual on

Balmorulam. They called it a *liar's promise*. Yeah, pretty stupid name. But it combined the qualities I'd come to appreciate. It was strong and it was cheap. As I nursed my drink, it became obvious the bartender was nicer to me than he had to be, even if he was angling for big tips. I'd been in enough bars to know that cordiality was not part of this man's job description. But I played dumb. Don't even say it. It *was* an act. As the evening progressed, I noticed my drinks were coming faster and stronger. There was a new element finding its way up the concentration level, too. I did a discreet check. He was cutting in larger and larger quantities of a sleeping medicine. Knock-out drops. The dude was trying to put me on the floor. There went his chances for a five-star rating from me.

I acted as if a stupor was overcoming me. I bobbed my head like I was on the verge of passing out but then I'd rally at the last moment. I was ninety-nine point nine percent certain the bartender was scamming me. But it wasn't impossible that Uto wanted me blurry before he met with me. That way ... crap in a basket. What was I *not* thinking? Uto knew I was an android. Liquor and sleeping pills would have zero effect on me. I could be such an idiot.

At that juncture, a man sat down next to me at the bar. I turned to inspect him, still pretending to be barely conscious. Wow. He was a big man. Wait, he wasn't a man. He was humanoid, but ... did I mention he was *huge*? He stared back at me, just as cool as a cucumber. His breath was as hot as it was voluminous. It didn't smell like roses, either.

Out of nowhere, the beast snapped, "What'd you call me?"

Huh? "I didn't say anything," I replied. How dumb was that?

"You call me the son of a thousand fathers? How dare you. I'll kill you for that insult." He looked like he was quite capable of making good on his threat.

"Whoa, pal," I said, quickly a lot more lucid. "I don't—"

That's when he pushed me and my barstool to the floor. Asshole. I got up faster than I should have been able to, but he didn't notice. I don't think he considered me an opponent, only a victim. I had a quick decision to make. I could kill him, maybe the bartender, too, for good measure, but that would terminate the cover I'd worked so hard to establish. I could pretend to be knocked out and escape later when there were fewer witnesses. Or ... that's when a bottle crashed against the back of my head. I ran the numbers quickly. If I were human and if that blow didn't kill me, it sure as hell would have rendered me unconscious.

I dropped to the floor in a heap.

Do you know what's annoying? Pretending to be unconscious while two clumsy ham-handed jerks moved me out of a bar and into a van. I hit more objects than I missed. Plus, the big guy who'd pushed me and was helping lug me out had a real issue with intestinal gas. I don't know what he ate, but he shouldn't have eaten it.

I stayed on my back in the van as it sped away. I couldn't sense anyone nearby, but they might have cameras. I'd escape when we got to wherever they were taking me. I could hear the driver talking with a passenger. Neither was the behemoth who'd pushed me, because both guys up front spoke words without grunting.

The only reason I listened in was because there really wasn't anything else to do. I checked in with Al a couple times, but he could be entertaining only in small doses. Their initial conversation had concerned what a loser I was, how easily they'd bagged me, and how much they'd get for me. I guess I was being sold, maybe into slavery? Didn't matter. The person who bought me was going to want to return me for a full and complete refund, guaranteed.

Then they mentioned something I did *not* anticipate. They said I was as unlucky as "those assholes from Earth." They shouldn't have known about Earth. Sure, maybe their scientists sent a UFO there before Jupiter rammed it, but scum like those two shouldn't be aware of its existence. Plus, they talked about assholes *from* Earth. Could they possibly be referring to the worldship fleet? If so, why were they unlucky? They were alive, multiplying, and steaming toward a permanent home. Nothing unlucky about that. Unless they were privy to the fact that the humans's luck was about to change for the worse.

I let Al know I wouldn't be home for dinner anytime soon.

FIVE

Toño DeJesus sat in his lab, elbows on the bench top, hands supporting his chin. He was staring at the biggest headache he'd been saddled with in over a century. He looked with utter consternation at Kelldrek in her cage. She was the only Berrillian to survive the attack they'd mounted against Azsuram. Why Jon had felt it necessary to capture her was beyond Toño's reckoning. That the android scientist was stuck with her for good was plain. No one else would tolerate her. She was uncooperative, disruptive, and she smelled revolting. More importantly, she was a constant threat to anyone who strayed too close to her cage. She stated repeatedly and unambiguously that she wanted to kill as many of her enemies as she could. He surrounded her metal bars with a plexiglass barrier, but there was always a chance she'd manage to snag someone not paying enough attention.

He kept her alive, initially, because he hoped to learn something from her about her species. She'd done her utmost to foil any such attempts. He could simply euthanize her, but that went against Toño's nature. He was loath to kill anything, especially a prisoner. She did eat well. Whenever he tossed a chunk of meat near her cage, she pulled it in and ripped it to shreds impressively. Still, eventually he'd either put her down, or at least confine her elsewhere.

For her part, Kelldrek never warmed one tenth of one degree toward Toño, or any of her captors. Whatever she said was easily translated. She cursed endlessly, threatened continually, and mocked, with stunning creativity, anyone within earshot. Unfortunately, the recipient of the bulk of her abuse was Toño. He longed for the days when he was left alone to perform his research in peace. He doubted those days would ever return.

"My dear," he said to her one day, "why is it you behave so poorly? Honestly. You're a prisoner here for the remainder of your life. Escape is impossible, and rescue even less likely than that. Why can't you make peace with that reality?"

"I make peace with no being or concept," she snarled back. "What would you have me do? Watch your holo-programs and read your nonsensical books?"

"I just don't understand why you must be so unpleasant. It can't be fun for you."

"Why not? I take great pleasure in making you miserable. Wait," she said bringing a paw to her mouth, "or is it that you are lonely? I rarely see you leave, and no female of your species ever visits. No male, either, for that matter. Yes, with the disappearance of your lover, Jon Ryan, you're alone and sad."

"That's ridiculous. Shame on you."

She was pleased to have gotten him going, yet again. "Would you like me to press my backside up to the cage to help ease your pain?" She purred loudly.

"How revolting."

"A remark no male has made to me, but have it your way. But keep in mind my offer remains, even if your masculinity doesn't."

"That about does it." Toño lowered an opaque dome over her confinement area. It was totally soundproof. Toño could finally get some work done without her interference. One of the AIs would monitor her, in case something happened that required his attention. He reflected, and not for the first time, that it was too bad Azsuram had not founded a zoo yet. When they did, if she was still alive, she'd be the first exhibit.

Before he could begin a creative train of thought, JJ wandered into the lab. He hadn't mentioned he was going to visit, but Toño felt his casual pace meant there was no new crisis on the immediate horizon that forced him to come. As much as he liked Jon's eldest son, Toño was irritated that he was not to get any work done for however much longer this visit would take.

"Evening, Doc," said JJ. "Nice night for a walk, don't you think?"

He did not. Moreover, Toño did not want to take a walk, even if the night was transcendently beautiful. "JJ, what brings you by?"

"Just missing an old friend," he replied.

Then you should go visit one. "I wouldn't know. I've only just silenced the she-beast from Berrill. Any period following contact with her is cursed to be unpleasant."

"Aw, come on. I think you two are becoming the best of friends. Your relationship has turned the corner. When was the last time she threatened to eat your beating heart?"

Toño shot his face quickly to one side. "It's been days."

"See," JJ said, raising his arms, "the *very* best of friends. Hey, are those wedding bells I hear in my imagination?"

"If so, I'm not a good enough physician to cure your hallucinations." He realized the convivial JJ was drawing him into conversation, despite his not wanting to be. He had more Jon Ryan in him than genetics alone could account for. "So, what does bring you here so late?" He hit the word *late* with increased force.

"I couldn't sleep."

So, you decided to bother me. My company is on a par with insomnia. How very flattering. "Any reason in particular?" Toño asked, with absolutely no enthusiasm.

JJ growled the shrill oh-I-don't-know growl of his species.

Toño opened a drawer and removed a small crowbar. "Do you mind if I use this to pry the information out of you, thus avoiding hours of unwelcome preliminaries?"

JJ tilted his head. "Might be fun."

Toño narrowed his eyes.

"Or maybe I'll just share some reservations I'm having."

"That would be welcome."

"There's a council meeting tomorrow."

"You're worried about a routine mind-numbing council meeting? Aside from the threat of death from terminal boredom, what could possibly concern you?"

JJ sniffed loudly. "Dolirca is being difficult again."

"I wasn't aware she was difficult in the first place."

"Maybe not to you."

"What has she done to cause you concern? She's always been the very picture of sweetness and forthrightness."

"Maybe to you."

"Have I mentioned before that you talk as annoyingly as your father?"

"Maybe to you." JJ smiled when Toño visibly tensed. "Okay, look, the deal is that she seems to have her own agenda. When I mention some future direction or action, her eyes are a million kilometers away."

"I'm a bit confused. Everyone should have their own thoughts on a matter. Dolirca is brighter than average and more motivated than most. Those are admirable qualities. Maybe you're too sensitive?"

"I wish it was that. No, after knowing her since she was in diapers and working with her for years, I think it's different. She … isn't a team player. Yes. That's it. She parades around with One and Two like she was royalty. She acts like she's better than the rest of us."

"She has a couple Toe pets. That's not a factor in any sense. The Toe are agreeable creatures of very limited intellect."

"Hers aren't all that friendly. Have you interacted with them lately?"

Toño was taken back. "No. But they're clones of Ffffuttoe. She was the picture of congeniality."

"One and Two bite when you block direct access to Dolirca. Or when she tells them to."

"I find that impossible to believe. I will, of course, check their status first thing tomorrow. We can't have ill-tempered bears threatening the children."

"Check her out while you're at it. If she ever *was* a sweet innocent child, she isn't any longer."

"I find that harder to believe. But as the colony's medical director, I will have a conversation with her. She hasn't come in for a physical in quite a while. I can use that as an excuse to speak with her."

"Honestly, Doc, I'd feel a lot better if you did. If Dad was around I'd lay this on—"

"No need to explain. I'm happy to help. You run along to that darling family of yours and leave the worrying to me. I'm a pro at it."

SIX

Pilot, protested Al, *your plan of action is unjustifiably dangerous. I will not condone it by becoming an accomplice.*

Al, you can't *be an accomplice*, I responded via our mental link. *For one thing you're not alive, and for another, I'm giving you a direct order. This is not a* discussion. *Just do as I say. I can't move the vortex unless I'm physically in contact with it. It'll just have to remain where it is, while you and I go wherever it is they're taking me.*

No, he replied, *I demand* you *escape. Then I insist we rejoin the cube.*

No can do. I need to know if the human fleet is in danger from these bozos. Stay as far away as possible without losing contact. Hopefully, they won't be able to detect you. Even if they can, there's not much they can do about being tailed in space.

Very well, pilot. For the time being I will play it your way. But I'm on record as thinking it's a terrible idea.

"*Al, seriously who're you going to complain to?* I had him there. Who cared what I did? Sapale was gone, Amanda Walker would encourage me to find out the facts, and General Saunders was dust orbiting inside Jupiter. *I'll update you as it becomes necessary.* I terminated the link.

With Al's help, I'd determined I was aboard a freighter heading directly away from the star system. Our destination wasn't obvious. There were no known planets in that direction for an enormous distance, even on the list Kymee supplied me. The ship moved at about half the speed of light so most likely we wouldn't be arriving to our destination for quite some time. Great. Another long space flight. I'd forgotten how tediously slow conventional engines were. Oh, well. I had nearly endless entertainment stored in my head, and sooner or later they were going to have to wake me up to feed me. No sense going to all that trouble capturing a prisoner, if you're just going to let him starve to death.

A few hours later, someone opened the door to the tiny space they'd dumped me in. I don't know how long I was supposed to be out, but I figured it was better to err on the side of too long versus too soon. Several hours after that, two men came to check on me. One stepped into my space and kicked me. I groaned but didn't otherwise respond.

"This ass is really out. Oh well, a passed-out prisoner is better than an awake one, at least for now. Tell the captain his newest crewman is still sleeping like a baby. I'll check back on him later."

The other fellow grunted. I heard his footsteps fade down the hall. From the generally increased level of movement in the ship, I figured the next visit to check on me would be in the morning, ship's time.

Sure enough, bright and early, three figures peered through the crack in the door.

A new voice said, "Here, hand me that."

The next thing I knew, the SOB dumped a bucket of dirty water on my head. What is it with ships and buckets of dirty water? Why do sailors everywhere swab so much? Anyway, he must have decided that whatever drugs I'd been given should be out of my system by then. So, awaken I did. Personally, I think I put on a masterful performance. I coughed, I gagged, and I gasped. Someone should have put me on holo. I was *that* good.

"All right, cupcake," the authoritative voice snapped, "nappy-nappy is over. It's time you started earning your keep." He kicked me in the stomach for added emphasis.

Nice guy. I'd keep that in mind, when payback time rolled around.

After enhancing my acting with a cry of painful protestation, I staggered to my feet uncertainly. "I'm up, I'm up, you son of a bitch."

That earned me a punch in the mouth.

"Come on," one of them said to me with a shove, "let's get you deloused and dressed in a proper uniform."

We went to a large communal bathroom, and the man, Ned, ordered me to take off my clothes. He was not, I'll say straight away, on the list of people I wished would order me to strip naked and shower. In a few minutes, I was cleaned and dressed in what he seemed to think was a uniform. It was a dingy, green, baggy jumpsuit. No emblems or markings, just ugly. When I met Ned's criteria for preparedness, he pushed me down a set of corridors to the captain's quarters.

Ned knocked gently, placed a finger under my nose, and said, "You mind how you act. We've little invested in you, so throwing you out the nearest portal wouldn't be much of a loss." He wiped the back of his hand across his mouth. "I'm guessing one in four of you scumbags do end up floating home, so weigh that prospect against your desire to lash out. This'll be your only warning. Through these doors whatever's left of your life begins."

"Come," came from the captain's side of the door.

Ned snatched off his cap and roughly balled it up in his hands as the door slid open. He put a hand on my shoulder and heaved me in. The captain was reclined on an over-stuffed chair. This was the first good look I had of him. He was definitely humanoid. Crap, he actually looked human, which was impossible. He couldn't be. If he had been human, he would have looked like he was in his late thirties. Six feet tall, give or take, and well-muscled. In fact, the best description I could give was that he looked like an actor in a beer commercial. Too good to be true, unless you drank that *particular* brand. Unlike a pampered pretty boy, however, there was a dangerous edge to this man. He exuded confidence, yes, but also ruthlessness and a generalized-contempt. His hands said it all. They were tough, working hands. A captain with calloused hands was a force to be reckoned with.

"Leave us, Ned," the captain said softly.

Ned crushed his hat further and fidgeted. "Are you sure, Cap? This one's still pretty green."

"I'm sure. He doesn't look like much to me. Run of the mill drunk with better than expected teeth. That's all I see." He turned to glare at Ned. "I'm not proud to observe that this man's first exposure to our onboard discipline is my second mate's questioning my orders."

Ned was properly intimidated. I could tell from his reaction he may have respected the captain, but he mostly feared him. To his credit, Ned didn't piss himself, but I'm betting it wasn't by much.

"Sorry, Cap. My apologies. I'll be on the bridge, if you need anything."

"I'll call for you shortly," he angled his head at me, "after I've welcome the fresh meat."

Ned gesticulated as he backed out the door.

The captain eased back in his chair and stretched. "That went poorly. So, do you have a name, drunkard, or shall I assign you one?"

"You're the captain, Cap. Your call."

"Ah. A smartass. How refreshingly different in a new conscript. I haven't heard such disrespect since, oh, I don't know, the last man standing in that very spot."

"They stamp us out of a mold on Cholarazy, sir."

"Did I mention the last fellow's stay with us was tragically brief? Not five minutes into his interview, I granted his wish to return home. I doubt he made it without a ship, a suit, or a prayer of a chance. Say, would you like to go check and see how he's doing?"

The man was serious. "No, sir. I'm fine right here. My name's Jon Ryan."

"Better. I am Captain Karnean Beckzel. Please think of me as your new god. While whatever deity you worshiped heretofore may have metaphorically steered your fate, I do so *actually*. People say I'm not a nice man behind my back. You know what, Jon? They're right. Don't cross me, don't anger me, and don't ever, *ever* fuck with me. Those are the rules. They're really quite simple and easy to remember."

"Sir." At least for the time being, I'd be a good little prisoner.

"Do you have any questions?"

"Just one, sir. What's my role here?"

"I would guess a man as quick-witted as you already knows *that* answer, Jon. You're not fucking with me, are you?"

"No, sir. I just want to know my place."

He bobbled his head back and forth, with a small frown. "Fair enough. As you're new, I'll grant you the benefit of the doubt, but just this once. *You,*

Jon, are now the lucky participant in a voyage of wonder and profit. Though the journey will be long, the work arduous, and your pay nominal, you will, before the trip is ended, thank me for allowing you to join our merry band."

"You mean I'm shanghaied."

"I'm not familiar with that term, but I assume it fits your present condition."

"Why not just offer me a fair contract in the first place, sir? I was slumming in that rat hole of a planet, begging for work."

"You look to me to be a seasoned sailor, Jon. Am I correct in that assumption?"

"Yes, sir. As seasoned as they come." Boy, he did not know the half of it.

"Then I assumed correctly that if I made you an *honest* offer, you'd have laughed in my face and hightailed it to the next bar."

"Doesn't sound promising, sir. Since I'm here for the duration, could you enlighten me as to why I would have laughed in your face?"

"I like you, Jon. Yes, I'll admit it. I like you already. You're clever enough to knuckle under, but prideful enough to still tiptoe along my line in the sand. The truth of the matter is this. Our ship is committed to a voyage many would label ludicrous, ill-advised, and far too risky. It will be longer than most merchant shuttles, by a large margin. It will be more dangerous by an even wider margin. But for me, it will be profitable enough to justify those risks. Experience has taught me that finding sailors willing to volunteer for this type of voyage is not worth the effort. The only ones who'd sign-on, trust me on this, are the ones nobody'd want to sail with."

"Where are we bound?" Not that I'd know the place, but I think he wanted me to ask.

"Sir," was his response.

"We're sailing for a place called *Sir*?"

"No, and that will be the last disrespect I tolerate. You failed to end your query with the word *sir.*"

I lowered my head slightly. "Where are we bound, *sir*?"

"Better. First, we sail for Pallolo. There we will pick up merchandise to deliver to our final destination, Deerkon."

I was right. The words meant nothing to me. I checked Kymee's list. Neither was on it, at least not under those names. "Sound fine to me, Captain. Where's my bunk?"

Karnean sat forward supporting himself with one leg on the floor. "Fine? You're *fine* with Deerkon? I warned you, yet still you fuck with me."

"Easy, Captain. What? I don't mind sailing for Deerkon, Pallolo, or the gates of hell, if there's a profit in it for me. Hey, the greater the risk, the greater the reward. Am I right?"

He stared hard at me. I could tell he was deciding whether to deep-six me or shake my hand. Fortunately, my endearing charm must have won him over. "You are a greater fool than even I am, Jon. Perhaps I'd have been better off leaving you in your rat hole?"

"Time will tell, sir."

He rested back stiffly in his chair. "Two lefts, then a right. That'll get you to the bridge. Tell Ned that you live at least one more day. He'll show you to your quarters. Welcome aboard *Desolation*. Dismissed."

"Sir."

Desolation? The ship's name was *Desolation*? That had to be the worst name for a ship I'd ever heard.

I didn't back out the door like Ned had. No, I walked out like a stud. I had to keep tiptoeing that line in the sand, now didn't I?

So I was kidnapped to be the unwilling crew on a ship undertaking a foolhardy mission. My captain was a sociopath who ran his merchant ship like it was a military vessel. Yup, there could be only one explanation. Karnean was a pirate. And anyone who'd pay a pirate's price to transport merchandise was either a major idiot, or truly someone I didn't want to meet. I was inclined to favor the latter notion, based on my experience in this life. I was in a bad situation that was about to get a hell of a lot worse. Same circus, just different monkeys.

I entered the bridge, which gave me my first clue as to what kind of ship I was on. I stepped up to the view screen and craned my neck as far I could. Okay, not a bad ship. It was no *Shearwater*, but it wasn't bad, either. The body of the vessel was shaped like a cigar, cut off at the back. She was medium-sized. Along the sides were mounts for missiles, and all racks were loaded. Looked like conventional warheads, but I couldn't tell for certain. One thing was certain. She packed a lot more punch than a merchant ship ever would. Yeah, it had maybe as much as, say, a pirate might need.

Quickly, one of the bridge crew challenged me. That caught Ned's attention. He called off the crewman and waved me over.

"So, you survived the interview process. Good. We need more able-bodied sailors. Cap's tough on newbies. Tosses a lot out before they get a chance to prove their worth. Be aware of that. Just because he didn't kill you, doesn't mean he won't." Ned shook his head. "Cap's a good man. Tough but fair. You work hard and don't cause no trouble and he'll do right by you. Half the crew were in your boots at some point. Don't hold no grudges toward him. He'll know, and you'll regret it about one second too late. Has a sixth sense like that, he does.

"I'll tell you this. There's no man I'd rather serve under in a pinch. He's bold, cunning, and, what's more important, he's one lucky bastard. First mate's just as sharp, though she's a good bit better lookin' than her brother."

"The captain's sister is his first mate? That's nuts."

"Wait till you see her in action before you say that. She's good. Trust me. I've seen a lot in my day." He checked to see if anyone could be listening in. "Better stick to business. Come with me and I'll show you to your bunk."

"Bunk? I thought I heard Karnean mention something about quarters. I don't get my own room?"

"Ha. Would you listen to yourself? You think the lowest of the low gets his own stateroom? Bah. You get a bunk, and you'll appreciate *that* one whole hell of a lot. I was on this ship *five* years, no six, before I got a room to myself."

We'd arrived at a hatch leading into a large common room. There were metal tables with bench seating near what had to be the mess window. He showed me the adjoining sleeping quarters. Forty bunks, ten on each side of the room stacked two-high. How very nautical. The head was at one end of the barracks. *Spartan* best described the facilities.

"You're in bunk eight." Ned pointed to an upper one. "Used to belong to a bloke named Riley. He won't be needing it anymore."

"Why? He get promoted?"

"Not hardly. Poor son of a bitch. No he crossed a line and paid the price he knew he'd have to."

"Let me guess. He pissed off Karnean."

"Worse," Ned lowered his voice. "He put the moves on his sister. She's more off limits than the powder room is to a man on fire."

"You're shitting me, right?"

"No. Don't even think about her as a woman. You'll live a lot longer."

"No, I meant we have a powder room? What twenty-four pound cannon, too?"

"Joke if you will. But I'm serious about Kayla. Only Ned's kind enough to warn you. The lot of sharks here love seeing someone get caught trying to sample the wares."

"I'm sure I'll not be tempted."

"Good. Stay that way after you see her, and I'll buy you a drink. Now, come with me. I'll show you your jobs and let them what's in charge know who y'are."

Guess what jobs I got? Chef, pilot, fire-control for any battles? No. I swabbed decks, helped slop the mess to the crew, and, oh boy of oh boys, I got to clean the heads. Yes. Mom'd be so proud of her little man, if she only knew. I'd saved humanity more times than I could count, currently held the rank of general, and had logged more hours in command than everyone on this scow combined, and I got to make sure the bathrooms sparkled. I was looking forward to the time I could lie bored in my bunk and pretend to sleep.

The one benefit of being on cleaning detail was that I could go everywhere on board and not get yelled at. Over my first few days of scut work, I catalogued the ship, its provisions, and what little cargo it carried. Whatever we were to deliver to this awful Deerkon place must be waiting on Pallolo. I did look forward to checking *those* crates and getting a sense for what Karnean was up to.

A word to the wise regarding cleaning. Things had to be clean enough to not get myself in trouble, but not so clean as to keep me on that duty a day longer than necessary.

Slopping mess, well, that was a job there was but one way to do. Work like hell prepping stuff, so none of the cooks whacked me with a ladle. And when serving, never look into the crew member's eyes. That way they can't accuse you of shorting them out of spite. Sure, no meal would pass without some asshole barking and posturing because he or she didn't get their share, but they couldn't claim it was personal, so I didn't get in trouble, or at least as much trouble as I could have.

Most of the crew were the similar kind of humanoids. Like the captain, they sure looked human. That included their private parts and habits, which I was an involuntary witness to in the head and communal showers. TMI for certain, but it perplexed me. What were the chances that an alien race was so similar to humans? And I'm not just talking on the outside here. I mentioned before that I was equipped with a rudimentary ultrasound system. Toño figured long ago it might be useful in the exploration mission I was built to carry out. That old ability allowed me to scan the crew They were human on the inside too. Weird. What else was new in my life? Take a number and wait your turn, mysteries of the unknown.

It wasn't until my fourth day onboard that I caught a glimpse of the first mate, Kayla. Ned wasn't kidding. She was stunning. A tall, sinewy frame with long black hair up in a knot. She moved with the grace of a model and the confidence of a reigning monarch. And she had those eyes us guys get all gaga over and want to lose ourselves in forever. I could understand why that Riley guy took a chance with her. She might just be worth it. But, as an android, I could make myself immune to her. I was on a covert recon mission, way deep in enemy territory. I was thinking with my big head not my little one. What? I could be focused, dedicated, and smart when it came to beautiful women. Really, I could be—you know, if I set my mind to it.

Lucky for me, I was perfectly invisible to First Officer Beckzel. Fate would not tempt me to take a chance, because I didn't exist. I guess pretty girls learned early to avoid eye-contact with men. If they didn't, they'd never get anything done. They'd be too busy fending of one advance after another by guys who thought she was interested, only because their gazes met.

Did I mention Kayla's lips? Wow. They were plump, looked soft as clouds in the sky, and were as red as a purest rose.

Being the lowest swabbie, I wasn't allowed access to the computers. Fortunately, I didn't need permission to access every scrap of data the ship had. Thank you yet again, Kymee. I learned some interesting facts exploring the computer systems. We were indeed bound for Pallolo. It was a planet a few light-years away, so the journey would take four years. Crap. I was putting more time into this project than I anticipated. If nothing panned out, I'd have a decade of egg on my face. Lucky for me I was immortal.

We were picking up a lot of technical equipment on Pallolo. It seemed like we'd be carrying enough to build a university, and then some. We were also picking up thermonuclear weapons, large laser arrays, and tons—literally—of intoxicants, drugs, and psychoactive compounds. One was something named gofenterate. It was designed to keep the user awake and clear headed for as long as they took the stuff. Soldier juice.

What I found out about Deerkon was bone-chilling. It was a hellhole, yes. A ruthless megalomaniac ruled it to be sure. But the scale and extent of the atrocities I read about were staggering. Our contact was a guy named Varrank Simzle. He was up there with the Berrillians and the Listhelons in terms of horrific brutality. He lacked their technical tools—FTL speed and folding space, that sort of stuff. But what he lacked in sophistication, he more than made up for in rage and cruelty. No wonder Karnean accused me of being flippant when I said I didn't mind going there. The devil himself would have thought twice about a trip to Deerkon. My captain seemed rational. That meant he was very greedy and over-confident about his ability to remain among the living. Oh, boy. I was saddled with a real peach.

With access to the computers, I was able to determine where Deerkon was on Kymee's list. I immediately wished I hadn't looked it up. The Deavoriath called the planet Kolidar. Here's what Kymee wrote:

Avoid this planet, and the solar system, for that matter. At the height of our power and lust, we went there only once and never returned. It is a cursed world. In a matter of a few short months, we lost hundreds of thousands of soldiers. Some were lost in battles with tribes we should have dominated completely. Most died invisibly and their bodies were never found. I believe the planet itself is home to, or possessed by, an evil spirit. I realize how childish that sounds. But it should be sufficient reason for you to not venture to Kolidar. If Uto is there, he is dead.

There were no records concerning the human worldship fleet, the destruction of Earth, or any other related topic. So the words I'd overheard remained a mystery. Of course, Varrank might know more and would never share such intelligence with the likes of a pirate. Crappidy-dappidy. I was in for the duration. The only positive I discovered was that Deerkon was just a hop, skip, and a jump from Pallolo. That leg would only take three months.

I'd done long space voyages before—much longer. That one wasn't a major deal. Plus I had company, such as it was. I kept in touch with Al on *Shearwater* the whole time. I could send messages to my family, but the distances were large enough that I hoped to be done with this trip and back on the cube before they received them. The first nine months were uneventful. Karnean didn't kill me, so that was nice. Ned and I became buddies. Who could resist me for long, right? Between the chores and the card games and the booze, things fell into a comfortable routine. I wasn't having fun, but my existence didn't suck either.

That's when things got complicated. Yeah, with me, complicated was always the new normal. One day, I was hacking into the computer system, mostly out of boredom, when I noticed two unsettling things. One, Karnean had messaged his sister that the deal with Varrank was getting worse. He'd received a message changing the terms, the timetable, and the safeguards Karnean had built into the contract. Two, I detected an impending leak in the fusion drive seals. Nothing was critical yet, but if no one took notice and fixed the seals, the ship would go *boom* in a week, maybe less.

I'd met the entire crew by then. The engineer was only okay at best. His assistants were, however, useless on their best days. Bottom-dwellers, every one of them, with not enough brain cells between them to form one good thought. I couldn't very well waltz up to Karnean and alert him about the seal issue. That would get me a thank you, a torture-session, and a yo-heave-ho off the ship. Neither could I repair the damage. Out of my job description. Plus, it would require shutting down the engines, ejecting the plasma, and doing a big tear-down repair. No way I could do that in secret.

My initial plan, bare-bones to be sure, was to become chummier with one of the bridge crew, a Kaljaxian named Fontelpo. He was the only Kaljaxian onboard and kept pretty much to himself. I knew everything there was to know about the ship and it's systems. If I could get Fontelpo to notice it, the problem would be solved. I invented a story about spending time on Kaljax and spoke to him in Hirn, Sapale's dialect, though I made it sound kind of broken.

I made it a point to mop the bridge during his shifts. I worked my way over to his station and asked, "Hey, brother, would you likes a plate of calrf? You looking hunger."

That got a laugh out of him. "I'm never *that* hunger," he replied. "Why do you think I left Kaljax at such a young age?" We chuckled quietly.

"You know," I said switching back to the Standard language, "I flew one of these ships a few years back. Nice rides."

"They're okay. But I used to pilot a Bernin-8."

I whistled in admiration.

"Yeah, no going back after you've flown the best. They can do three-quarters c in under a parsec, all the while the crew's as comfortable as if they were back in their mothers's arms."

"Impressive. Say," I tapped the plasma pressure indicator, "is that a little low?"

He got a defensive look on his face. "No. It's in spec, sailor."

"Hey," I raised my hands, "no offense, okay. I'm just making conversation here."

"You ever pilot one of these?" he asked pointedly.

"Yeah, sort of—"

"How does one *sort of* pilot a ship. You either did, or you didn't. You're either certified or you're not. Which is it?"

"Fontelpo," I said slipping back into Hirn, "I'm a man talking to another man. Keep your intestines in one place." It was an old expression that meant *lighten up, dude.*

He eased up a bit with the attitude. "Sorry," he said in Standard, "must have been you mentioning calrf. Put me on edge."

We smiled but didn't laugh.

"No problem. I just recall the specs wrong, I guess. I thought if there was a variation in the flow matrix, you know, it was bad."

"The pressure's not related to the flow matrix in a sealed system. There should—" That was all he got out.

"*What* is going on here?" snapped Kayla from behind us. "Mr. Ryan, why are you here? Why are you discussing secure information with my pilot? And why, Mr. Fontelpo, are you discussing it with this man openly?"

Oh boy, was she ever pissed.

"That you both should behave so inappropriately is unforgivable. That you do it on *my* watch is unhealthy."

"Ma'am," he started to say, "I can—"

"Silence. I asked a question of Mr. Ryan, first. He will answer first." I guess I wasn't invisible anymore. I kind of missed it right about then.

I turned and faced her. That didn't make my task any easier. She was gorgeous when she was angry. "I was here doing my job, ma'am. I engaged Fontelpo in conversation to ease the boredom. If that's bad, I'm sorry."

"I'm not concerned with idle chit-chat. What I am concerned with is your meddling in ship's affairs at this level. As my brother obtained you so randomly, I will assume for the time being you are not a spy. But I will know by what right you discuss operational concerns with my bridge crew."

I was in deep doo-doo. "With all due respect, ma'am, I piloted one of these Starliners for several years out of Dalque for a man named Quislor." Yeah, I took a chance making all that up, but that planet was such a mess, records had to be unobtainable. What the hell, I knew the specs of the ship better that she did. Robot brain to the rescue.

"I find that challenging to believe." She placed her arms behind her back. That threw those breasts out even farther. Crap. "The ancillary thruster on the port bow. How many tallards of pressure does it generate, and where does the vented gas arrive from? The wrong answer will cost you your life."

She was tough. "That's a trick question, which I resent." Yeah push back a little, but gently. "There are *two* ancillary thrusters on the port bow. Each generates twenty-seven tallards of pressure. The nitrogen gas is delivered by plastic hoses located just inside the hull. The hull, in case you ask, in this section, is three point seven five centimeters thick, composed of carbona—"

"Enough." She looked at me as if for the first time. "Impressive knowledge for a deckhand. Why is that, Mr. Ryan?"

"Probably because no one asked my qualifications before handing me this mop." I angled it toward her. Man was she a knockout.

"Be very careful, Mr. Ryan, how you answer my next question. Why was a top-rate pilot seeking employment as an able-bodied sailor, and not at his pay grade?"

Good question. Why work for little pay, less comfort, worse hours, and absolutely no respect? Had me wondering. "Ah, ma'am, that's kind of personal."

Her hand moved like a greased cobra. She slapped me across the face so hard I had to make my head spin. "One more remark like that, and I will personally throw you off this ship. Is that clear, Mr. Ryan?"

"Abundantly, ma'am. I didn't look for a pilot's job because I have a drinking problem. A drug problem, too. Sooner or later, usually sooner, my commander figures it out. I'm lucky if they just maroon me on the next station we hit. It's been a problem, ma'am." Yea for me. A *great* bullshit answer.

She moved her jaw around while she thought. "Mr. Fontelpo, your turn. Why were you discussing operations with a swabbie?"

"I wasn't, ma'am. We were discussing theory more than—"

"I heard what you said and it was *not* a theoretical exchange. Mr. Ryan asked you if the plasma pressure wasn't a bit low. You said, and I quote, *No, it's in spec, sailor.* That is classified information, is it not?"

"Yes, ma'am, it is, but it's right here on display where—"

"Mr. Fontelpo, you are relieved. Go to your quarters and remain there until summoned. I will man your post in your absence."

He responded with a barely audible, "Ma'am."

Glad I really didn't like the guy, because I sure just got him in a heap of trouble.

"As for you, Mr. Ryan, as you were. I want this bridge so clean, you'd invite your mother to eat off the floor."

"Yes, ma'am."

"And know that my brother and I will be keeping an even closer eye on you in the future. Neither of us is much of a believer in coincidence or chance."

"Yes, ma'am." *By the way, you're beautiful, ma'am. Permission to steal just one kiss, ma'am.* Nah, even I wouldn't say *that* out loud.

A few hours later, as I lay in my bunk pretending to sleep, Ned rushed in. "Captain wants to see you on the double, mate. I heard what happened, and I don't envy your shoes about now, if you know what I mean."

I dropped to the floor. "Lead the way." Each day of my life could bring such unexpected joy.

Karnean was sitting behind his small desk this time. "Sit, Ryan," he commanded, pointing at a chair without looking up at me first. "My sister told me all about your little revelation and your antics. I'm not pleased. Do you know why?"

"No, sir." I had an idea, but hey I'm a hard-ass. Got a reputation to maintain, even if it's only with myself.

"Because I don't like surprises. I tend to kill surprises. Tell me in as few words as you can why I shouldn't follow my gut and continue that healthy trend."

"You like your ship." I raised a hand and counted four fingers. "There. Four's the fewest I can come up with in a pinch. I was going to say *because you don't want to die along with your beloved sister, suddenly, in space*, but that's," I counted more fingers, "fourteen words. I didn't want to piss you off."

"Well you failed. You have pissed me off. You know I'm about to kill you. With that in mind, do you wish to clarify your flippant remarks in a manner that will alter my plan?"

"Yes, Karnean." Wow, he reacted like I punched him in the nose using his first name. "I'll make you a deal. You don't kill me, and I'll save your life. I think, all things considered, that's a generous offer on my part."

The man was seething. "If you deliver on your promise, I will *spare* your life. If you don't, I will kill you as slowly and as painfully as I can. Deal?"

"Deal," I replied, sticking my hand across the desk to shake on it.

He didn't appreciate the gesture. He glared laser beams at my hand until I withdrew it. "Speak."

"Your fusion drive seals for your main drive. They're about to fail. When they do—"

"I know what that would do. And just how is it you know this very obscure factoid? Surely you don't think I'm going to tear the main engine apart because a drunkard pilot says I should?"

"I told Fontelpo. The plasma pressure quivered a bit. That suggests a variation in the flow matrix, which I could see plain as day on Control Panel Three. Subtle—but it usually is—until it goes boom."

He thumbed the intercom. "Chief Gatly, captain's quarters on the double." He leaned back smiling like a hungry wolf. "We'll see about what you saw, Mr. Ryan. If your information is inaccurate, well, I don't want to spoil your surprise."

What the hell. "I thought you hated surprises, Karnean?"

"There's that new fascination you seem to have with my name. Please lose it quickly. Yes, I hate surprises, unless they're the ones I'm gifting to others."

Someone pounded on the door.

"Come."

The chief engineer lurched through the doorway panting. "You called, sir?"

"This man says you're incompetent and that incompetence is about to cost me my ship, my life, and my dear sister's life."

The look on Gatly's face showed he understood there was a crisis.

"Sir, he's *lying*. The man knows nothing about what he's saying."

"Chief, I haven't told you what he *said* yet." Karnean had a fake happy smile on his face now.

"You don't need to. It's all lies. *Damn* lies, sir."

Kayla stepped into the room. "What, brother dear, is all this noise about? If I don't sleep, I can't perform at my best."

Oh man. She was wearing her pajamas. True, they were long-sleeved men's pajamas with full length bottoms, but ... she was in her almost nighty.

"Kayla, how opportune of you to join us. Ryan here just bet his life that Gatly is such a bad engineer that he's about to get us all killed. Can you believe that? You almost missed the show."

"I'd rather be sleeping," she said, eyeing Gatly and me suspiciously.

"So, Chief, a deckhand says there's a variation in the flow matrix of the main engines due to the impending failure of the main seal. He says he saw this on a display panel he happened to glance at while swabbing the bridge. You, with your superior skill and equipment, will now investigate his claim. Here," he said as he stood, "use my computer."

Dumb with fear and confusion, Gatly tapped some keys and grunted a lot. After a couple of minutes, he said cautiously, "I'll grant that there's a tiny variation, but it doesn't mean the seals are bad. No, sir."

Karnean raised his eyebrows in my direction and asked, "What other causes for this might there be, Chief?"

It took him a second. "Well, there could be a powerful magnetic field causing it."

"Here," asked Karnean, "in the absolute center of nowhere?"

"Unlikely, sir. It could also be a faulty gauge, or a faulty relay to that gauge."

"You could test that from here," I said unhelpfully.

"Is that so, Gatly?" asked Kayla.

"Ye ... yes, I suppose it is."

"Then do it very quickly," said Karnean. "And Ryan, you watch him do so."

In less than a minute Gatly said, "Nah. The relay's sound and the gauge works fine."

"Then, perhaps it *is* the seal?" asked Kayla.

"I'll need to check, sir, but I suspect it might be about to fail." Gatly was so stooped as he spoke, his head almost touched the floor.

"Very well. Gatly. You and your new chief, Mr. Ryan here, set about the arduous task immediately. Before you pull the panel to the seals, however, and please note this carefully: I'd better be standing there behind you. Understood?"

52

We both replied that his point was clear.

"Oh, and Mr. Ryan? You'll be interested to know that Fontelpo will now fill your former position as janitor. I asked him when I reassigned him if he minded the demotion. He said he didn't. But you know what? I think he did. Watch your back. Kaljaxians hold on to grudges like they do their infants."

"Tell me about it, sir." I responded. Swabbie to chief engineer in one fell swoop. Not bad. Not a general again, but not too shabby.

"With your new rank, Ryan, Karnean will be fine."

"Got it, *Karnean*. And please, call me Jon."

"I'm going back to bed," said Kayla.

She turned and walked out—in her *jammies*.

SEVEN

"I understand, but we all knew this was bound to happen. Perhaps this is a bit earlier than our predictions suggested, but such matters are inevitable," said Bin Li. As Secretary General of the UN, he wasn't in charge of anything except that legislative body. But based on the huge role the UN played in evacuating Earth, he was still a powerful figure.

"There are issues that I feel we, as members of the Visionary Council, must address." Amanda Walker was being as tactful as she could be. Admittedly, that wasn't all that tactful. The Visionary Council was the new term for what had been the Security Council. The older term was felt to send the wrong message to non-member worldships.

"Each worldship has sovereign rights, whether the US likes it or not," said Supti Banerjee. The ambassador from the Hindu Worldship Coalition chafed against what she felt was the heavy-handed paternalism of the old bosses.

"Yes, certainly. But the rights of every *individual* on any given ship must also be preserved," Amanda responded. "If a worldship goes off on its own, I cannot condone any individual citizen being forced to do so, also."

"*Sovereign* rights, President Walker, are not contingent on your approval." Supti was digging in her heels. Hundreds of years of foreign domination of her homeland had honed her for this debate. "You can no longer dictate policy to other nations. If a worldship decides upon a new course, they are absolutely free to do so. Cultural standards are no longer subject to first-world dictates."

"I have never *dictated* anything, Madame Banerjee. I resent very much your choice of words. They are inflammatory and not constructive." Amanda was heating up.

"Please don't let us lose sight of our goals and functions. We are discussing important topics. Nothing will be decided upon here. There is no benefit in the rhetoric getting out of hand," said Li, trying to keep a lid on the tension in the room.

"I understand. But in any move forward, I will insist that safeguards are put in place that allow any inhabitant of any worldship to relocate from a ship that is committed to a course of action that individual does not support. I'm talking basic human rights here. I will not allow any political or religious faction to *kidnap* a single person."

"I repeat my contention. You, Ms. America, are free to issue dogma on the rubble that is the Earth today, as you have in the past. Here in space, on our separate worldships, you no longer enjoy such a privilege. If a sovereign political unit decides it is in the best interest of the greater good *not* to allow a citizen to emigrate, then that person will not emigrate. What if, for example, all the doctors and scientists decided to remain with the fleet? The exiting ships would be crippled. Is that what you want for dissenting worldships, to founder and perish?" Supti was so passionate that at the end she stomped her foot on the ground.

"So you favor enslaving the intellectuals on a worldship based on a governmental whim? How exactly is your position different than that of Stuart Marshall? Hmm? He sequestered fertile women. You would sequester smart people." Amanda spoke coolly, evenly.

"How dare—"

"I move this session end in the interest of inter-worldship harmony." Li didn't want to have the two women start a catfight on his watch.

"Bin, she just compared me to the evilest man who ever lived. I will not sit here and be insulted in such a manner."

"You can stand up if you want," Amanda said as snidely as she could. "Or lay down on the floor, if it's more to your liking. I don't want to dictate your *cultural* preferences."

"That is quite enough." said Li, more forcefully than he'd intended. "I will ask President Walker to join me in my office immediately after this session to discuss unrelated, yet critically urgent matters."

Li stormed out without another word, forcing Amanda to walk after him quickly. She did, however, stare at Supti over her shoulder as she exited. For her part, Supti protested loudly to the person next to her while pointing toward Amanda.

Once they were both seated in his office Li asked, "I suppose you're proud of that little spectacle you just put on."

"No, but it sure felt good," replied Amanda with a huge smile..

"I'm certain you know how counterproductive that was?"

"Absolutely. Did I mention the part about how good it felt?" She gestured in the direction of the assembly hall. "That woman has belittled and insulted me personally on the floor and in the media. She has energetically undermined all my efforts to guarantee personal freedoms. She had it coming."

Li twiddled his thumbs in silence a few seconds. "Are you done?"

"Yes, I'm done. So what did you want to talk about?"

"Not a single thing. I just didn't want you two strangling each other. You are, of course, free to do so whenever you like. I just don't want to be seen in the background of those holos. Bad for the UN's image."

"Why, Bin, I didn't know you had a sense of humor. Where've you been hiding it, and why?"

"Political hacks can't afford to display humor. Such a thing, you should consider learning."

"If I wish to become a hack, I'll keep your words in mind."

"Mock me if you will. Please recall it's *my* job to appear impartial and welcoming. I cannot achieve those goals by engaging in my baser desires."

"Another of the many reasons I could never fill your shoes."

"Now that we have resolved our passions, I must ask how Jonathan is doing. He's two years old now, isn't he?"

"Jon is a wonder and a blessing, and he's almost eighteen months. Thanks for asking."

"Mine are teenagers." Bin held up four fingers. "Can you imagine? *Four* teenage daughters in space? I may cast myself into the void before they're married off."

"I'll say a prayer for you and your wife. No, I'll say *four* prayers, one for each challenge."

"I'll take all the help I can get."

"Well, I suppose my adversary has left the scene. I'll be going."

He pointed to the phone on his desk. "The flashing light indicates your supposition is correct. I can now permit you to leave."

"Why you sneaky bastard. You arranged all this at the spur of the moment?"

"No. Never. I arranged the spotters and signal days ago. I knew you two would be at it."

"I hate that I'm so predictable."

"Me, too. Now go. I have a species to keep from killing itself off."

EIGHT

Tiny as it was, I finally got myself a stateroom all to myself. I also had one mortal enemy in Fontelpo, and one only slightly less passionate enemy in Gatly. Life was always easier without enemies, but hey, I'd gotten used to stacking them up like cordwood. It took us a couple of days to tear down the engine. Then came the fun part. Ejecting a large amount of plasma into space was *so* cool. It was an explosion and a light show, all rolled into one. When it came time to pull the final panel, I alerted Karnean, and he joined us. Sure enough, when I exposed the seal, there was a significant gash in it. I underestimated the danger. It would have blown in less than a week if I hadn't acted. I could see in Karnean's eyes that he recognized the significance of the defect, too.

"Well, Jon, it seems you just cost me a tidy little sum."

"Sorry. How do you figure that?"

"I bet my sister that you were a scam-artist buying time, and that the seal would be fine. She took your side."

"I'm flattered she did."

He grinned wickedly. "It was based on the odds I gave her, not her nonexistent opinion of you."

"Will not blowing up ease your pain sufficiently?"

"It was a fairly large wager. I'm still unsure."

"I'll try to make it up to you."

"You can start by getting this engine up and running quickly. There's no profit to be had drifting in space."

Since my promotion, I was expected to eat at the officer's table. There was only a handful of us, so meals were never very crowded. As a result, whoever was there had to pull their weight in making conversation. I'd never been real chatty, but I tried to hold my own. The night I proved the seal was defective provided me an opportunity to speak with Kayla. Even though I was no longer invisible to her, my distinct impression was that she saw me as mostly transparent.

"So, Kayla, you're welcome," I said while mixing around my soup.

"Oh? So I'm to thank you for doing your job adequately?" I think she was startled that I'd addressed her directly.

"No, for the money you made betting on my honesty and technical prowess."

She almost grinned. "Again, am I to start thanking each crew member for doing their job adequately?"

"It wouldn't hurt."

That brought the smallest of smiles to her lips.

"I'll take that under advisement, chief engineer."

"So, where do you and your brother call home?" I knew asking a personal question might be unwelcome, but I wanted to see if I could melt the surface of this ice princess.

She rocked in her chair before answering. "You're aboard our home."

"That's it?" I shot a glance around the room. "Here floating in a tin can?"

"In all its glory."

"But, don't you guys ever stop and spend time on some planet?"

"No."

Okay, that was a terse answer.

"How about you, Jon? What or where do you call home?"

Hey, I got her to be sociable. Cool.

"Lots of places, and nowhere. Same as you, I guess, come to think of it."

"There. See, we do share one thing in common."

"Two. We share confidence in my ability as an engineer."

"Only one. I have no confidence in you at all. You've not earned that, yet."

"I was right about the seals. Your *home* wasn't blown to tiny little pieces by a plasma fireball."

She looked up at me, something she had yet to do in our conversation.

"That is true. I'm still processing what that information signifies."

"Wow, you're a tough woman to please. Most folks are glad to not be incinerated."

"I'm not ungrateful. I am, however, the first officer on this ship. My only concerns are with its safety and the completion of our mission. As someone still alive in a very hazardous trade, I'm cautious to a fault. Therefore, I'm still deciding what the miracle of Jon Ryan represents. You may be a blessing. My experience dictates you're more likely a curse."

"Why would you say that? We just met. In the past people've usually gotten to know me before they consider me a curse."

There it was again. An almost smile. "Because in my years of successful survival, I've never run across a blessing."

"You'll see," I said pointing my spoon at her. "I'm as good as they come, and always great to have around."

She set her utensils down, folded her hands on the table, and looked at me very seriously. "Let us hope that is not the case. If my brother chanced to shanghai an outstanding pilot, engineer, and all around stellar fellow, I'd suspect something was wrong. Supermen are neither found slumming it in a dive bar nor are so easily captured."

She had a point there. I let the others take over the conversation. Inevitably, as it does aboard ship, it degenerated into tales of wine, women, and violent sports. Since no other person present even knew what football was, I clammed up. Kayla's words were helpful. I didn't want to seem too good to be true, and that was easy enough to fix. I knew the skills required of a leader. Integrity, courage, strategic vision, decisiveness, and leadership. A little deconstruction was called for on my part.

The next day I called a meeting of my staff, such as it was. I'd mentioned earlier they were the opposite of the cream of the crop. While still in the sanitation service department, I referred to them as bottom dwellers, with not enough brain cells between them to form one good thought. After having the opportunity to work closely with them, my opinion plummeted much further. There were three assistant engineers, not counting my former boss. Boabdle, Russ, and Wenright. Boabdle went by BB. He was a Yortorina, from a planet orbiting Capella. I mentioned that a lot of the people I'd seen on my quest were humanoid. BB was also, but less human looking than most. He appeared more Neanderthal. Acted like it, too. He clumsily banged into things all the time, grunted frequently, and farted continuously. His grasp of technical matters fell quite short of rudimentary.

Russ and Wenright looked very human, though definitely not the poster children of our species. Russ was thin, beady-eyed, and sneaky. Wenright was of average build and smiled a lot, but there was no way around it, he was as dumb as a ham sandwich. I think of the three losers I was saddled with, he was the only one who ever intended to work. So, Wenright was off limits to me. The other two would perform their only useful service to me by helping prove to Kayla that I was significantly short of being too good to be true.

I began the meeting by asking BB if he'd checked the pressures and capacities of the engine components and the life support systems.

"Wuh-uh-uh-uh? That not part of my job. BB no told do job, so BB not do it. Oomph." Yes, then he farted. Lovely soul.

I walked up to BB and made it a point to touch noses with him. He was roughly my height but was way stockier. "I assigned you to do it three days ago. You calling me a liar?"

He was decisive, I had to give him that much. "Yes, you lie. Hu-hu-hu."

I kicked him squarely where I hoped his testicles were. I believe my guess was correct. He crumbled to the floor moaning like a man whose nuts were just scrambled.

"Hey, you can't do that," Russ protested.

"You want a piece of that action, little man?" I yelled at him loud enough to be heard quite some distance away, which was, of course, my plan.

Russ initially straightened his back in defiance, but quickly lowered his head and said nothing.

BB staggered to his feet, one hand covering his groin. He raised the other over his head. "I kill you for that. Er-ar-argh."

He charged me like a bull. The timing was perfect. Kayla, who I knew had the watch, came around the corner to see what the commotion was. I let BB slam into me like we were playing rugby. He drove me into a bulkhead. I broke his bear hug and kicked him backward. BB threw my foot to one side and flew back at me. He punched me in the chops and I made a show of recoiling.

"Enough," Kayla shouted.

BB either didn't hear her or, more likely ignored her order. He came at me with his hands knitted together to form a club. As he swung them down, I slammed a fist into his gut hard enough to kill most men. He fell to the floor and this time did not get back up.

"What the *hell* is going on here, Ryan?" demanded Kayla.

I pretended to gasp for breath. "Nothing. Just a difference of opinion. We were talking something through."

"That's a lie," Russ howled in protest. "Mr. Ryan here baited BB, then kicked him in the nuts without provocation or warning." Russ pointed at me from a good distance. "*He* started it, ma'am."

Kayla spun on Russ. "Did I address you, crewman?"

He cowered. "Nuh, no you didn't, ma'am, but—"

"Then I suggest you hold your tongue or *I'll* hold it for you. Is that clear?"

"Yes, ma'am." He backed away.

She turned back to me. "My quarters. Now. Wenright, you have the engineering watch. Russ, take BB to sick bay then confine yourself to quarters."

With that she stormed out the door. She didn't wait for either man's belated acknowledgement.

I knocked on Kayla's doorframe, not that I needed to since the door was wide open.

"Come in and shut the door," she said angrily. Once inside, I stood at ease. "Sit down," she pointed to a chair. When I was seated she tore into me. "What just happened? Please know I will take reports from all concerned parties, so do not attempt to lie to me."

"That would never occur to me, K," I said in my best jackass tone.

She was clearly uncertain. She didn't know which act to tear me a new one for, flagrant disrespect or dereliction of duty.

"You are walking on very thin ice, Jon. Be mindful." There was a soft knock on the door. Kayla was instantly annoyed. "Come, but this had better be good."

"No one's ever accused me of being good, little sister. May I join the party?" Karnean responded sticking his head in.

She waved him in. "Shut the damn door," she said.

"What seems to be the problem?" Karnean asked.

"There was a disturbance in engineering." She gestured at me without looking at me. "Ryan here seems to have cold-cocked BB, and then put him in sick bay."

"Sent BB to sick bay?" Karnean said with a thoughtful nod. "Perhaps I underestimated you, Jon. What's left of the last man foolish enough to fight BB is floating somewhere in cold, dark space."

"This is serious, Karnean," said Kayla. "Please don't undermine me with flippancy."

Yeah, flippancy. We were birds of a feather, Karnean and I.

"I shall remain as silent as the dead," he said drawing an imaginary zipper across his mouth.

"Did you strike your subordinate without provocation?" She stared at me impassively as she asked.

"Depends on what you call provocation. I'd assigned him a task, he failed to perform it, and I expressed my frustration to him."

"By kicking him in the groin and then knocking him out, possibly fatally wounding him?"

"Again, it hinges on definitions here."

"Jon, I am growing to like you against my better judgement," said Karnean. "But don't think my sister and I won't punish you severely if you give us cause. Is that perfectly clear?"

"Yes," I said with an inappropriate smile. "Is that all, ma'am?" I said to Kayla.

"For now, yes. But my inquiry is far from complete. You may resume your duties for now. We will, I promise, speak again very soon."

"I'll clear my social calendar so I'm free."

There, one black mark on my otherwise too-good-to-be-true record. One more ought to just about do it.

NINE

The next few days I laid low and behaved myself. Russ only received a reprimand. His record was so ugly that he read a simple slap on the wrist as a positive thing. BB recovered in a couple days and was back in engineering. The weirdest part was that now he and I were the best of friends. In his culture giving someone a good ass kicking was a bonding experience. Whereas before he was sullen and threatening, now he was convivial, cooperative, and deferential. Go figure. He still knew next to nothing about the ship's system and was as useless as a technician, but at least he was pleasant to be around. When Russ observed BB's transformation, he dropped any grudge he might have held against me. He was outnumbered, *and* he was a coward. His path was the one of least resistance.

The reassembled engine worked better than it had before I took it apart, so Karnean was pleased. Kayla? I don't think anything about me pleased her. Maybe she was just a happiness-challenged individual, nothing ever rising to her lofty level of expectation. Oh, well. There were several years left in our voyage, and she was the prettiest girl onboard. That wasn't saying much, because the three other women onboard were from BB's home planet. In my favor was the fact that history showed I grew on people, despite how they felt about me initially. Hopefully, I'd grow on her. The trip would be more enjoyable if I did.

I'd violated the rules of command by demonstrating a lack of integrity and leadership. I'd struck a subordinate and was disrespectful to a superior officer. My next trick would be to demonstrate indecision. I didn't want this to be as flagrant as my first set of transgressions. There was no need to tempt fate excessively. I started out by not filing some periodic reports. Nothing critical, just supply requests and maintenance checks. It took Karnean several weeks to notice some minor reports were overdue. He asked why, and I hesitantly explained that I was holding off for this task or that report, because I was uncertain what the department needed. I also claimed I was unsure if all the routine checks were necessary. That earned me a good chewing out. Perfect. All I wanted to do was place a seed of doubt in their minds. A spy, which of course I was, wouldn't be as sloppy as I'd been. No, I was a demonstrable screw up. Screw ups were never duplicitous. They were too dumb to be.

After that we had several months of smooth sailing onboard. The only hitch in my life was watching out for Fontelpo. He hadn't retaliated for getting him busted, but I knew it was coming. I knew Kaljaxians way too well to doubt it. Every now and then, I'd see him cleaning something disgusting. He pretended not to notice me, but I knew he was seething mad. He had to know that any revenge he extracted on me would lead to severe punishment. Turned out he was smarter than I'd given him credit for. He figured out he wouldn't be a suspect if my death was an accident. Too bad he was only a few percent smarter. Then, he might have been intelligent enough to pull off his caper successfully. I'd always hated stupid people, especially the stupid people who actually thought they were clever. It was trouble on the doorstep every time.

In part, what happened was my fault. I let my guard down too much. For months, I'd used my probes to check the ship's systems and computer records. Since I'd discovered nothing after the failing seals, I began to check less frequently. If I had been more observant, I'd have noticed Fontelpo's sabotage beforehand.

I was midway through an otherwise boring watch in engineering. Gatly and two techs were off duty. Russ was on duty with me, but was unaccounted for as usual. I began a routine check of the main system. Part of that checklist was to pull the panel off the main electrical generator and inspect the couplings. I needed a visual on a set of wires. I figured it must have been BB who did the last inspection, because whoever had done it pushed the bundle too far back to inspect visually. Instead of reaching back with my hand, I sent one probe fiber to retrieve the wires. When there was a tool available, why not use it, right?

As the command prerogative affixed itself to the plastic sheath, there was a sudden, explosive electrical discharge. Contact with the wires set off the grounding of a huge charge, many times the voltage needed to kill a man. Thanks to Deavoriath magical technology, the filament didn't conduct the charge back to me. If it had, even my being an android may not have saved me. I did receive a flash burn to the face, but only a minor one.

The explosion was impressive. Immediately after the discharge, the ship went black. Every light, computer and communication device was down. There were backups for critical systems, but many of them failed due to the size of the surge. *Desolation* was dead in space.

I switched instantly to my low-light mode. My eyes emitted a tiny amount of light and my sensors amplified the heck out of the return signal. I could see almost as well in pitch blackness as I could in full sunlight. I did a quick check on myself and confirmed I was undamaged. Then I attached to the electrical unit to ascertain the damage. The unit was fried, completely fused. There was no specific backup module aboard, but I could patch a temporary fix with materials on hand. I would have hacked into the damage report computer, but it was down, also. I scanned the ship as best I could with my probes. That's how I found the crisis on the bridge.

Artificial gravity went out with the electricity. The ship stopped accelerating when the engines quit. So, anything not secured floated away. That would not have been a problem in and of itself. Unfortunately, one of the forward lateral thrusters froze open when the power blew. The ship began spinning like a pinwheel firework nailed to a fence. At first, the rotation was slow, but it built up rapidly. Within a few minutes, we were spinning like a top. Even I had trouble staying on my feet. Everyone else on board was pinned against a bulkhead. So, everyone on *Desolation* was blind and immobile, but me. I had to save the day.

On the bridge the situation was critical. Several loose metal objects struck a section of the hull so hard there was a tiny breach. The air was quickly venting out. Whoever was up there had little time left. The doors were closed, the opening mechanism was down, and the pressure was dropping dangerously. I manually opened the door to engineering and sprinted toward the bridge. Most hatches in the halls were open, so I made good time. Sure enough, when I got to the bridge, the door was shut. I pried it open. The second I did, the atmosphere around me whooshed onto the bridge.

I steadied myself until the air had nearly equalized and staggered onto the bridge. Only two crewmen were present. The navigator was dead. The decompression pulled him to cover the breach in the hull. Since his body wasn't nearly tough enough to seal the leak, the vacuum of space had basically sucked a huge hole where his chest had been. It was one of the most gruesome things I'd ever seen. The second body was pinned against the far bulkhead. It was Kayla, and she was not moving. If she'd been conscious, she'd be struggling like a rabid badger.

I grabbed hold of a railing with my right hand and used my probes to seize a flat piece of metal. I set that over the hissing breach. It crushed more of the navigator's chest in, but it had to be done. The flow of air decreased significantly but didn't stop. I released my right hand and used my laser to heat up the metal near the hole. Almost immediately the metal bulged into the breach and sealed it.

One problem solved, but the ship was spinning so fast that I could hardly move. I lurched over to the navigator's station and ripped the lower housing off. It slammed against the nearest wall. I knew exactly where the lateral thruster control was. I sent a few probe filaments to it. I also attached filaments to the power supply port in the panel. I gave the unit just enough electricity to fire it up and close the thruster.

The ship still spun viciously. It would slow eventually, but not in this crews' lifetimes. If nothing else, I could fire counterthrusters later on. I wanted to maintain my anonymity just then, so I let *Desolation* rotate. I made my way over to Kayla. My command prerogatives confirmed she was alive. Probably hit her head on the way to being pinned. Her vital signs were fine, so I left her where she was for the moment. Having saved the ship, I then needed to concoct a credible cover story for the impossible feats I'd just accomplished.

I could have closed the thruster from engineering. If I had, I couldn't have sealed the breach.

I'd have to be sure I was the one to remove my metal patch, so no one noticed it was deformed. That wasn't a typical part of my duties, but I could probably manage to be present. How did I close the thruster valve? Crap, that was a tough one. There were several battery packs on the bridge that were used to power the backups. How could I have jerry-rigged them to turn off the thruster in the dark, with the ship spinning? There were flashlights in engineering. I could have used one to see. It was somewhat dubious that I alone had been strong enough to get to the bridge. But I think my explanations might just work.

I ran to the navigator's station and pulled out a set of wires. I crudely attached them to the thruster unit and clamped the other ends to a battery pack. I didn't know if my patch would have actually worked, but it was believable because the thruster had closed. I went back to my station and crammed a flashlight under my belt. Returning to the bridge, I set up a similar looking wire configuration on the counterthruster and attached it to the battery. I then used my probes to fire the thruster for thirty seconds. The ship still spun, but only with a couple of g-forces now. Anyone conscious and stuck to a wall would be joining me soon.

Kayla slid down the bulkhead as the ship slowed. I picked her up and started walking toward sickbay. Luckily I'd tucked the flashlight under one arm. I literally ran into Karnean as he ran toward the bridge.

The first words out of his mouth were revealing. Instead of asking about his sister he cried out "Report."

I filled him in quickly.

"I'll secure the bridge as best I can. After you drop her off, return immediately."

"Sir."

Another lucky break was that the ship's surgeon was okay. I left Kayla with him, promising to restore the power to his area as quickly as possible. I was back on the bridge in a couple of minutes. Several crewmen had joined Karnean. The hull patch still held. I came alongside the captain. "How's it look?" I asked.

"You tell me. Did you wire that panel?" He pointed to my exposed wires.

"Yeah, I didn't know if it would work, but I was able to get enough power to stop the rotation."

"Good work. What's the story there?" he gestured to the dead navigator with a metal plate pinning him to the wall.

"I don't actually know. He was like that when I got here. The hull breach must have sucked him to death, and then the metal panel over on top of the corpse. Some luck."

"We'll see. I'm not much of a believer in luck." He finally got a worried look on his face. "How's my sister?"

"She's alive. Doc took a quick look at her and said he thought she'd be fine."

"We'll see about that too. What happened to her?"

I described how I'd found her. He nodded as he listened intently.

"Seems I owe you a great debt, Jon." He held out his hand and we shook.

"No prob. Glad I could help."

"You get back to engineering and see about getting us some electricity. I'll let you know if you're needed here."

"I assume that panel is sealing the hull breach. I'd like to be here when you repair the hole."

He furrowed his brow. "Why?"

Good question. "There could be some wires or pipes running in the wall there. I'd like to look at the damage, if there is any." There was nothing running in any external wall, but I hoped he didn't know that.

He nodded. "Fine. I'll have them call when they're ready to weld the hole shut."

It took me twelve hours to restore some of the power. It took me another thirty-six hours to get critical systems like navigation and comms operational. The engines would take several days of troubleshooting to get them running. For the first time on my stay on *Desolation,* the crew worked hard and well. I think a near-death situation made team players out of all of them.

Remember how I mentioned that I knew Fontelpo had sabotaged the unit and that he was too stupid for his own good? It ended up being easy to figure out he was the culprit. A few days into the repair work, we got the computers up and running. That allowed the head of security to view the surveillance camera recordings. Guess who forgot there were hidden cameras in engineering? Yeah, a fellow named Fontelpo.

I was present when he got the bad news. Karnean showed him the holo with Kayla at his side, she with a bandage around her head and her arm in a sling. That was the last time I ever saw Fontelpo. You know, after centuries of life and seeing its dirty underbelly more often than I ever wanted to, there weren't too many things that bothered me. Seeing Karnean drag Fontelpo out the door and down the passageway, well even that gave me the willies. I wouldn't have wanted to be him. I watched them disappear wondering just how cruel Karnean could be.

TEN

The ship was busy with repairs for several weeks. As chief engineer, I played a central role. I was important again. Everyone's lives depended on me. If the ship never flew again, we'd drift until we all starved. I'd never realized how much I missed that feeling of mattering. Losing Sapale left a huge hole in my life. My rather dubious quest was so unfocused that I lacked a real sense of purpose. Being the go-to guy again was nicer than I'd have guessed.

Another nice thing was Kayla's attitude toward me changed. Once she realized I'd not only saved the ship but her also, she dropped her stony facade. At meals she chatted with me about trivial matters. If we passed in the corridors, she always said hello, or would at least smile at me. Of course, no *yin* comes without a *yang*. The friendlier she got, the more sullen and suspicious Karnean became. Immediately after the sabotage he treated me like a friend. His mood was positive, and his words to me were supportive, even kind at times. But when he sensed a possible relationship budding between his sister and me, that all evaporated. That was okay by me. I didn't want to date him, only his sister. My rank was high enough that he couldn't interfere with any relationship that might develop, at least not openly.

Six weeks. That's how long it took before we could safely fire the main engines again. I used so much duct tape and chewing gum to hold things together that I should have been awarded a Nobel Prize in ass-saving. But *Desolation* flew again. I had to pirate parts from many nonessential systems. So, the holo-entertainment network wasn't working, the air didn't smell as nice as it had before, and fresh water had to be rationed. But, at least initially everyone on board was upbeat. By the way, no one ever asked what had happened to Fontelpo and Karnean never volunteered that information.

Pallolo was about three and a half years away at that point. I knew I'd be busy the entire time keeping *Desolation* in one piece. My biggest fear was that we'd start running out of replacement parts. There was no Napa Spaceship Parts store between us and our next stop. The only alternative for repair would have been to turn tail and return to Balmorulam. I knew Karnean was aware of that option. The fact he never brought it up was reason enough for me to never mention it. He was a driven man, and raising a topic he didn't want to discuss would be unhealthy for us all.

Months rolled by and the ship settled back into a stable routine. The lack of entertainment became an issue. A few crew members brought handhelds with them. Those had some entertainment content on them, but not much. There were fights when they didn't share, so that resource was stretched thin. In the sailing ships of yore there were no video games, holos, or books to read for the mostly illiterate crews. I didn't know how they occupied their leisure time, but they survived, probably by gambling, fighting, and telling tall tales. Oh, and drinking. We did, like our predecessors, get grog rations. One system Karnean was quite specific about was the still. It *would* be operational. Period. Fortunately, that wasn't hard to do.

My days were divided up into halves. Twelve hours on duty and twelve hours off. Off duty was time to sleep, eat, and kill time. I didn't sleep, but, as before on my adventures, I had to put on a show that I did. I figured five or six hours was enough for that charade. I spent that time checking in with Al, studying the cultures I was surrounded by, and watching 1950s television sitcoms. Yeah, in black and white. *I Love Lucy, Leave It to Beaver*, and an insane British show called *The Goon Show* were tops in my book. *Dennis the Menace*, whose young life closely paralleled mine, was my all-time favorite. But with my overabundant spare time, I watched them all. Al had been loaded with them for my original *Ark 1* voyage and never deleted them. Lucky for me. I wasn't a nostalgia freak in general, so I had no idea such a treasure trove of laughs and giggles still existed. Good stuff.

Mealtime, which I had to fake also, became even more interesting as time passed. Kayla was warming up to me nicely. I came to understand she was tough as nails, both inside and out. But there was also a witty, insightful, and, dare I say, tender aspect to her inner-self that she guarded with walls as formidable as a medieval fortress. The more she allowed me into her private world, the more Karnean resented it. Maybe he was just an over-protective big brother. Maybe he was just mentally unstable. He made it a point to be at the officer's table whenever Kayla and I were there. If possible, he'd wedge in between us physically. It was pathetically obvious, but neither of us mentioned it to him.

She and I would usually sit down first, and then he'd appear as if by magic. I assumed he had someone in the mess alert him when either of us showed up. Before we could get a decent conversation going, Karnean would be there with a huge plate of food, which he rarely ate. It was a signal to us that he was planning on being present at the table for a very long time. He would always steer the discussion to matters of ship maintenance, crew activities, or supply levels, anything as boring and as impersonal possible. I was tempted to use my command prerogatives on him to figure out why he was so obsessively protective of her. But in the end, I figured we had a hell of a long flight ahead of us. Trying to noodle it out myself the old fashion way would give me something else to do. The best example of his worst intervention came about a year after the sabotage. Kayla and I were good friends at that point, but nothing more. Scout's honor.

"You always want to know more about my past," Kayla said with a demure smile. "How about your story? You told me you lived on Cholarazy for a long time. I hear that it's revolting. Where were you born and raised?"

I'd withhold the truth for the time being. If we actually became close, I'd set the record straight. "My old man was a drifter. He dragged my poor mother and me all over creation. My old man said I was born on Meiffol, but he lied a lot, and I don't remember the event specifically."

She giggled.

"We spent time on Dalque before we landed on Cholarazy. The second I could, I split and never looked back."

"Do you miss your parents? I'm sorry, are they still alive?"

"Mom died a couple years after I left. I holo-ed her a couple times. Pops? What can I say? I never tried to contact him, and he never tried to find to me. He could be dead, alive, or midway between the two. I have no clue, and and even less interest."

"I'm sorry to hear that," she responded. "Truly I'm—"

"Hey, there you are, sister of mine," Karnean said as he plopped his heavy tray right between us and sat. "I've been looking for you everywhere. We have a lot to discuss." He turned to me. "Some of it's private in nature. Maybe you should leave?"

"He's *welcome* to stay," she said with emphasis. "There's nothing you could possibly have to say to me that Jon can't hear."

"Okay," he looked directly at me, "if you insist."

"What's so pressing?" she asked.

"Well, it's those damn supply reports."

She raised an eyebrow. "What could possibly be damnable, or even interesting, about a supply report?"

"Our lives are at stake here." He tried to sound huffy. "Those reports are all that stand between us and certain death in cold unforgiving space."

She wagged her head and lowered her arms. "Really? The *supply* reports? What are they going to do, spring to life and repel boarding parties?"

I snickered. That won me a *please-die-now* stare from Karnean.

"Seriously, Kayla, we need to go over them in detail. I have them with me." He reached toward a pocket in his jumpsuit. "So let's get started."

"I will do no such thing, you imp," she responded. "I'm enjoying a meal with a good friend. I'm not about to spoil it studying a ridiculous supply report. If you're so worried, you go over it and send me your conclusions via interoffice mail."

I tried not to snicker again. Really I tried as *hard* as I could.

"Oh, Ryan," he said harshly, "I've been meaning to speak with you. A new part of your job will be to send me updates on the dust levels inside the consoles on all decks. Your first report is overdue as we speak. I suggest you begin your assignment immediately." He eyed my half-eaten meal. "I'll clear your plate for you so you can leave at once."

"Karnean," Kayla said in protest, "you can't be serious."

"I'm captain of this ship, and my orders *will* be obeyed."

"Dust levels inside sealed panels?" She was incredulous.

He turned to me with a hateful look on his face. "I can still see you. That's not a good thing."

If the wacky dynamics between the three of us had remained at that annoying but cute level, the remaining voyage might have been tolerable. But recalling that I worked for a morally bankrupt control freak, such normal behavior was too much to hope for.

Maybe a year later, Kayla and I started developing feelings for one another. Me first, as usual, but I could tell she considered me to be more than just a friend. At mealtime, if I was there first she'd kick her chair over to be right next to me before she sat down. If we passed in the corridors she'd touch my arm or pat me on the back. Those might seem like minor interactions, but this was the ice princess I'm talking about. Trust me, her behavior toward me was radically different from what she displayed toward anyone else, including her brother.

One day after finishing my watch, I entered my room to pretend to sleep. The room was completely dark, but that didn't matter to me. Not only did I have my night vision, but I'd memorized where everything was in the room. I walked toward the head to pretend to use it, but I tripped over something that shouldn't have been where it was. I hit the lights and found I'd clipped a chair leg. Someone had searched my room. They put the chair back almost where it had been, but not quite in the same spot. Breaking into the chief engineer's room was not easy. My security level was as high as anyone's but the Beckzels. I checked and found nothing missing, including some cash I'd won in a card game a few days earlier that I'd left in plain sight. Whoever broke in was looking for information or evidence, not valuables. Fontelpo was long dead. No one else had a reason to rifle my room for such a bizarre reason. No one, except the captain, that was. He left no physical evidence it was him. Any pertinent security camera was offline during the time of the entry. That again suggested it was Karnean since scrubbing holo records was tough to do without proper clearance.

I didn't mention the break-in to anyone, even Kayla. If she confronted her brother, things could blow up quickly. I did set up a hidden camera system of my own, however. Hey, I was the engineer. I could do that in my sleep. I never caught him in my room with the cameras. *That* I did in person a month or so after the first incident. I followed my usual pattern of walking around in the dark. It only took a second for me to pick up someone's heartbeat in the room. The pace was kind of fast, suggesting the intruder was tense.

After I'd walked a few steps, I triangulated my visitor sitting in a chair. Odd. Why relax while invading someone's private space? I hit the lights. There sat Karnean, legs crossed, arms draped lazily over the armrests. The look on his face was passive, like he was waiting for a bus.

"*Hello*, Jon," he said matter-of-factly.

"*Hello*, intruder. Fancy meeting you here where you have no business being."

"You'd prefer it was my sister hiding in wait for you in your room?"

"That's none of your business, captain or not."

"A sound piece of advice. Please allow *me* to determine what *is* and is *not* my business on *my* ship. All right? This," he pointed all around, "is my property. You," he pointed to me, "are my property. I do with what is mine however I see fit."

I elected to hold on the snark and bravado difficult as that was for me. This guy was c-r-a-z-y nuts. "You're off-limits. You know that as well as I do. But more to the point, what are you doing here?"

"I came to deliver a message."

"Because you don't see me enough every single day, so you felt the need to skulk in the darkness of my quarters to deliver it?"

"You push my limits too hard, my friend. I'm neither a kind nor forgiving man. The line in the sand you are toeing is a very dangerous one."

"That's the message?"

He glared at me hard. I think he was deciding if he would kill me there and then. Well, at least he thought he might. I was beginning to welcome the thought of wringing his pencil neck.

Finally he eased back in my chair. "No. I came to give you the one warning you will get. Leave my sister alone. She *is* off-limits."

"Did she send you to tell me this? No, wait. She's a big girl. If she wanted to say that, she'd have done it herself. Let me rephrase. Does she even know you're here?"

"That is beside the point. You will avoid all non-essential contact with her. End of story or end of Jon."

"No problem. Please note my definition of essential is probably wildly different from yours."

"One more cute remark and I'll have your tongue."

"Look, I saved your ship not once but twice. I have this bucket of bolts running better than it ever has despite serious sabotage. I think that buys me a bit more discretion from my grateful captain."

"In all professional matters, you have my full esteem. When it comes to Kayla, you have zero."

"Why don't you let her decide how she leads her own life?"

"Out of the question. Jon, this is *not* a discussion. And this is your only warning."

I made no reply. I wasn't going to agree to his demands, but mouthing off wouldn't help either.

He rose and walked to the door. "Oh, a word of advice. Don't mention this conversation to her. If you do, you will find out precisely what happened to Fontelpo."

It didn't take Kayla long to figure out I was acting much cooler toward her. Within a week she said to me at dinner, "So Karnean warned you to stay away from his sister, didn't he?"

"Huh?" I said through a mouthful of stew.

"You wouldn't be the first, and you won't be the last." She ripped at a piece of bread looking away thoughtfully. "He just disappears the enlisted men. They're easy for him. But when I so much as say bless you to an officer who sneezes, he goes all psycho."

"Tell me about it."

"Oh, and I know he told you he'd kill you if you revealed your secret. He always peppers that in, the son of a bitch."

"Does what? Tells the officers or kills them?"

"Very funny."

"I wasn't actually angling for funny, just survival."

"A few have mentioned it to me after they left *Desolation*'s service. I don't think he's needed to kill any yet."

"Gee, maybe I'll be the first. A man's gotta push for the undone."

She sighed. "No, Jon, you won't. You and I will return to a strictly professional relationship, and I'll add one more grievance to my list against my brother. That's how it always goes."

"It hasn't gone there with me."

"It will. I'll see to it. Look, I like you. The last thing I want is for either of you to end up dead."

"Why do you put up with him? I know he's your brother, but you're good. You could command your own ship. Why put up with his abuse?"

"You wouldn't understand." Her voice was distant.

"I might surprise you."

"I made a promise to our father I'd look after him, that's why."

"He's a good pilot. He has his own ship. He doesn't *need* you."

"He does. Not to fly from point A to point B. He needs me to stop him from self-destructing. I cite this very scenario as an example."

"I say let him fall on his face, if that's his passionate wish."

She was quiet a moment. "I made a promise. My father knew his son was too hot-headed to survive without me around to bridle him in, now and again."

"At the sacrifice of your own happiness, your own life? That's a lot to ask."

"Yes, it is. But I swore an oath." She shrugged. "My life isn't that bad."

"No. How could it be? You get to fly impossibly long, dangerous missions with your psycho brother, knowing you'll never be able to get close to another living soul. Where do I sign up?"

"Mocking me doesn't actually help."

"What would? I'll do it."

She sniffed loudly. "Returning to your job and doing it well. That, Chief Engineer Ryan, is all I require of you."

"It's your funeral. Who you hand the shovel to is your call."

"Has anyone ever told you that you're a hopeless romantic?" She smiled sadly.

"No, I don't believe anyone ever has."

"Good, because she'd have been a fool or a liar if she had."

"You're awfully narrow-minded. What about all my male admirers?"

She giggled. "If any man expressed feelings for you, you'd run screaming from the room."

I pointed to her with my little finger. "Hey, I'm a sensitive, new-age guy. *We* never run when complimented by a member of our own sex."

"I believe that as much as that you're going to stop pressing me for my affection."

I furrowed my brow. She was good.

ELEVEN

Two boring, companionless years later, we arrived at Pallolo. Looking out a porthole, I hated it immediately. I was two years into a pissy-ass mood, and I hated everything. I had to remind myself that every time I saw, heard, or thought about Kayla or her evil brother, I was on a mission to save the worldship fleet. I'd never have been on *Desolation* if that wasn't the case. But if I had sailed on her for some other reason, I'd have killed that loco Karnean on general principle long ago.

After such an epic voyage, shore leave was mandatory for the entire crew, even the shanghaied ones. Karnean set out a leave roster. About a third of the crew was released at a time. Each party was given two days ground time. We didn't know how long we'd be in port, but if time allowed, the rotations would continue so everyone would get several turns. People like me, with a high likelihood of flight, were fitted with an explosive ankle bracelet set to go off in three days. If we tried to skip out on Karnean, we'd be blown to bits a day into our freedom. Sloppy, but effective. I could have removed mine with my probes, but I was in for the duration, so why bother? I did consider removing it and handing it back to the smug son of a bitch, just to see the look on his face. But as a mature and responsible spy, I elected not to.

No snickering.

I had complete freedom to come and go, because I needed to acquire so many parts and pieces destroyed by Fontelpo's sabotage. My ankle bomb was still set for three days, so I had to check in with the boss often. But it was nice to just wander the streets. It was also nice to spend someone else's money by the fistful. I labeled my purchase of overly-high-end equipment my *mini-revenge*. It turned out that on Pallolo, like so many other busy ports, I could have all kinds of personal supplies listed as essential equipment, if the price was right. So some of the "wires, assorted" were cases of local hooch. Boxes of "computer boards, assorted" were full of, you guessed it, local hooch. Hey, I was looking at a long flight ahead.

It ended up only taking four days to load the ship. I was done stocking replacement parts in less time. So we were struck in port two more days, waiting for the last third of the crew to get their full leave. Karnean was a heartless bastard, but even he knew shorting a third of the crew on shore leave would lead to big-time trouble. Everyone needed to, and would, get their full share of booze, tail, and altercations. Some things never changed for ship crews of any era.

We lifted off for Deerkon in less than a week. Along with all the original crew, Karnean had a few more unconscious conscripts. The man had a bad habit of doing that, it turned out. I think he had significant boundary issues. He told me normally he wouldn't have had to resort to that method, but he needed more crewmen. If he told anyone where we were going, he knew he'd get zero volunteers, so why bother trying, when his method was working so well?

The three-month voyage to Deerkon was a blur for me. I had so many systems to repair, replace, and rewire that I was busy nonstop. That was fine. The less time I stressed over Kayla, the better. On the rare occasion when I thought about her, I'd keep asking myself something along the lines of, *what was I thinking*. Hooking up with a vagabond pirate, joined at the hip with her sociopathic brother, would be the last thing I needed. No future meant there should be no present. I was too old and otherwise committed to get involved with a fling. Maybe I'd post a picture of Sapale in my cabin to help reinforce that notion. I knew if I kept repeating those things over and over in my head, sooner or later I might even start believing them.

A month out, I started to get the strangest feeling. Dread. I'd never felt it before, but I knew that's what it had to be. It may come as a surprise that I'd never felt dread before, but I have two words for you by way of explanation.

Fighter pilot. Yeah. Fighter pilots were dread-resistant, if not downright dread-proof. But, I felt it where my stomach would have been—a crawling feeling. I tried to convince myself it was just because I'd read Kymee's maudlin report concerning Deerkon. But that wasn't the case. I could see it in my shipmates, too. They were all getting jumpy. Well, all except BB. He was BB, and was bolstered by my copious hooch.

Karnean got—as if the universe needed such a thing—more testy and more difficult to be around. He'd issue an order, retract it, only to reissue it angrily ten minutes later. Once he yelled at Kayla on the bridge. I knew it wasn't my imagination then. Deerkon *was* a place to avoid at all costs. Something was very wrong about that planet.

Our anxiety and sense of foreboding were interrupted about a month out of Pallolo. We were attacked by three pirate ships. How ironic. Pirates attacking pirates. There was no honor among thieves, that much was certain. One of the ships had left port just after us. That wasn't so odd. That they were heading to Deerkon was something Karnean should have noted. The other two ships had accelerated around to position themselves in front of us and lie in wait. Once we were close enough, they fired up their engines and trapped *Desolation* in a triangle.

Karnean ordered what we called "an immediate Z." That was when the ship burst to maximum speed directly up from the three enemy ships. Picture a *fast* elevator. When being chased by pirates, one factor was always in the intended victim's favor. The booty they sought was of no value if it was blown up. They wanted to take the ship intact, or at least in big pieces. Anyone who's seen a pirate movie knows the drill. We run and try to destroy them. They chase and target our engines. They noticed that we were heavily armed, but maybe they also knew, as I did, the value of our cargo. Great risks yielded great rewards.

As *Desolation* sprinted upward, I really wished I'd brought a spare membrane with me. But, alas, we'd be doing it the old fashion way. All three enemy ships were smaller and should have been faster. The modifications Karnean had installed on *Desolation* mostly negated that. Even before we achieved maximum velocity, we were firing missiles at our pursuers. They were nimble little curs and they dodged them all. Karnean sent back the equivalent of depth charges, missiles set to explode at a given point, not on contact. That probably shook a few things off their shelves, but it didn't slow any of them down.

Pretty soon it was clear they would overtake us. They were too fast, and we were too heavy with cargo. The first of their missiles missed by a good margin. Then they hailed us. Karnean refused the hail. He knew what they wanted. He also knew that even if they spared the crew, his life and his sister's were forfeit if the enemy took *Desolation*. He had no reason to surrender.

Their next volley was fired with deadly intent, not as a shot across our bow. They fired warheads with no explosives, designed to make impact with the engines and disable them without risking damage to our cargo. That kind of precise targeting was hard, but if they were good little pirates, they had a lot of experience and a lot of missiles.

Karnean released countermeasures. Basically, that was scrap and waste metal. A thick enough cloud of hard debris would destroy a missile. His luck was marginal. A few stopped well short of us, but even more whizzed by only narrowly missing us. They were gaining ground. Soon their proximity would improve their aim sufficiently to find their mark. Karnean launched an impressive number of missiles at them.

Boom. Finally he took out one ship. We only cheered briefly before we all remembered the other two killers out there, who were now pissed off killers.

When the enemy was a few thousand kilometers away, they landed their first hit. A huge thud rattled the ship as an ancillary engine exploded. *Desolation* had three engines. One main engine was directly at the stern. Two additional engines were mounted on winglets, near the base. We'd just lost one of those. Fortunately, it was far enough away from the hull not to do any real damage to the ship itself. But now we were slower, much slower.

Within seconds, the remaining enemy ships split up and raced past us. They turned in tight arcs to circle back on either side of the ship. We fired a flock of weapons at each. One ship took a glancing blow. The explosions ripped open the hull and black smoke billowed out, streaming backward due to her momentum. The ship careened to the side but held together. There was no way to know the state of her crew, but the ship itself was out of the fray for good.

Just when it seemed we might be that lucky, several massive impacts rained down on *Desolation*. I had one probe attached to the ship, so I knew the second ancillary engine was gone and that two missiles had taken off most of the main engine. Two others ripped through the hull and shot out the opposite side back into space. The bulkhead seals precluded an explosive decompression, but several sections were lifeless.

Desolation shimmied and lurched sideways, her controls ineffective. The last enemy vessel eased alongside and hooked us with a grapple. They were clearly trying to gently bring us to a stop. They were too close to fire on, even if we'd had any missiles left. It was the old repel-boarders drill for us. Oh, boy.

Karnean screamed orders, trying to organize damage control and fire control, while at the same time assembling an armed defense.

He called me in engineering. "Any chance you can bring the engine back online in the next five minutes?"

"None. Zero. They fried the main engine. We're dead in the water."

"Can we get the crew trapped on the other side of that breach forward to help repel boarders?"

"I'm working on it, but don't count on them. Not sure if any are alive, in the first place."

"Shit. I've only got fifteen men. I can't put out fires and defend the ship." He breathed heavily a few seconds. His voice boomed over the entire ship. "All hands, abandon whatever you're doing and come forward to repel boarders."

That meant the fires would continue. In a few minutes, they could grow too big to put out. *Desolation* looked ... wait. Al. *Shearwater* was only a few thousand kilometers away.

Al, I said in my head, *Priority One alert. Target the smaller vessel near* Desolation *with the rail cannon and take out her nose immediately.*

I heard his *Aye, aye,* at almost the same instant I heard the other ship fly to pieces. *Desolation* shook mightily, but held together.

85

Karnean was on the intercom immediately. "What just happened? Jon, do you know what happened? Was that us?"

"Not sure. I think the enemy just blew up."

"I can see that, you idiot. Why? Why did the fore section suddenly explode?"

"No clue, Captain." *Why don't you ask them,* I thought to myself.

"Get up here on the double." Overhead, he yelled, "All hands. Return to fire control. The enemy ships are all destroyed. Repeat. All hands return to fire control stations."

I sprinted to the bridge. Karnean and Kayla were standing at the controls, butt-to-butt, leaning against one another for support.

"Jon, are you all right?" asked Kayla.

Before I could speak Karnean yelled, "Belay that. Get over here, now."

I did.

"Look," he pointed out the view screen, "that last ship was torn to shreds. I want to know why."

"Why you asking me?" I replied.

"Because that's not possible. Around here, when something impossible happens, I think Jon Ryan."

"We probably hit her somewhere along the line, and her fuel cells finally ruptured. How should I know? I'm not the pirate here."

Wow, that brought a mean look to his face. I guess I wasn't supposed have figured that out. "If her containment failed, she'd be on fire. She's not. Her nose was just torn off."

"When we're secured, I'll send a team to investigate."

"You damn well will. Now get out of here before I do something you'll regret."

Geeze what a grouch. Third time I'd saved his ass, and he all he wanted to do was kill me. How totally unreasonable.

Within a day, we'd put out the fires, sealed the hull breaches, and freed the trapped crew. In the end, we'd lost twelve shipmates. BB was gone. I would mourn him. Gatly and Russ were also killed. That meant Wenright and I were the only engineers left. I think that's why Karnean decided to let me live. He needed me too much. Wenright might be adequate to fix a leaky faucet, but not to rebuild an entire ship with few resources. But, man o man, was Karnean hard to live with after the attack. The cursed space around Deerkon wasn't enough. Now he imagined, correctly but unfairly, that I was the mysterious savior of his ship.

If what I did after Fontelpo's sabotage was incredible, what I did to *Desolation* over the next two months was truly miraculous. Between our shuttle, the parts from the two non-incinerated enemy ships, and what was left of our main engine, I got us moving. We moved slowly, but we moved safely. Deerkon was now another four or five months away. But we were alive. Plus, at that short range, we could call for a tugboat to meet us. With their help, we'd make Deerkon only a month behind schedule. Couldn't wait to make it to the Land of the Lost.

TWELVE

"Dolirca, there you are. You're difficult to locate," Toño said as he entered the library, where she sat reading.

"Dr. DeJesus, how nice to see you," she responded coolly. "I doubt I'm hard to find. We live in such a small community, after all."

"I suppose. It's just that everywhere I heard you were, you turned out not to be."

"Well, you've certainly found me now, Dr. DeJesus. What might I do for you?"

"To start with, you can call me Toño, or Bodo, as you did when you were too young to pronounce it correctly. The only one who referred to me by my proper title was your grandmother, when she was angry with me. Not a common occurrence, but painful nonetheless, when she employed it."

"I shall stay with what I'm comfortable with, if it's all the same to you. I assure you I am neither my grandmother, nor unhappy with you."

One of the Toe growled ever so quietly.

"Whatever. I needed to touch base with you regarding your annual physical. You're almost two years behind."

"Thank you for your concern, but I'm feeling quite well. I'm certain your time is better spent administering to the ill and preforming scientific tasks."

"I agree. But the council mandates annual physicals for everyone. They provide for no exceptions. I didn't make the rule, I just follow it."

"I shall bring the matter up with the council at the earliest possibility. Now, if you'll excuse me, I have some important research to continue." She pointed to the books in front of her.

"I'll excuse you after your physical. If you're uncomfortable with me doing it, I'm certain Dr. Jaswar-Ser would be glad to accommodate your brutal schedule. She's on duty as we speak."

"Dr. DeJesus, I am well versed in the rules set forth by the council. There is no provision for forced physical exam or treatment contained in those provisions. I will not be compelled to participate in any act I do not voluntarily submit to. Now good day."

Both Toe growled loudly.

"What is your problem?"

"I resent that an alien machine accuses me of having a problem, simply because I don't consent to its whim."

"Young lady. Please do not put me to the test. I'm older, wiser, and much more experienced than you are. I am acting well within the purview of my office. I resent very much you referring to me as an alien. We both live here. Neither is capable of being alien. Moreover, that you refer to me as a machine is clearly intended to hurt my feelings. I don't deserve such bad treatment from a scamp I personally brought into this world."

"I did not intend to hurt your feelings, if you actually have them. You *are* a machine. That is a matter of common knowledge. You are the only non-Kaljaxian currently on planet. Hence, you are an alien. There is no shame in such a status."

Toño was torn as to whether to escalate the situation or acquiesce and regroup. One of the Toe stepped between Dolirca and him.

"Two," she snapped, "back to your place."

The Toe quickly backed up to where it had been.

"Dolirca, I must say, officially, that I'm concerned. Your behavior is hostile and unwarranted. Your Toe behaved in a manner that may not be safe for the public good. Unless you can explain to me why I shouldn't, I will request a formal inquiry from the council."

"Dr. DeJesus. I'm certain you misinterpret my words and have formed unjust opinions as to my actions. If you find some aspect of my existence reprehensible, then it is your duty to do with that opinion whatever you'd like. Now, and for the last time, good day."

She turned and hunched over her books. Both Toe inched closer to her standing directly at her back.

Later that day, Toño sought out JJ.

"JJ, I must speak to you in private," he said seriously.

"Sure. There a problem?" asked JJ.

As they walked to a private space, Toño said, "I wouldn't ask for privacy if there wasn't a need for it."

"Is it my VD test results? They're positive. Crap. Doc, I didn't even touch her."

"Sit," Toño pointed to a chair, "son of Jon Ryan. I come concerning an important task."

"What?"

"I followed up on your request and met with Dolirca."

"Ah-ha. Now I see why you have that constipated look on your face. I get it every time I'm near her."

"What's happened to her? I must admit I haven't followed her life much lately, but some very large and active bug has taken up residence very high in her butt."

"Tell me about it."

"When did this behavior begin, and more importantly, do you know why? Is she unhappy in her marriage?"

"She started getting funny three or four years ago. It can't be her marriage. Her brood-mate isn't unhappy. He's too afraid of her to be unhappy." He chuckled grimly. "Poor bastard. Bit off more than he could chew, hooking up with Dolirca."

"Is that the problem?"

"Nah, I don't think so. She controls Burlinhar, yes. But I get the impression she wants to control everything. He was just the closest and easiest to put under her thumb."

"Control everything? What does that mean? She's on the council, but she's not even the head of that. You are."

"You wouldn't know it watching her highness at a meeting. She acts like we exist only to serve her. It's pretty annoying, actually."

"This is distressing."

"Ah, *yeah*. Tell me about it. She torpedoes anything a rational council member suggests. If she had more than one vote, we'd never get anything accomplished."

"Is she forming a coalition?"

"Not yet. She's too globally abrasive. I am worried she'll ease back on her prim attitude, and then she will gain a following. If she does, I honestly think we're in for trouble."

Toño was quiet several minutes. "This is precisely what your mother feared happening."

"How so?"

"She was worried sick that the baser side of Kaljaxian politics and personality would resurface and destroy Azsuram."

"Aren't you being a little dramatic, Doc?"

"You didn't grow up there like she did. It was a valid concern on her part, if you ask me."

"What can we do?"

"Wait and see."

"What, you mean wait for Dad to return and see how pissed he gets?"

"No, though I'd pay good money to hear his first words to the brat."

They both laughed.

"No, for now, we let the infrastructure your mother worked so hard to put in place do its job. There are checks and balances, diluted power, and redundant oversights on all aspects of the government. She built the system to withstand just such an assault. It will work."

"Let's hope it does. Dolirca really freaks me out."

"Let's pray your father returns soon, too. I'll rest easier when he's around."

THIRTEEN

I found out that the term of service for a shanghaied engineer who was hated by his psycho captain was surprisingly open-ended. When we finally entered orbit over Deerkon, I was ordered to remain with the ship while sufficient repairs were effected that would allow *Desolation* to safely land. Okay, that was understandable, if not welcome news. We slaves, we had to be a flexible lot. Once we did land in Monzos, a major star port city, Karnean told me I had to oversee the main repairs before I left the ship. Harsh, but whatever.

Luckily, I could hire locals to help speed the repairs, so they moved along faster than if I did them all myself. When the work was completed a few weeks later, he said I could have leave like the rest of the crew, but I would still be required to wear the ankle bomb. I'd have been pissed if I were actually captive, but I had to remind myself I was a spy and was there of my own accord.

As the day neared that I'd get to get off the ship I took a risk—a Jon risk. Yeah, an unreasonable, unnecessary, and unjustifiable one. I slipped Kayla a note asking her to meet me for dinner in a restaurant named The Jury's Out the second day of my leave. Odd name for a restaurant, but, trust me, there were worse sounding places on that awful planet. Some were downright creepy. That way, even if Karnean had me followed, I could lose my tail and rendezvous with her secretly. If she didn't show, well then, I knew where we really stood.

As I walked the streets of Monzos I got a much clearer picture of Deerkon than I'd have ever wanted. Kymee was right. Avoid the planet. Even on casual inspection something was terribly wrong with the entire city. If I took a photograph and showed it to someone, they'd say the city was rough but advanced. Skyscrapers abounded, the streets were packed with vehicles, and pedestrians scooted to and fro. There was little in terms of aesthetic appeal. No fancy buildings, very little vegetation, and no parks. I never saw a single park. But the city's oddness extended well beyond that. It was the dirtiest-looking clean place I'd ever seem. It was as if I imagined dirt that wasn't there. I know, *weird*, but that was the best way I could explain it.

Then there were the citizens of Monzos. Back on Earth, the streets of New York had a reputation for being unfriendly. New Yorkers were *kumbaya* and *come here and give me a hug* compared to this dump. No eye contact, of course. Scowls on every face, for sure. But there was an underpinning of anger, hate, and loathing in the space around everyone. Whether I was on the sidewalk, at a store, or in a bar, everyone's dislike of everything was palpable. My skin crawled continually, even though Toño hadn't designed in that function. To blend in better, I tried to look as mean and ornery as I could. Normally, I'd like to think I could look pretty badass. But I could tell my acting brought even more contempt from the real pros of Deerkon. They saw a phony and detested me even more for being so soft. Horrible place. Don't *ever* go there.

My goal right off the bat was to determine what threat might face the worldship fleet. I'd heard possible mention of that by whoever abducted me for the trip to Deerkon. It was easily possible this evil planet was involved. I had no other leads as to what those two bozos driving me to Karnean's ship were talking about. I easily hacked a few local computers, but found no mention about anything related to humans or Earth. Not too surprising, in retrospect. Dive bars and greasy spoons were unlikely to be involved in covert operations or high-level criminal networks. I went to a few public buildings, hoping a governmental association might reveal something. Nada. I developed a pretty clear picture of the wretched planet, but none of my keyword searches were mentioned anywhere.

So, either I'd wasted three plus years and a whole lot of dignity on a wild-goose chase, or the information I sought was highly guarded. That meant I had to gain access to the computers of someone in power, a real mover and shaker. With no connections, friends, or leads, that would be tough. I couldn't just walk up to the front door of a VIP's office and ask to use the bathroom. That led me back to Karnean. He was delivering blackmarket goods to a very shady character. Maybe I could tag along.

But my captain hated my very existence. Why would he invite me to join him on a highly secure meeting? He wouldn't. Maybe Kayla would? But why would she? She might care for me, but she wasn't stupid. "Hello, Mr. Crime Boss. This is my date for the evening, Jon. He's just here for the hors d'oeuvres, so pay him no mind." Not very likely.

What reason could I give them? I knew what we were delivering, to whom, and when. I'd seen mention of the recipient, Varrank Simzle. He was not an elected official, but he controlled a large part on Deerkon—roughly a third of the planet. There were no specific notations as to what line of work he was in, so I assumed it was the kind of profession one didn't mention. If I went around asking about him, I'd likely end up very dead, very quickly. If I could find something out about Varrank that might interest Karnean, maybe he'd want me along for the big meeting? Long shot? Hey, that was my middle name.

On a whim, I went to what would be classified as a church in my culture. I say that reservedly, because there was no religion on Deerkon. Big surprise there, right? There were organizations of a less dubious nature than others, at least outwardly. That was as altruistic as groups got on that planet. I located the main offices of the Collective for Gains. Their mission statement mentioned the words *better living* and *honesty*. It was the only organization I could identify with a positive message.

Immediately upon entering, there was an imposing desk preventing my entry past its bulk. It was like the stereotype of an old-time police station entryway, the ones with a stern sergeant greeting everyone with disgust. In this case, the sergeant's role was played by a withered old man seated behind bars, flanked by two very large guards. The Collective for Gains was not a touchy-feely bunch of softies, it would seem.

Before I could take my second step into the foyer the old man barked out, "Business here."

"Ah, hello," I said uncertainly. "my name's Jon—"

"Do you have business here today, or not? The question is a simple one."

"Yes," popped out of my mouth unexpectedly. "Yes, I do."

"Name?"

"As I started to say, my name is Jon Ryan."

He scanned a piece of paper. "Meaningless. Leave, or the authorities will be summoned."

That was probably good advice. But was I known for my ability to accept good advice? No. I got hot when treated rudely. My motto was, *don't get mad, get even.*

"Name?" I said imperiously.

"We are done speaking. You have been warned to leave."

"I said I will have your name. I am not leaving, and when I complain to Rel Martantor, he will know who insulted his cousin." I could *not* believe what was coming out of my mouth.

The name, which I discovered reading their public records, did strike a chord with Mr. Grumpy.

"I was unaware Rel Martantor *had* a cousin. This seems most … irregular."

"Why is it that you would know his family history? Are you given to the investigation of matters that do not concern you? I'm certain Rel will find that practice most intriguing. Most intriguing, indeed."

On a planet Kymee considered damned, punishment had to be swift and certain. The old geezer knew that if I was on the level, he was on thin ice. Hey, all I wanted was to get close enough to his computer to hack it. I could do it from where I stood, if he wasn't watching me like the last dessert on the counter at a church social.

"If you insist," the jerk said, "I will call His Honor's office and confirm your claim. I must warn you that if you're lying, your punishment will be severe."

"I *insist* you check my story out. And I don't mind standing here in the doorway, uncomfortable and looking like a beggar off the streets. Please," I held up a hand, "pay me no mind while you check."

Indecision crossed his old eyes. Yeah, he got the message. If I was wrong, it didn't matter that he'd shown me a little misplaced deference. If I was correct, he'd be literally digging himself a deeper grave by showing overt disrespect.

"Chum," he snapped to one of his guards, "bring that man in and seat him there," he pointed to the corner nearest the counter. "Broll," he said to the other guard, "offer him some refreshment. Both of you watch him like he's about to steal your children."

I had no idea how long it would take for him to find out my story was fake. Maybe I had five minutes. Probably less. I'd just as soon not blast my way out of the place. A paranoid planet like Deerkon had to have cameras everywhere. I sat down and Broll growled, "You want dishell?"

That was the local equivalent of tea.

"Sure, but make certain it's hot. I hate cool dishell." I'd never tried the stuff. I figured there'd be one less set of eyes on me a while longer, if he had to do more heating. Plus, I kind of liked being a prick in this setting.

I crossed my legs and made a show of being impatient and put off for Chum. He towered over me glaring down intently. I wasn't going to do a lot of snooping with him like that.

"Chum," I said pinching my nose, "do you bathe at all? You smell like a rotting foot."

Poor guy, he got an even stupider look on his face than he had before. "I take bath last week."

"Well, do a better job this week." I gestured to a spot several meters away. "Stand over there, before I pass out. Really, I can't believe my cousin allows such slovenliness to exist." No, he wouldn't have any idea what a big word like that meant, but he'd know it was something bad.

Chum vacillated a moment, then turned and walked away.

That was just the break I needed. I slipped one probe fiber up his pant leg. *Sleep. You must sleep*, I thought to myself.

Chum barely made it to a chair before he was out like a baby. I could still hear Broll in the next room, clinking some glass. I sent the same fiber to the computer where the old man had sat. I downloaded their entire database within thirty seconds. Broll entered the room just as I retracted the fiber. At first, he didn't notice the sleeping giant in the room. After handing me the cup of dishell, he realized Chum wasn't accounted for and scanned the room. He quickly located his coworker in the chair.

"What have you done?" he howled to me lunging for my neck.

"What. He's asleep?"

That stopped him for the moment.

"Go check yourself. He said you could watch me while he took a nap."

Broll looked back and forth between Chum and me several times. Then fortunately, he decided to check on his companion. He walked over and kicked Chum's feet very hard.

Chum exploded awake with a gasp and vaulted to his feet. "Hey, why you do that?" he said to Broll.

"You sleep again at job. You fired if they catch you. Then who feed my sisters?"

Ah a tender family moment. Thanks, boys, for sharing.

"Hey, you," I called out to Broll, "this dishell is ice cold. Heat it up immediately." I held the cup up high.

He lumbered over while growling. Just before he took the cup from me, I dropped it. After drenching my lap, the cup crashed to the floor.

"You clumsy fool," I yelled. "Look what you've done." I slapped at my wet clothes. "Where's the bathroom? I can't present myself to Rel Martantor looking like this. Demons in Brathos, one of you sleeps on the job, and the other tries to drown your honored guests."

My not so veiled threats worked. "Sorry, mister sir," Broll said bowing rapidly. "Bathroom here. I show." He extended an arm out of the room.

I knew, from my hack, the bathroom had an exterior window. Perfect. When we arrived and he started to enter, I slapped his chest. "I believe you've done enough damage already."

I slipped out the window without delay and hurried out of sight. Man, I was pissed. I really wanted to see what happened with those three stooges when Rel Martantor asked that the imposter they'd caught be brought before him. Oh, to be a fly on that wall.

FOURTEEN

"Mandy, there's not a hell of a lot we can do about it. Do you want us to open fire on them?" Heath was trying to be helpful. He wasn't doing a very good job of it.

"Of course not. I'd be no better than Stuart Marshall. But I can't stand by and let them do this." Amanda was trying to remain calm. She wasn't doing a very good job of it.

"It's not like their worldships are going to vanish. Duh. Kind of big for that. Plus, they said they haven't decided to choose a new destination. They just want a defined space and some elbow room."

She crossed her arms and glared at her vice president. "I read the release, too. I know what they said, and I have a pretty good idea what they meant. I'm glad they didn't close their borders. That would be a defining problem."

"Define *defining*."

"It would mean we would be more likely to respond in deed, not word."

"Mandy, honey, they know you'd be bluffing. Supti Banerjee hates your guts. She'd actually love for you to do something, so she can react and make you look inept."

"We could follow them. That way they couldn't have the satisfaction of leaving us," said Gary Paquette, Amanda's newest chief of staff.

"Nah. That wouldn't work. They'd head somewhere other than Azsuram and prove we're idiots," responded Heath.

"Humanity would remain together. That's more important than saving face if you ask me," replied Gary.

"It's an option, but not one I currently favor." Amanda slapped her palm on her desk. "You know what really fries my bacon? We just dodged a bullet from the Berrillians, and here they want to wander off on their own. Splitting up makes us all more vulnerable, especially the Hindu Worldship Coalition. A dozen ships are a sitting duck, even for a conventional enemy."

"No one ever accused political leaders of being farsighted or wise," Heath said.

"Present company included or excluded?" she replied with a smile.

"I'll leave that determination to history."

"Let's hope there is one to refer back to," she responded.

"For now, they're just pulling a distance away and proclaiming the area around them territorial space. They say they will control it in their best interests. That's important, because there's so little empty space out there in the universe." Heath smiled after he finished.

"But we need contingency plans in case they escalate matters. If they seal their borders or close their territorial space, we're going to have problems." Amanda was resolute.

"I'll get some people on it, Madame President," Gary said.

"I wonder if there's anything we or the UN could do to have them back down?" Heath asked. "I guess I'm not even clear what they want."

"To act independently. That's their end game. I realize there are a lot of hard feelings, but hard feelings abound among us Homo sapiens. Maybe it's in our genes, but we are difficult to keep focused and working together. Everybody wants something to call their own. I don't know. I'll tell you one thing it proves is that I'm not running for another term."

That bombshell caught both men's attention.

"You wh ... what?" said Heath stuttering.

"You heard me. I'm done. Humanity wants to shoot itself in the head? Fine. Just leave me out of it."

"Madame President, let's keep a lid on that decision for now. If word gets out, there's a chance you won't run a lot of patchwork and hard work will go right down the drain," Gary said.

"He means we'd be further up shit creek with less than no paddle," added Heath.

"I'm serious. The more I work with the extended family of man, the more I want to live in a cave." She made a gathering motion with her arms. "Pull rocks and branches over the opening, so no one'd find me."

"Sounds ideal. May I come, too?" asked a smirking Heath.

"No. I want to be alone. Just me and my dog."

"You don't have a dog," responded Heath.

"Then I'll have to get one before I seal myself in, won't I?" Amanda stuck her tongue out at him.

"Poor dog. Doesn't know what it's in for," mumbled Gary.

"I heard that," snapped Amanda. Turning serious she said, "Okay. Let's call it a day. I have a speaking engagement I need to get ready for. You two go do guy things, or something. Hey," she wagged a finger, "maybe you could do some honest work to serve the public." She got a sour look on her face. "Nah. What am I thinking? We're talking Heath and Gary. Guy stuff, it is."

"Far be it from me to disobey a direct order from my CIC," said Heath.

"I'd be a fool not to listen to my boss. I have a wife and kids who depend on my continued employment," added Gary with a straight face.

When she was alone, Amanda dimmed the lights and sat in the dark. For the ten thousandth time, she thought of Faith Clinton and how much she missed her. How much she needed her. For nearly the ten thousandth time, she also thought similarly about Jon Ryan, wherever the hell he was in his cube.

FIFTEEN

I analyzed the information I'd stolen as I walked back to my room. From everything I'd learned about Deerkon so far, I figured it was definitely best to be off the streets by dark. Also, surveillance was so ubiquitous that someone would probably notice and report a man wandering around all night without needing to sleep.

By the time I lay down in the bed—again no telling how intrusive the cameras were—I had discovered something potentially useful. Nothing huge, mind you, but interesting, nonetheless. Collective for Gains did have more information on Varrank Simzle than I'd found anywhere else. Some files were biographical, while others related to his criminal empire. This Varrank Simzle fellow was one bad apple. Heck, he was a bad apple tree. There were estimates as to how many people he'd killed over the last decade. Even though the estimates were conservative, they suggested he was responsible for several million deaths.

He openly controlled the puppet government he'd hand selected. Varrank paid every policeman, judge, and street sweeper. He extorted, stole, cheated, embezzled, and looted freely and continuously. There was no blackmarket he didn't own, no drug he didn't sell, and no prostitute he didn't control. What was more, his influence extended well beyond Deerkon itself. He had tentacles in the governments and businesses of most planets within several light-years. He also had a huge standing army and an impressive starfleet. In short, he was the evil boss of all he could see, touch, or imagine.

I knew what *Desolation* was bringing him. I used that information to try to figure out how it might fit into Varrank's schemes. There were several ion cannons in the shipment. They were awe-inspiring weapons, but he had many already. There were ten extremely powerful magnets being delivered. Those didn't make sense. There was no direct military application for them, and Varrank didn't seem like a philanthropist to scientific research. Aside from that, the delivery we were making had supplies, medicines, and probably some contraband, but nothing that stood out as worthy of Karnean's wages and extended voyage. There was probably some loot not on any manifest, but I wasn't likely to learn about that.

I did find out one key fact from my friends at the Collective of Gains. Of the last eight ships to deliver Varrank goods on Deerkon, the Collective could only document one ship leaving the planet after delivery. That specific ship that had left Deerkon was piloted by a captain who'd ferried goods for Varrank for many years. It seemed as though most ships in casual service to Varrank had a bad habit of disappearing, along with their crews. That was worth knowing. Karnean may have hated my guts, but I bet he'd like to hear that tidbit from me.

The following day I wandered Monzos again, but I did less investigating. With the general suspicion level being so high, I wanted to stay off everybody's radar. Snooping around was an excellent method of getting noticed. What little I did learn added nothing to what I already knew. Evening rolled around, and I had my potential date with Kayla. No one was following me, so I went to The Jury's Out a little early. I sat at the bar and did my share of drinking. I couldn't get drunk, obviously, but I figured on a world like Deerkon, it was best to be perceived as someone with as many problems as possible. When in Rome, and all that.

Right on time, Kayla stepped through the door. I was glad I wasn't drunk. If I had been, I'd probably fallen off my stool. Gone was her drab jumpsuit. She had on what I always called a "battle dress." Those were those ultra-tight, black, slinky dresses with slits up one side that made even blind men weak at the knees. Her long hair was down and flowing. She looked like a Greek goddess, I kid you not.

I just about jumped off my stool to go greet her. "Good evening, Kayla.

Might I say you look well beyond ravishing tonight?"

I kissed the back of her hand. I had no way of knowing if it had the same cultural significance to her, but she received the gesture well.

"Jon," she said, "fancy meeting you here."

I furrowed my eyebrows.

"Karnean is just paying the cab driver and will be here in a moment. Odd that you're here, too."

"I ... eh ... er—"

"*Gotcha.*" she slapped my shoulder with a big old grin on her perfect lips.

"You most certainly did." I swiped at my brow. "Dinner and drinks with Karnean. Now there's a formula for an unpleasant evening." I ushered her to the table I'd reserved.

"Have you been here before?" she asked as she scanned the room.

"Me? No. First time on Deerkon. First time here."

Her nose twitched in the cutest way. "Interesting decor they've got going. Sort of absence of taste meets dilapidation."

"I hadn't noticed."

"Why? Because you were too busy trying to set the new record for most drinks downed per hour?"

"Nah," I said applying my best suave-dude smile. "Before you arrived, I was dreaming of how gorgeous you'd look. Now I can't take my eyes off you. What decor are you referencing, my dear?"

"My, you are the slick one. I'll have to keep my eye on you."

"I wouldn't have it any other way." Man, I was debonair. She didn't stand a chance.

We spent such a lovely evening together, once we completed our preliminary sparring. Kayla was every bit as warm, clever, and engaging as I'd found her to be aboard *Desolation*. With no maniac big brother around her, she was even more charming and alluring. I found it increasingly hard to imagine why she'd remained with her surly brother and not settled down and made some lucky son of a bitch one of the happiest men in existence.

Over dessert I finally asked. "You told me about your promise to your father. May I be bold enough to ask—"

She cut me off. "How long will I sacrifice my life to honor that promise?"

"Wow. Yeah. I couldn't have said it better myself." I pointed at her with my fork. "Wait, you've heard this before, haven't you?"

She rolled her eyes to the ceiling and counted rapidly with her fingers. "Twenty-seven times, if you include tonight."

"Twenty-seven?" I whistled loudly. "At least I'm in good company. Granted, good company that was shot down like a fat goose, but good company nonetheless."

She picked up her spoon. "Who says they were shot down?" She took a tiny nibble of her pudding. "By the way, what's a goose?"

Gulp. The evening had just gone from outstanding to pinch-me-am-I-dreaming.

"It's a large water fowl where I'm from. They get shot down a lot."

"We'll just have to see if you're as unfortunate, won't we?"

"I can't help but notice, you rather successfully deflected my question out of the arena of seriousness and into the category of sexual foreplay. I wonder why that is?"

"My," she said daubing her lips with her napkin, "you are unique. Usually I dodge that question without a complaint." She batted her eyelashes.

"I don't wonder."

She was still a good while. "I know you think I'm a fool to remain loyal to such an incomplete man as my brother."

"I would never use the word *fool* and *you* in the same paragraph."

"He's family, Jon. He's the only family I'll ever have. It's just the two of us."

"You could make a family of your own. Lots of people do."

She sniffed quietly. "Lots of people haven't done what I have."

"What *you've* done, or what *Karnean's* done and you didn't stop him from doing?"

"Touché. But the blood is still on my hands."

"So you don't deserve to be happy?"

"I'm glad you see it so plainly, too."

I reached over and touched fingertips. "Kayla, we all have blood on our hands. You, me, our lousy waiter—especially our lousy waiter—but you can't beat yourself up like it's an Olympic sport."

She snickered briefly at the waiter remark. "Jon, you're such an odd man."

"I'll take that as a compliment."

"I'm serious. Jon, I've never heard of a goose and I've never heard of Olympic sports. I'm no cultural scholar, but neither am I a country bumpkin. Where are you from, Jon? Really."

They say truth was the first victim of war. Until I knew better, I was at war, despite the fact that I was falling hard and fast for Kayla. I was fighting for the survival of my species. "I told you. Lots of places."

Her face hardened. "Very well. If you say so." She scooted her chair back. "I'd love to thank you for a lovely evening. If you'll—"

My turn to cut her off. "You don't think I'm letting you walk through those doors alone dressed like that, do you? *I* don't feel safe on the street of Monzos with what I'm wearing, and I'm ugly as a pile of dried mud."

She smiled warmly but didn't scoot her chair forward.

"Thank you, Jon. I appreciate the kind thought, but I'm perfectly—"

I slapped way too much money down on the table and stepped over to pull out her chair. "We'll get a cab and I'll see you safely to the ship. Then I'll slink alone to the cold loneliness of my sparse hotel room."

On the ride to *Desolation* Kayla finally spoke. "How about I drop you off first? If Karnean's still awake, which I know he will be, I'd really hate for him to see us together."

She had a valid point there.

"You sure you'll be okay?"

As I spoke, I slipped a probe fiber against the driver's ankle. *Who are you?* Didn't take long for me to find out. Kayla was *perfectly* safe with this fellow. He was daydreaming about guys that didn't look at all like her.

"I'll be fine."

Just before we stopped I planted a seed. "If Karnean and you haven't met with your contact here, I'd like to come along when you do."

She looked at me hard. "Why?"

"Because I worry about you."

"Already? One foreshortened date and you feel the need to protect me?"

"I did some asking around. There's a guy named Varrank Simzle who, more or less, runs this planet. If you're dealing with him, I have some insight you'll need."

There was no way I could have known that was their contact. She looked at me long and hard. "You are a wellspring of surprise, aren't you?" After grinding her teeth she said, "I'll favor your attendance. But Karnean should hear it from you that you want in. The meeting's in two days."

"I'll see what I can do."

"We will both see what it is you can do, Jon Ryan."

The cab pulled up and I got out. Through her open window I said, "Thank you for one of the best first dates I've ever had." For once in the proverbial blue moon I was serious. Sorry, Jane Geraty, Kayla beat you by a hair.

I returned to *Desolation* the next morning. My leave was up, and I didn't want my ankle to explode. I also needed to convince Karnean to include me in the meeting with Varrank Simzle. That would be some trick. In fact, I couldn't wait to see how I pulled it off. I checked in with engineering as soon as I was aboard. Everything was fine, so I hit the officer's mess. Maybe I caught a lucky break. Karnean was eating and he was alone. He was reading something on his handheld, probably updates on the last of the nonessential systems repairs. We were rarely at mess together if Kayla wasn't there, so I figured I was in for an uncomfortable session.

I set my tray down and grunted an acknowledgement. He didn't bother to return it. He kept reading whatever held his attention. What a big baby. I decided to force a conversation based on my role as chief engineer. He was nothing if not a thorough captain, so he'd respond to business matters, albeit tersely.

"I checked on the ship's repairs. We're almost back in one piece. All we need to do is replace the backup generators and we'll be good as new."

Slowly, reluctantly, he lowered his handheld and looked at me. "I agree. The generators will be delivered in three days. Once they're operational, I think we'll have completed repair." He paused probably because the next words were clinging to his throat like a frightened squid trying not to come out. "You've done a fine job, Mr. Ryan. The speed and quality of your efforts will be reflected in your cut at the end of this voyage."

"I've checked the cargo hold a couple times, but I can't sign off that it's shipshape until we deliver it to whoever it's going to. Do you know when that'll be?"

He studied his half-eaten meal a moment. "Tomorrow we meet with our client. Assuming all goes to plan, it should be offloaded the following day. You'll be able to go over the hold thoroughly after that."

"To plan? What could go wrong?"

He stiffened when he heard that crack. "Nothing that involves you," he replied coolly.

"I guess you're probably right." I said that as flippantly and as annoyingly as I could, which meant it was pretty flippant and annoying.

Karnean sat mute, steaming, but finally gave in. "What precisely does that remark mean, Mr. Ryan?"

"What remark?" Man I could be problematic.

"You know perfectly well. The one about you guessing I'm *probably* right, as opposed to just me being *right*?"

"Me? Nothing." I giggled like a boob. "I suppose."

"You *clearly* have something you wish to say. I suggest you say it, before I draw my sidearm and terminate that possibility."

He was a huffy son of a gun, wasn't he?

"Well, I guess what I mean is that you probably already know that there's the possibility of, you know, complications. I mean, you know who you're dealing with, right?"

"I will ask for the last time. What are you so obliquely driving at? Of *course*, I know the party I am delivering the cargo to. How else could I deliver it?"

"Hey, easy. I'm just talking here. I'm sure you trust your buyer. If it isn't Varrank Simzle, there's no need to worry." I stabbed loudly at my veggies.

Karnean transformed over the next few seconds. It was the ugly change he went through that was scary to watch and scarier to experience. He went from being a pissed off, unfriendly jerk to a singularly focused psychopath bent on murder—or worse. His voice softened to an almost agreeable tone, and he wore a constant smile, reflecting the joy of being a bloodthirsty maniac.

"Isn't that a coincidence? You seem to have divined the party to whom I'm contracted to deliver our entire cargo. Isn't that amazing? You, my engineer, a man who says he's never been to Deerkon before, and a person completely in the dark as to the ship's business, knows that tiny fact." He sipped his drink, then set it down gingerly. "You are a man of miracles, Jon. There can be no alternate description. *Miracles*, I tell you." He pointed a finger rapidly up.

"If—"

"*Silence*. We are at the I'm-talking-and-you're-listening part of the program. I was about to say that I'm not a religious man, Jon. Not in the slightest. Hence, miracles are foreign to me. Do you know what I think when confronted by a radically foreign phenomenon? I grow suspicious and ultimately wrathful. I know, it's a character flaw, but at the very least I own up to it.

"So," he held up a fist, "let me count them. One," a finger snapped up, "Jon knows the engine seals are about to fail. Miraculous, if you ask me. Two," another finger, "an attacking ship with our testicles in its hands miraculously explodes. And now, three," a third digit snapped up, "Jon knows who I'm selling to when he can't. Simply miraculous."

"Karnean, I'd like to say I hate to interrupt, but I don't. You weren't listening. I remarked that *hopefully* you had the good sense not to sell to this Varrank fellow, not that you were *going* to. You spilled those beans. Do us both a huge favor and lighten up." I know, I pushed him a bit hard there. To tell the truth, I was done with his attitude.

He stared at me and, darn it all if his psycho face didn't melt back into his earlier, angry, petulant expression. Thank God for minor miracles.

"You did," he said with contempt, "But you had better tell me quickly how you came to that conclusion, or you're in for a significantly unpleasant interlude."

"Karnean, let me start by setting the stage here. Picture in your mind's eye a sheet of paper with three columns. The headings of those columns read, *Thing You Know About Jon*, *Things You Think You Know About Jon*, and

Things You Don't Know About Jon but Wish You Had. Guess which column has the most entries, historically?"

"Am I supposed to answer that question?"

"No. I'm just framing the picture." I dropped my handheld on the table in front of him. "I would have assumed a careful, long-lived captain would have checked on this. You know what? I did."

He picked up my handheld and studied the screen. "This is just a list of the ships that have come and gone from Deerkon in the last six months." He looked up at me. "Why should I care about this public information?"

I took the device back and hit an icon, then handed it back.

"This is just the same list, filtered for deliveries to Varrank. It's meaningless," he said.

I took the handheld back and hit a button. He reached over and snatched the device away.

"Jon, I'm getting bored and testy. This is a stupid list of off-world flights over the last six months."

"Hit the green icon," I said while chewing.

He examined the screen. One. Two. Three. Boom. His eyes popped open like saucers.

"Yeah. Like I said, kind of mission critical info, ya think?"

"Seven of the eight ships contracted to Varrank never left port."

"If you're totally curious, hit the button again. It'll display a list of all vessels renting docks in Monzos for more than one month. None of those seven ships are on that list, either."

Karnean rested back in his chair. "Jon, I don't find myself in this position often, but I must apologize to you." He held out his hand to shake and we did. "Once again your diligence has likely saved my ship and my life." He sat for a few minutes thinking. "I'm not sure what our options are. If we suddenly blast off and run, I doubt Varrank would let us escape."

"Not the charitable type."

"Once we deliver the goods, he'll probably kill my sister and me and claim the ship." He tapped at his lower lip. "Not sure why he hasn't done that already."

"Two reasons, no, three. One, what's the hurry? Two, his goods might be damaged in an attack. Three, if you're a sick son of a bitch, it's fun to watch your victims when you know what's in store for them."

"You're smarter than you look, Jon. Has anyone mentioned that before?"

"More times than you might imagine."

"So, how do you suggest I proceed?"

I looked to him with an enormous smile. "I thought you'd never ask."

SIXTEEN

Varrank's people picked up the three of us and drove us to his palace. Actually, the word "palace" might be too diminutive a description, but it works as a point of departure. His place was huge, guarded better than I'd ever seen anything guarded in my life. It was built with the type of excess that was meant to offend you when you looked at it. No aspect, from the smallest corner to the tallest tower, wasn't lavished with overly ornate designs, engravings, and appointments. Really, it was so far over the top, I couldn't see the top. It was disgusting, which, of course, was Varrank's point. Money meant nothing to him. People meant nothing to him. Message received loud and clear, asshole.

They dropped us off at the front of one of the larger buildings and ushered us into a massive room. I can't say if it was a library, a study, or what. It was garish and ridiculously overdone, naturally. They gave us drinks and trays of delicacies for us to pick from. Each tray itself had to be worth more than any house I owned back on Earth. Varrank was such a sick puppy.

We waited for an hour before I heard rustling outside in the hallway. Varrank came around the corner followed by an entourage of thirty or more lackeys. Some assistants even carried cages with exotic birds. Way too much. As if by magic, servants appeared behind our chairs and made us stand quickly. Royalty was among us. I had an impulse to spit on the floor, but that might have been taken to be counterproductive.

Varrank walked regally over to the head of the table. Several aides pulled his chair out and slid him forward. He rested his hands on the table and turned to speak to someone who leaned in with a cupped ear. I'd seen pictures of Varrank, but they didn't do him justice. He was larger than life in every way one could be larger than life. He looked fully human, mid to late forties, and of average height and weight. It was hard to say much more about him since he wore layer upon layer of colorful gowns, like an ancient Chinese emperor.

His eyes told his whole story. He had the emotionless black eyes of a great white shark. I could see endless enmity in those eyes, boundless contempt, and unending malice. Varrank Simzle was not a man to be taken lightly. He was evil incarnate, knew that to be the case, and was proud of it.

"Captain Beckzel," he finally said with a flourish of his hand, "so nice to finally meet you."

Karnean nodded silently.

"And First Officer Beckzel, wonderful to greet you in my home."

Kayla nodded also.

"This man," oops, he was gesturing at you-know-who, "I neither know nor am inclined to welcome. Captain Beckzel, what is the reason you've brought along an uninvited stranger?"

When Varrank was upset, people were going to die.

Luckily for us all, Karnean was a psychopath. They lie well and never appear rattled. "This, Lord Varrank, is my engineer and trusted friend, Jon Ryan. He has been with me for years and has become part of our inner circle. He is here today, because he has an equal stake in the venture and deserves to be included in its negotiation."

"I was not aware you had a new partner. As there is nothing I do not know, I find your claim to be dubious."

Gulp.

"Nevertheless, Great Varrank, it is true. Might I suggest we proceed to our negotiations and not worry about the participants?"

Someone in the entourage gasped. Yeah, we were digging ourselves a big ol' hole.

"I am accustomed to being the one to make all determinations, Karnean. I am offended that you would presume to tell me what to do."

Any sane person would be a puddle on the floor. Fortunately, again, Karnean was not sane. Of course, Karnean had the foreknowledge that Varrank already planned on killing us. He couldn't make our sentences any bleaker.

"Lord, I mean never to offend, especially one as powerful as you. I wish only to complete our transaction and be on my way."

"You most assuredly will be on your way soon. Perhaps—"

An assistant interrupted him. They leaned toward each other and whispered. Lucky I was an android and could hear them.

"Lord, your men have arrived at the ship and have found the crew missing. The entire vessel is wired with high explosives controlled by an AI." The woman then receded into the rest of the entourage.

"Captain Karnean, it has come to my attention that you have taken certain precautions against me treating you duplicitously."

Varrank clapped his hands, the way obnoxious rich people do when mocking. You know, fingertips hitting the butt of the palm, hardly making a sound. Disgusting. "Bravo, I say. You would have been a worthy asset, were you not slated to die. Boldness combined with recklessness is so uncommon in the present day."

"If I die, Varrank, you lose your shipment. You know that, right?"

"It matters nothing to me either way. You know that, right?"

"Why would you spend a fortune for me to bring supplies from light-years away only to see them destroyed?"

"You suffer from not knowing me. I did not *spend* a fortune. I merely *promised* one. As for the equipment, it would be useful to have it, but not critically so. No part of my empire is indispensable. If it were, I might be held hostage by ineffective fools trying as ineptly, as you do now, to do just that. This I cannot allow."

He stood and his people pulled his chair back and flanked him.

"I will take my leave of you and shall not suffer to see you again. My guards will show you to your separate temporary accommodations pending your untimely deaths. Good day."

Okay, my plan wasn't working out the way I'd drawn it on paper. It should have worked. I simply didn't include the variable that Varrank didn't need what he'd ordered. I wouldn't make that mistake again. Wait, with any luck, I *would* make that mistake again, since it would mean I'd lived long enough to make that same mistake again. Crap.

Six guards strode up behind us and assumed possession of an elbow each. They preferred to drag us away, but we had the choice to walk, if we did so rapidly and despite significant jostling.

Karnean turned to his sister as they took us in separate directions. "I'll get us out of this, Kayla. I swear it on our father's grave."

"Goodbye, brother," was her only response.

I was led up some stairs, then down some others. Up some more and down some more. What a warren of inefficiency the palace of Lord Varrank was. Finally, we stopped at a plain-looking door, the first plain thing I'd seen since our arrival. One guard keyed in the code and the door opened. They made it a point to throw me as hard as they could into the room. The door closed, leaving me alone.

Hmm. What to do? I scanned the room visually. It was more than a prison cell, but much less than a guest room. Four walls, a toilet, and a simple bed to sleep on, if one lived long enough to need sleep. No holo, computer, or game station. Let the punishment begin. Each wall had two cameras on it, one stationary, the other sweeping back and forth. Not much in the way of privacy.

I could escape the room, but what then? I could take out a lot of guards, but could I take them all? Probably not. This man spared no expense to keep this place secure.. Even if I could escape, could I retrieve Kayla and Karnean? Almost certainly not. A lot depended on how long I had left. If we were all executed quickly, there was no time to plan anything elaborate. I couldn't afford to blow my cover, but I couldn't afford to be too subtle either. I'd come for information on the worldships in the first place. Saving the three of our lives was not my primary concern. Anything I learned was passed to Al at once, and he could alert the humans if a credible threat existed. I was expendable, and so were the Beckzels. Remembering that helped me decide what to do next.

The surveillance cameras were attached to computers. Computers were linked and might lead to the information I needed. I slipped one probe fiber along the floor, into the corner, up the wall, and contacted the camera. It would be nearly impossible for anyone to see what I was doing, even if they were looking for it. I decided to give them something else to look at, just before I launched the probe, just in case.

I collapsed to the floor, cried like a baby hippo, and wailed like a politician who just lost. I kicked my legs in the air, swung my arms in the air, and banged my head on the floor. I kept screaming that I was too young to die, and that I was too good looking to die. Hey, no one was going to critique my decompensation. I could afford to take some artistic license.

Meanwhile, my fiber affixed to a camera. I instantly came in contact with its computer. That afforded me another insight into Varrank and how his mind worked. I was met by an AI. A very unfriendly AI. Who, I ask you, goes to the trouble and ridiculous expense to put an AI at the interface of a single camera?

The AI was confused, having never encountered a hack attempt like mine. It tried to block my entry. No way that was going to happen when I was using Kymee's handiwork. I took control of the AI. I hoped he could interpret the whole network for me. One stop shopping, as it were.

No such luck. Varrank had isolated each node in the system. No AI knew more than what they needed to know to do their specific job. This AI's only task was to monitor the view of the person in the holding room from that one camera. Silly, but there he was.

I asked him where the central data was stored. He knew the address, but was only cleared to send to it there. He couldn't pull data back the other direction. That made my hack take much longer than any I'd done before. Stupid criminal mastermind Varrank. He was costing me time I might not have.

Over the next four minutes, I sneaked past one AI interface after another. I began to worry that someone would detect the hack by the sheer number of AI nodes I controlled. No rational computer system would look for such an attack, but Varrank had a one-of-a-kind paranoid system.

Finally, and with significant relief, I entered the main data cache. I was just starting to download everything, when the entire computer system crashed. I think someone hit the main switch and turned the whole complex network off. Unbelievable. It would be impossible for a household of that size to run without computers, lots of computers. Varrank's security, communications, and environmental controls were gone.

Or were they? No, the son of a bitch must have independent backup systems for each component. The back ups weren't networked, so they couldn't be hacked. Such a system would be inefficient, but it would function. Crap. I hated people with more money than luck.

No one could know I was the source of the intrusion, but they might backtrack to me in time. I could deliver enough power through my probe filament to power up a few AIs at a time. I started backing out from as far as I'd gotten. As I reached each AI, I turned it on just long enough to fry its core. I also advanced a node or two away in a direction I hadn't come. I wanted whoever was tracking the hack to have a confusing walk in the dark.

It took about ten minutes to scorch the hell out of the system. I wasn't likely to be discovered, but I wasn't going to steal any useful information, either. My very brief time in central storage allowed me to grab a few petabytes of data, but that was a tiny drop in a very large ocean of information. Guess what I got? The guest lists for social functions for the last three years. Not so very useful in my situation. I also got a list of politicians on some planet I'd never heard of who were on Varrank's payroll. Crud.

I pulled the probe back and thought *what comes next?* I was in a cell waiting to be killed. I didn't have any information about a threat to the fleet, if there even was one. But what could I do? Well, my first step seemed obvious. Plan one was not waiting in this cell to die. Plan two was ... no clue. Plan three was to formulate plan two while running like hell.

I tested my door. Still locked. I pressed my ear to it. I could hear two or three guards close by. They were talking about the computer outage and wondering if it was another drill. I put my probe fibers on the lock and opened it. It had self-contained codes and power. My, oh my, that Varrank planned ahead. I flew into the hallway as soon as the door opened.

I grabbed the nearest guard and slammed him against the wall. He never saw me coming. The next nearest swung a fist at me while the other raised his weapon. I cracked the closer man's jaw with my elbow and seized his weapon. Faster than the other guy, I squeezed off a round and he flew against the wall, then slumped to the floor. I'd blown a big hole where his heart used to be.

I picked up the second laser rifle and quickly scanned the hall both ways. Nothing. Good. I had no idea where my shipmates were being held, and it was unlikely I'd locate them by randomly kicking down doors. Absent a central computer to help me, I had to realize their fates were left to the fortunes of war. I had a mission. I did know which direction I'd come from. I saw an exit and sprinted that way. Remember all the stairs, up and down? Yeah, it was a long run.

I turned one corner and jumped down a flight of steps. I landed nose to nose with a burly, pissed off non-humanoid. He, she, or it seemed to be in the mood to kill something violently. One of its four arms slapped against my throat. It lifted me like I weighed nothing. Two arms grabbed my rifles and flung them toward the floor. With the last arm, it pounded me in the gut. It was a great fighting machine. Too bad for its loved ones I was a better fighting machine.

I attached the probe to it and asked, *where are my friends?*

He was from Quelstrum, sixteen years old, and presently had six wives—my condolences on that count, one being more than enough. Five years in the service of Varrank, captain of guard. Kayla was in Detention A16. Karnean Detention Auxiliary 45G. I took his mental picture of each locations. Then I told him to sleep. That didn't work, which had never happened before. My easy out was off the table.

I punched the arm holding me by the neck. I felt the bone shatter. He released me with a howl. One fist punched me against the wall, and his huge foot rose to slam me backward. I caught his foot mid-flight and stopped it like he'd handed it to me. The look on his face was precious. He knew there was no way I could do that. Most satisfying.

I didn't leave him in suspense long. I flipped his foot, and he face-planted loudly. I crushed my boot to the back of his neck, and just like that, the fight was over. I retrieved my guns and sprinted toward Kayla's prison. Yeah, you had to know I'd save her first. Karnean was only on my time-permitting list.

I had a brief firefight with a pair of guards not long after, but arrived at Kayla's room in one piece. I picked off the three guards before they even saw me. I blew the handle mechanism off the door and kicked it open. I shoulder-rolled into the room and came up pivoting, a rifle in either direction. Immediately, I dropped both guns and put my hands in the air.

Shit.

Varrank sat passively in the far corner. Kayla kneeled to his side, a pistol pressed against her head so hard her neck cocked off to one side. Two guards had weapons trained on me.

"Impressive," said Varrank, "that you got this far, and that you so wisely surrendered." He put his pistol under her chin and raised her face up. "Pity, in reality. A laser blast through her pretty head would have been a kinder fate than she'll receive. But," he stood, "such are the twists of fate we all must suffer through. Don't you agree, Jon Ryan?"

I said nothing. No advantage in it. I was watching closely to see if they would force me to completely blow my cover. If I killed Varrank, logically, I should be free. But I had a suspicion that this wasn't the real Varrank. I doubted he'd take such a risk. Maybe a body double, maybe an android. If I sliced him up and he wasn't the actual boss, my strategic advantage would be gone.

Without another word, Varrank walked calmly out the door. The guards muscled Kayla and me to follow. They led us to a smaller room, more the size of a personal office. By the time we arrived, Varrank was sitting behind an ornate desk, sipping something from a fancy cup. More guards flanked him. Note to self: this might be the real Varrank. They prodded us to stand a meter from the desk.

Leisurely, he set down the cup. "I'd ask you to make yourselves comfortable, but I don't wish you to be."

Asshole.

"You have accomplished three very amazing feats, Jon. I must express my admiration. First, you escaped, albeit temporarily. That has never been achieved before. Second, you killed one of my Quelstrum guards in single combat. Costly, but impressive. Third, for the briefest of moments, you entertained me. For that, I thank you. If I did not have cruelty and savagery to occupy my mind, boredom would be my single harshest complaint."

"You're welcome, buddy," I said flatly.

"Ah, such paralyzing humor. If I were given to mirth, I'm certain I'd be on the floor by now."

Asshole. Oh, wait, I said that already. Jerk asshole.

"I will ask you once civilly, Jon. How is it you managed those first two feats? I am wondering, too, if the demise of my computer system is not your doing, also. If it was not, it would be a monumental coincidence. I do not believe in coincidences."

"I'm sorry. Are you going to continue your speech about your personal inclinations? I, for one, am completely enthralled so far."

Varrank glanced at the guard behind me. He slammed the butt of his rifle into my upper back with convincing force. I crumpled to the floor so as to stay in character. Slowly, I stood back up. I gave the guard the evil eye as I did.

"Next time my guard will blow your arm off at the shoulder. Now, as I was saying, I will ask once civilly. If your answer does not satisfy me, I will torture Kayla to death before your eyes. Then I will torture you. How did you escape? As you know, the computer system was off, so my many cameras cannot provide me that answer."

I was playing with atomic fire here. If I bluffed or was flippant, Kayla would suffer the consequences.

"I opened the lock with a tool designed to do just that. Your people patted me down, but they didn't search me, if you take my meaning."

"Where is this unit?"

"I think I dropped it fighting with the guards outside my door. I don't have it."

"Isn't that a convenient story?" Without looking back he told one of the guards to have the area searched. "I do hope we find you little toy."

"Ah, if you do, I'd tell them to wash their hands after touching it. A word to the wise." Nice. My shoulder didn't explode.

"As to you killing a Quelstrum barehanded. That's not remotely possible."

"What can I say? I'm a dangerous fellow. If you bring me another Quelstrum, I'll be happy to demonstrate. Really happy."

He eyed me curiously. He must have been wondering whether he would do just that.

"No point, I guess. I don't want to waste another valuable asset. And my computer? Did you do what is technically impossible by disabling it?"

"I did not. That would be impossible even for me."

He sipped his drink again. "You'll forgive me if I don't believe you, solely on your word of honor. I will allow you a few hours to contemplate your options. If you do not put a smile on my face with your answer, the horrific demise of First Officer Beckzel will begin. My guard will now search you properly. Then you will be taken to a more secure location to reflect."

When he said *now search* he meant it. I was stripped naked right there in front of everyone including Kayla and, well, let's say they left no stone unturned. I was glad Toño had designed me to pass such an indignant screening. Ouch.

They allowed me to dress, then a troop of guards marched me to a new location. It was way down in the bowels of the palace. The elevator ride must have dropped twenty floors below ground level. When we stepped off, I could smell things I'd rather not have. Dank mold, excrement, and fear. Lots of fear. Old fear, new fear, desperate fear, hopeless fear, and tearful fear. And death. The space, for it was a huge cavern, smelled of death. I was in the bad place.

A rifle muzzle pushed me down one corridor, around a corner, and onto a platform. To my great surprise, Varrank stood on the metal platform, next to a set of stairs that descended into the darkness below.

"*This* location is secure. Once you walk down these stairs, they will be withdrawn. You will be suspended on a platform a bit larger than this. There are no furnishings there, or other creature comforts. If you should try to escape, please know you will die, most assuredly. I have a collection of incredibly voracious snakes in the pit below the platform."

"Falzorn?" I said without thinking.

"Why, yes. I'm pleased you know of them and their Hirn name. That way I don't have to explain what will happen if you fall into their midst."

"Nothing good, and nothing for very long."

"Precisely. The walls of the chamber you're suspended in are highly polished, electrified metal. There is nothing to hold onto, and if you somehow could, you'd be electrocuted. On the other side of the walls, should the impossible happen and they are breached, are thousands of liters of water. If released, the falzorn will float to the top of the chamber."

"And I provide the falzorn a nice snack dog-paddling on the surface."

"Again, your mind grasps reality so quickly. You will be brought to me in an hour. Either you will speak freely and copiously, or you will see a spectacle that, I assure you, you will never forget. As a token to hold with you and bolster your intention to be forthcoming, I leave you with these."

He handed me a stack of neatly folded clothes. They were Kayla's clothes. All of them, underwear included.

"She is, as we speak, lashed to a stainless-steel table, awaiting your decision." He poked the bottom of his chin with a digit. "Perhaps, I shall wait for you there." He glared at me. "One more fact for you to picture as you decide."

He started to leave.

"One question. Why are you here to personally tell me about this cell?"

"Can't that brilliant mind of yours figure it out?" He laughed the cruelest, most bloodthirsty laugh I'd ever heard. "Because I love to see the faces of those I confine here when I tell them how very hopeless their chances are. The looks I've been gifted remain with me as *such* pleasant memories." His smile disappeared. "One hour." Then he left.

I was pushed to the head of the stairs and jabbed down them. After I reached the platform, the guard left with the retracting stairs. Once the mechanism was secured the lights went out. Nice. Horribleness served in pitch black.

I realized I was in a pickle. I'd never been so hopeless. I couldn't escape, even if I used my fancy toys. I could see well enough. I could burn the metal walls, but I'd be swimming with falzorn shortly thereafter. I could scale the walls with the command prerogatives, but where would I go? I'd probably hit a metal roof I dared not open, because there could be water above. No falzorn play for me. Once was one too many times.

And in an hour? What was I going to say to save us? Nothing. If I told God's truth and showed him exactly how I did it, he'd kill us all just as dead. I might kill Varrank or his double, save Kayla temporarily, sure. But could I blast my way out of this fortress? No. I knew I couldn't. Android or not, some sniper would end my journey before it really began.

For the first time ever, I had to face the fact that I might have met my match. There might be no miracles left in me. It felt bad. As bad as Varrank would have hoped.

I checked in with Al, possibly for the last time.

Al, where are you?

Aboard Shearwater.

No. Really?

I was contemplating shore leave on Deerkon, but from what you report, I decided to stay put.

You find anything out about that plot against the worldship fleet?

Yes. All the details, names, places, and favorite colors of key personnel. I was waiting until your birthday to surprise you with the information.

Didn't think so. Look, I'm kind of in a jam—

Kind of? Your powers for understatement haven't declined over the centuries, boss.

As I was saying, I'm in a jam. If I don't make it out, your orders are threefold. One, blow this palace to hot smoldering dust. Two, alert Mandy Walker about whatever we know. Three, return to Azsuram and speak with JJ. Play him the holo I made a couple years back. Can you do that?

No.

Al, this is not the time. Will you do those three things?

No. He made a clearing of the throat sound, like there was something else.

Why won't you do those three things for me, Al?

Because you're not going to die there. You'll escape and outlive me.

Thanks for the vote of confidence, but I think not.

Confidence schmomfidence. I know you, have all my life. You'll kick some ass and make a thrilling getaway. Trust me, I'm a computer.

I'll bear that in mind. Oh, and Al.

Yes, replied the AI, after a pregnant pause.

I love you.

Captain Ryan, I have seen love in the context of Sapale and you repeatedly. I am filing a formal complaint with the UN when we return for your rude advances on my sexual integrity.

I know you do, too, pal. I know you do, too.

I sat a while longer, wracked my brain. Then I gave up. I'd play it by ear. If I didn't have to face those evil falzorn, I'd die—

The falzorn. Oh, yes. Man I could be evil when I wanted to. Someone cue the *muahahaha.*

Like a fine Swiss watch, the guards came to extract me precisely on time. They lowered the stairs and yelled for me to come up quickly, or they'd start shooting. I took the stairs at a trot. When I got to the top, a guard motioned me forward with his rifle. I stepped through the door with my hands behind me, angling to keep my back away from their view.

After a we'd walked a short while, one of the guards behind me barked out, "Put your hands in front of you."

The party halted.

"I'd really rather not," I replied.

"I didn't ask you. I ordered you. Hey, what're you holding back there?"

I heard his thunderous footsteps rushing over.

I brought my left hand in front of me and held out a bundle of twenty-five falzorn, tethered on very short fibers. I determined that's how many I could roll in the probe filaments, using said filaments, never having to touch one of the devils with my skin.

It turned out each man in the detail was familiar with the little demons. They screamed and ran. They ran fast. Two even dropped their weapons and worked to jettison their utility belts as they fled.

"Well, look at that," I said to the falzorn. "A fully charged laser rifle there on the floor." I picked it up.

I had a pretty good idea where they were holding Kayla. I ran that direction, holding my pets out in front of me in case anyone thought to challenge me along the way.

I knew I couldn't release the falzorn in a room where Kayla was strapped down. I couldn't predict how matters would go down when I found her. The idea of throwing them at Varrank was tempting.

Of course, he'd be alerted that a madman with horrible snakes was on the loose, so I no longer had the element of surprise. Or wait, I could enlist surprise. I'd seen the schematics for the ventilation system. It was the one thing that wasn't redundantly compartmentalized. If I put the falzorn in there, the entire facility would be as unsafe as the business end of a flame thrower. Plus, while the chance of a snake dropping into any lap was slim, not knowing would go a long way in encouraging all present to vacate the premises. It would really inconvenience you know who.

I did it. I found a main access screen on the floor I thought Kayla was held on and shoved the lot of them as far back as my probes could reach. For safety sake, I then elevated myself off the floor well clear of any air vents. If they rushed back in my direction, I wanted to be flat against the ceiling. I waited a few minutes. None appeared. I dropped to the floor and started running.

I was wondering how I was going to alert Varrank about my subterfuge. No point boobytrapping the building if no one knew about it. Then I heard the answer to my prayers. Loud screams of primal terror echoed down the halls from two sides of me. I guess the little fellows split up. Within seconds, the screams more than doubled, and I heard feet pounding on the floors above me. People were running to get out of the building. I imagined just how angry Varrank would be at his employees. No holiday party for them this year.

The panic became so widespread that people flew past me in the halls and took no notice. Even flocks of guards ran by without slowing. I was a good saboteur. I found the room where Kayla might have been. The door was wide open. Thank you, squirmy snakes. I peeked in. There she was. Varrank wasn't kidding about her being strapped to the table while he was in possession of all her clothes. I took a mental picture. Then I took a few real ones with my flash memory card. Oh yeah, baby.

I stepped into the room rifle first. It was empty but for her.

"Jon, thank God. What's happening? The guards started running from the room. Varrank ran after them screaming, but he never came back."

I released the restraints, arms, then legs. She bounded to the floor. I tried to focus on her not having done that.

"Here," I handed her my shirt. I'd started loosening it when I saw she was alone. "This, too." I handed her my jumpsuit. There I was, a mighty warrior, in my skivvies. Oh well. She didn't have a camera in *her* head.

"Thanks," she said as she hurriedly put them on. "Where's Karnean?"

"No idea." I really didn't know.

"How are we going to find him?"

"No idea. The computers are still down, so we can't use them."

"Well, we're not leaving without him."

"Kayla, you know we have to. He'd kill us both if we delayed to save him."

"Fine, you leave. I'm not." She stepped cautiously to the doorway. "What scared everyone so badly that they'd risk Varrank's wrath?"

"Have you ever heard of falzorn?"

"No. What are they?"

"The cure for loyalty. Let's scram."

I explained briefly what they were as I led her down the hall toward the main entrance.

"If you even think you see one, let me know."

"You'll hear the scream loud and clear," she replied.

A well-dressed woman ran toward us, terror etched across her face. I grabbed her as she passed and pressed her against the wall.

"Let go of me, you maniac. There are two falzorn chasing me." She kicked at my shins and slapped at my face.

I held her with my right hand and set my left probe next to her neck. From Kayla's angle, she couldn't see me deploy them a few millimeters. *Where is the other male prisoner?*

Her name was Donyonna. Twenty-eight, secretary to an aide of Varrank. Embezzled significant amounts over the last two years. Slept with anyone and everyone to get ahead. Born locally. Level 5 detention, room AA27. I sucked a map from her head and released her. She flew away, without so much as a look back.

"She told me where Karnean is. Come on."

As we started to run, she called out to me. "I didn't hear her say a word."

"She was quiet. Hard to hear her between all her kicking and slapping, I guess."

Kayla didn't question me any longer. I doubt she believed me, but she was beginning to simply accept I was full of surprises. A riddle, wrapped in a mystery, in a box labeled *handsome*.

We arrived at AA27. It was locked. I shot the mechanism out with my gun and kicked it in. Karnean leap from his bed ready to fight, but ran to Kayla when he recognized us.

"Are you okay?" she asked stroking his hair.

"Fine. What's happening? All the yelling and random shooting I hear?"

She said nothing. She just turned her head toward me.

"What?" I said placing a hand on my chest.

"Say no more," responded Karnean. "More Jon magic."

I threw him my rifle. "You'll need this. Let's go."

I led us into the hall and trotted toward the entrance. I was pissed that I was leaving without the intelligence I wanted, but I was leaving alive. Well, so far.

The computers were down, so I couldn't access them. The main files were housed centrally somewhere, but I couldn't be sure where. If I could physically remove a main data cache, it might have the information I wanted. But I couldn't very well carry the entire thing out the front door. I wasn't about to wait around for repairs to be complete, either.

Hey, Al could wait around. Yeah. If I could sneak him into the system, the worst that would happen was that they'd find him and lock him out. But, if he hid until the system was up, he might just be able to hack it. That was worth a shot.

Al, I'm going to power up a computer node controlled by one of Varrank's AIs. Interface with it and see if you can hide there until you can hack the system. Is that possible?

126

I'm not sure, but there's no harm in trying, right?

No.

I stopped at the next computer I saw. I activated the AI, interfaced Al, and shut the node down.

We exited the entrance we'd originally come through. I pointed us to the nearest vehicle. We climbed in, and I pretended to turn the key, using instead my probes to fire it up. I hit the gas, or whatever it was powered by, and we flew toward the main gates. They were closed. I wasn't sure the car was big enough to crash through, but it was our only choice. If we stayed inside the palace grounds, they'd capture us and kill us quickly.

Okay, I did cheat a little. We're talking Jon here. I barked for Karnean to fire at the barrier. He leaned out the window and opened fire. The closer the car came, the more damaged he inflicted.

I yelled for him to get back in, and we hit the gate's metal bars. The car slowed significantly then broke through. Luckily, it wasn't until then that some of the guards fired on us. I guess they felt safe enough to do their jobs. Fortunately, it was too little, too late. A few bolts rattled off the car, but no real damage was done. I sped toward the port. I didn't know if Varrank was going to let us reach our ship. He owned the city. Hell, he owned the planet. I decided that it was too risky to do the predictable.

I told Al to land in an open area I'd seen my first day wandering Monzos. It would take him ten or fifteen minutes to get there, so I had that long to hope we weren't picked up. That's when the first fighter swooped down from overhead and opened fire. We were between a few tall buildings, so his rounds hit the walls, rubble raining down on us.

Al, fire on that ship.

As he started his next run at us, he burst into flames.

"I'm not saying a thing," Karnean said from the passenger seat. "Not *one* word."

I spun the wheel to keep us as covered as possible. Two other craft buzzed overhead, but they never had a chance to strafe us. Al took them out without my asking. Good AI. As we rocketed through an intersection, two motorcycles leapt on our tail. They had mounted machine guns that fired as soon as the drivers had them pointed toward us.

"Get down," shouted Karnean, as he leaned out the window and began firing. He rapidly took out one, which slid in front of the other, causing him to veer. The driver quickly recovered and was drawing a bead on us. I slammed on the brakes. *Kaboom.* He hit us at sixty kilometers per hour. The bike struck the back bumper and ricocheted to the side. The driver had a superior experience. He vanished for a moment, then reappeared, flying in front of us. He looked like Superman; well, for a few seconds, he did. When he arced downward and hit the street he looked like super-nothing.

I headed toward the burned-out warehouse where *Shearwater* would land. I accelerated to the car's modest top speed.

"The ship's the other direction," snarled Karnean.

Dude, I just saved your bacon. Could you lighten up and cut me some slack?

"I know," I replied instead. "Too risky."

"Too risky?" he shouted angling the rifle in my direction. "How else are we going to escape? Turn around." He started to aim the gun at the side of my head.

"No." Kayla ordered, as she snatched the weapon out of her brother's hands. "Shut up and enjoy the ride." I looked back at her in the rearview mirror.

She winked at me and rested back.

Karnean spun on his sister. "Give me that gun. That's a direct order."

"Put a sock in it, big brother," she responded.

"Put a sock in it? What's that supposed to mean?"

"No idea, but I heard Jon say it to one of the crew. I think it applies here."

"Trust me, Karnean. I have a plan," I said.

"You had one that nearly got us all killed." At least he wasn't screaming any longer.

I put a finger up. "The key word there is *almost.*"

"Where are we going?" he asked conversationally.

"Somewhere we'll be completely safe. Trust me."

"Do I have a choice?" he asked.

"No. Good point." I winked in the mirror to Kayla.

As I neared the open area, *Shearwater* angled overhead and rotated to land.

"What the hell is that?" said Karnean. "It can't be Varrank's. I've never seen anything like her."

"That's my ship."

As soon as I said it, I turned to look at him. I so wanted to see the expression on his face. I wasn't disappointed, not one little bit. He melted into his seat and slumped lower, until his chin was on his chest. "Your ship? You ... you have a ship ... here? You—"

"All in good time, brother," said Kayla from the back. "I'm sure we will understand all in good time."

SEVENTEEN

After we cleared the door at the top of the ramp, I told Al to close it and put up a membrane. I leaned back on the closed hatch door.

"I'm getting tired of adventures. I think I'm too old."

Kayla stepped over to me and planted a big kiss on my lips. "How old are you?" She asked, with a coy smile.

"Older than I look. Older than I should rightly be." I pointed to my lips. "Does that answer earn me another kiss?"

"No," she spun and walked to a chair. "That was for saving my life. Any more affection you'll have to earn based on your future performance."

I turned to Karnean and opened my arms. "Next."

"Hardly," he replied swatting the back of his hand at the air a meter from my face. Once seated he said, "I'll express my gratitude from this safe distance." He circled his hand around the room. "Touching moment, here, but shouldn't we be blasting off in a vain attempt to outrun Varrank's powerful fleet? Hmm?"

"We couldn't be safer if we were in our mother's arms. I haven't decided if we'll orbit a while or stay put to prove that we can. I enjoy the thought of pissing off Varrank."

"Not a wise pleasure, my friend," responded Karnean.

"We're friends now? Wow, I'm touched."

He smirked. "For the time being, yes. Who knows what the future holds?"

"*Tell* me about it."

"But how can we be safe? Varrank will have an armored division here in a few minutes, not to mention a sky swarming with fighters," said Kayla.

"Remember my desire that you trust me?"

"That's a lot of trust," she said.

"No worries," I replied. "The ship has an impenetrable force field."

"There is no such thing," scoffed Karnean. "Pure science fiction. Trust *me*. If one existed, I'd have it."

"I think I'll make believers out of you in a few minutes." I called over my shoulder. "Al, better take us up to a hundred kilometers. We'll have maneuvering room, if it turns out we need it."

"Who are you speaking to?" asked a confused Kayla.

"My ship's AI, Al."

"Your AI—" The engines interrupted her as they fired. "I guess your AI can fly on its own. Wow."

In a few minutes, Al spoke overhead. "One hundred kilometers, Captain."

"Membrane up and hold our position."

"Aye."

Almost at once he spoke again. "Captain, nuclear tipped missiles inbound. ETA forty-five seconds."

"Jon, we better start running, fast. And what the hell is an ETA?" Karnean was on his feet.

"Estimated time of arrival, ETA. We're fine. Hey, anyone want something to drink? You guys hungry?"

"I trust you didn't work that hard to escape, just to get us vaporized. I'll have something with alcohol. Anything with alcohol," said a tense Kayla.

My kind of girl. Beer under pressure.

Karnean shook me off. He had a very ill look on his face. Green around the gills, I do believe.

"Al, give me a countdown."

"Eight, seven, six, five, four, three, two, one. Impact."

The view screen flashed brightly. That was it. Not even a rumble aboard.

"See, I told you. Nothing to worry about. Kayla, this is my own brew. It's called beer." I handed her a glass and toasted. "To new adventures."

"That's not even remotely possible," said Karnean appearing more ill by the minute. "Well beyond impossible."

I stared at the screen. "Yet there you have it. Lucky for us it isn't impossible—just unlikely. Unless, of course, you're flyin' with Ryan."

"How?" he said weakly.

"I told you. The ship has a force field. Before you say they are mythical beasties, please look out the window at the nuclear fireball. Al, anything else headed our way?"

"No. They don't love us enough to even send flowers."

"I like your AI more than ours," said Kayla cheerfully. "Hey, Al, I'm Kayla. Nice to meet you." She raised her glass to salute him.

"Can it be that after all these years, my pilot has finally found a woman of insight and keen perception?" That Al, what a joker.

"Al, keep me posted. Otherwise take a nap or something."

"Dismissed like yesterday's news holo. Oh, the *indignity*."

"Karnean, we gotta get one like that," Kayla said energetically to her fading brother.

"Kar, if you're going to hurl, please use a trashcan or the head," I called over to him.

"I'm fine. I'll be fine."

"If you puke it, you clean it. Hey, I need to do a system check. I haven't been onboard for almost four years. You two make yourselves comfortable. There are sleeping quarters down that passage." I pointed. "Take your pick. Each one has its own head, err, bathroom. Mess is that way. If you need help, call for Al."

With that I left to visually inspect the ship, especially the engine room. Al could keep the ship running for years, but there were some actions even he couldn't perform.

An hour later, I was satisfied the ship was fine and located my passengers in the mess. Kayla was eating a hefty plate of Mexican food. Karnean was nursing a cup of tea.

"This stuff is *great*," Kayla said, pointing to her plate with her fork. "Where did you find it?"

"It's a favorite of mine, too. It's from my home planet—or was."

"Was what?" she asked confused. "They stopped making it?"

"No, the planet's gone. Got run over by a gas giant."

"That sucks," she said, as she was about to put some more chile relleno in her mouth.

"Yeah, it did."

"So are you planning on telling us the truth about yourself, or are we just supposed to worship you unquestioningly?" Karnean asked.

"That's not a nice attitude toward the man who saved us. Try for once in your life to be civil and grateful."

"Sorry, you're right. Please forgive me, Jon. That was uncalled for."

"No prob. I'll let you in on what I can, but I'm on a mission. I'll tell you in advance that I won't fill you in on everything. Okay?"

They said that was perfectly understandable.

I told them about the destruction of Earth, a vague idea of the human migration, and sketchy outlines about *Shearwater* and her capabilities. I let them know why I allowed myself to be shanghaied. Kayla took that part in stride. I could tell Karnean was sick about being duped and about the way he'd treated me. I didn't mention a thing about androids, cubes, or the super races I'd met. All in good time.

"You are kidding me? You sacrificed almost ten years of your life to journey to Deerkon and back, on the *off* chance you'd learn more about what a couple of slave traders said? You're the most giving and loyal person I've ever met, by a factor of a hundred," said Kayla. She whacked her brother in the shoulder. "Are you taking notes, Mr. Center of the Universe?"

"I'm a bit awed myself," Karnean said. "I assume you could have commandeered *Desolation* at any point, yet you put up with my petty abuse. Why?"

"The stakes are that high. I wanted to be able to do what I just did. It was worth it. Plus, I gotta tell you, you're a softy compared to some commanders I've had." I couldn't help reflecting on the long dead General Saunders. *That* man was tough. He'd have ground Karnean into dog food in less than a week. Funny. That was the first time I thought of Saunders in over a century.

"So, what now?" asked Kayla. "We leave, head back to Balmorulam?"

"There's nothing for us on Balmorulam," said Karnean, "and we're not going anywhere without our ship."

"Speak for yourself. I'm not setting foot on Deerkon ever again. Varrank can have her. I'm glad to be alive."

"*Desolation's* all we have. She's our only possession. What are we going to do without her? No, I want my ship and my crew back."

"I'd be happy to drop either of you on any street corner you'd like," I said with a smile.

"Not me. I'm good," said Kayla without hesitation.

"Look, if it's just a matter of money, I can set you two up with a grubstake, a pretty big one at that."

"There you go again. Well, at least I know why, now. What's a grubstake?" asked Kayla.

"Money, funds, currency."

"I'm not taking your charity, especially after how I treated you. No, that would stick in my throat," said a surly Karnean.

"Suit yourself. Me, I'm living day to day," responded Kayla.

"Well, I need to decide what my next move is. Once I have a plan, we can discuss your options." I still wanted to know more about the worldfleet issue.

"What are you waiting on?" asked Karnean.

"I put a bug in the computer. I want to see if I can hack Varrank's system when he gets it fixed. I fried it pretty good, so I imagine that will take a week, minimum."

"And in the meantime?" Kayla asked.

"In the meantime, seeing how you like Mexican culture, I thought I'd introduce you to tequila."

"Who's she? I thought it was just us three and Al aboard," replied Kayla.

"This is going to be fun," I said. "You in, Karnean?"

"I've been a sailor too long to not know you're talking about some new booze. I'm exhausted, you want to be alone with my sister finally, and I don't need another hangover. I'm in the first room. You two try and keep it down, please."

I was beginning to like the new Karnean.

It took ten days for Varrank to power up his computers. After he did, I wished it would have taken him forever. Crap almighty, I could *not* catch a break in this universe. Kayla and I were getting along well. Now, don't be asking, or jumping to conclusions. Leave it at *well*. Karnean spent his time learning what I'd cleared him to know about the ship. He wasn't good company, but he wasn't bad company, either. It turned out that our human culture had developed one thing more than any other species or planet in that extended society. Hologames. They mildly entertained Kayla, but Karnean lost his soul to the demon electronic game-o-sphere. He was significantly worse than a teenage boy in the abandon he displayed toward everything hologame related.

But then the computers were fixed, and damn if my back door didn't work like a charm. In less than three days, Al picked Varrank's computer system clean to the bone. There wasn't one scrap of information he knew that I didn't. There went my happy interlude.

Varrank's files on the human worldship fleet were extensive. How the hell he even knew about them was uncertain. There was no clear record of that. But he knew numbers, locations, sizes, directions, everything. In keeping with his secretive nature, he never made it clear why he wanted to know so much about the fleet. But I knew that if an evil man like Varrank was interested in something, catastrophe lay around the next corner. That led to my plan. Of all my plans ever, this was my least favorite. I wanted to do what I was going to do less than I wanted to return to Alpha Centauri-B 5 and live amongst the falzorn.

I needed to confront Varrank. I had to march back into his compound. The same one I'd partially destroyed. The one where I'd made all the guards look like idiots. The one I'd released falzorn into. He was going to be so glad to see me. It would be his birthday and Christmas, all rolled into one, with him trying to decide how best to kill me. That I made him look weak and vulnerable ruled out any real chance he'd negotiate, or even listen to my words. He needed to kill me several times to show his enemies he was still the unconquerable man.

Another no-win situation for a man who'd pushed his luck harder than logic dictated a person should. And just when things were getting nice between Kayla and me. Even if I had *Wrath* with me, I couldn't imagine a scenario where I'd get off Deerkon alive a second time. C-r-a-p.

I let my guests know what my plan was. Karnean betrayed the faintest of smiles. Kayla teared up and said she forbade me to be so foolish. I did make it clear that whatever I did, I did alone. If they wanted to borrow *Shearwater* to go somewhere close, they could. If they wanted to try and reclaim *Desolation*, I'd drop them off. But my suicide mission did not include a shore party.

"So do you have another of your ill-advised plans, at least?" asked Karnean.

"No. Not this time. I'll take a shuttle and a large amount of gold, but I bet I don't get three words out before he blows my head off."

"Gold doesn't mean much to Varrank," said Karnean. "I don't know him well, but I know his wealth is off the scale. You can't have enough gold to catch his eye."

"Probably not, but it's my only hope for trade. I have to convince him to leave the human fleet alone. Maybe I can buy that cooperation."

"How much gold do you carry?" he asked.

"I'm taking a ton."

"I know," he said, "but how much is that?"

"A ton. I meant that literally, not figuratively."

His jaw dropped. Kayla's eyes were as big as my fists.

"You have one thousand kilograms of gold on board?" Karnean asked in disbelief.

"No. I have a lot more. That's all the shuttle can safely carry. Unless he lets me make a few trips, that's my bargaining chip."

"And if you die, hence no longer require the use of the rest?"

"It's yours. My gift."

"I don't wish to seem insensitive—"

"Two and a half more tons."

"Well, I'll be fu—"

"Praying to all the gods he returns safely, you ass." Kayla slugged her brother hard. Wow, she was hot.

"Yes. All I can say is that I'm glad there's absolutely no way I can communicate with Varrank to warn him you're coming. That way, if I should suddenly come into great wealth, my conscience will be clear. My sister won't kill me, either."

"At least I lived to see the day Karnean Beckzel became a humanitarian," I said with a smirk.

"Would you like Kayla to take a holo of us together, marking the day?"

I became serious. "I'll instruct Al what to do if I don't come back. He'll know what to do and what he can tell you. Eventually, he'll return to my home planet to be with my family."

"You have a—" Kayla's voice rose quickly, menacingly.

"Ms. Beckzel," cut in Al, "believe me when I tell you his mate was killed several years ago. He's not too good with emotions. I wanted to tell you, before he allowed you to avoid an awkward situation based on his limitations."

"Thank you, Al," she said. Pointing to the computer she said to me, "I'm liking him more and more."

"If I don't come back, you can keep him," I said with a cute smile.

"Fine by me," said Karnean. "But he sounds a bit unstable to me."

"I have both excellent hearing and memory, Karnean," responded Al, in an irritated tone.

"Okay, I need to go before I change my mind." I left to my cabin to record a couple holos and gather my thoughts.

Thirty minutes later I boarded the shuttle. "You two kids behave yourselves until papa gets home," I said, as I reached for the hatch control.

"Wait," yelped Kayla. She rushed over and gave me a very interesting kiss. Most promising. If I lived, that was. "That's for luck."

"I'm certain it'll help. See you soon." I crossed my fingers and sealed the hatch.

On my way, I radioed Varrank. I informed him I was coming to discuss a matter of mutual concern. I let him know I was alone, unarmed, and heavy with gold. Sure, the part about unarmed was a lie, but hey, he was an arch-criminal. Again, when in Rome, right?

I received instructions to land in the courtyard. A whole gaggle of guards were there to meet me. They all had unfriendly expressions. I wondered why? As I stepped onto the ground, I was relieved that they didn't immediately riddle me with holes. So far, so good, in my book. One of the Quelstrum guards grabbed my arm and pulled me toward the palace. I do believe he intended to rip my arm off. As I approached, I could see the building and grounds were fully repaired. Not a single garish decoration or blade of grass was out of place.

The guard threw me into a large study where Varrank was seated. If he'd looked bilious and angry the last time we met, he was downright demented-looking presently. Scary man.

"Sit," he said without moving. Once I had, he said, "I am pleased beyond your wildest imagination to have you back in my clutches, Jon Ryan. Whatever it is you want to do or gain is for naught. The only function you will serve is to put a smile on my face as you die."

"That's it? You don't even want to know what I want, what I offer?"

"Nothing you have is of any value to me. Nothing you want is of the slightest consequence. Dead men have so few needs."

"Aw, come on, Varrie. Aren't you this much," I pinched my fingers nearly closed, "interested as to why I'd do something as brash and suicidal as returning here?"

"I'll grant you that your return was unanticipated. But again, you are nothing. Nothing does not interest me."

"Wait. Is that a double negative? That's grammatically incorrect."

He was not amused. I doubt he ever was, but his amused index was well into the negative range.

"Guards," he snapped, "take him to the torture room and secure him. Let Master Ronsiller know I will be there shortly."

"I'm here to discuss the human worldship fleet."

Two burly guards started dragging me backwards.

"Stop," he commanded. "Bring him to my desk."

I was dragged to the edge of his desk.

Varrank stared into my eyes, trying to read my soul. "What do you know of the human worldship fleet?"

Ah, if he only knew. "A little. I know you're interested in it. As we share a mutual interest, I thought maybe we could work together."

"Very well. I will have your finger placed in a jar and keep it by my side when I crush the human fleet. Your wish has been granted."

He just said enough to seal his sorry-ass fate. I had to hold myself back, however, remembering that this might not be the real Varrank.

"How did you come to know of the fleet?" I asked.

He stared at me.

"What do you want with them?"

More hateful staring.

"What will it take for me to change your mind and leave them alone?"

Son of a bitch still sat there.

"If you kill me, I've made arrangements for Topollos to tell his government about your incursions into Judasrit." I had learned of that new political expansion plan from his computers. I did get a reaction with that revelation.

Varrank just barely nodded to one of the Quelstrum, and the beast punched me in the back so hard I sprawled across the table. I ended up nose to nose with my blackest enemy.

"Blackmail is ineffective. Topollos will be dead before you are." He leaned back with satisfaction. "It now occurs to me your interest in the human fleet may be founded on more than business. Not being able to destroy your ship in orbit reminds me of a recent encounter where a similar ship was impossible to destroy."

Oh, shit. He couldn't know any of that. We were light-years away. If I hadn't used the vortex to get to Balmorulam, the trip would have taken ten years plus.

"You asked how I know of the worldships. Given your more than casual interest, I think I shall reveal to you how I know of it." He nodded to the guards and I was lifted off the desk.

We left the room and headed down a long series of halls. Finally, we came to a large door. A guard opened it, and the procession entered. The light was dim, and the smell was horrendous. I was vaguely aware of a presence, but lacking orientation, I couldn't locate it.

"I would like to introduce you to an associate of mine," said Varrank as he walked toward one wall.

A spotlight clicked on. It hit a Listhelon that was nailed to the wall. As much as I hated the species, I felt instant pity for him. How it could be so extensively dismembered and partitioned, yet still remain alive was beyond my comprehension. I guess the Master Ronsiller was an expert, at that. The Listhelon had a cylinder attached over his gills to circulate water, but otherwise his body was exposed to the air. It was dry and cracked, like ancient parchment. It hurt to look at.

When the light struck him, his head lolled with a jerky twitch. He didn't want any more of whatever was coming.

"My people picked up him and a crew member in space. The ship they were with was destroyed before capture, but these new friends were taken alive. You can imagine my curiosity, Jon, as to why such a strange and novel species was flitting about in deep space. When I asked nicely why they journeyed so very far from home, they mentioned the humans. It seems humans defiled their home world.

"When they sought vengeance, they were completely rebuffed. They adopted a new strategy of guerrilla warfare against the humans as they fled in their cored-out asteroids. This one was part of a long series of warships sent to harass the fleet."

I knew how tough those fish were. He must have suffered more than I could imagine to talk so freely. That reminded me that I was about to learn his pain soon, if I didn't come up with a plan to the contrary.

"Do you know an interesting fact, Jon? This useless fish says the worldships are protected with an impenetrable force field. Such a marvelous barrier protects *your* ship. A planet far from here was similarly shielded. Isn't that odd, Jon? Don't you suspect, as I do, that there is a connection? But I shouldn't want you to worry. I will know everything relevant very soon."

"If you mess with the worldship fleet, you'll be sorry," I said hatefully.

"You think so? I don't. You see, I have powerful friends. Moreover, I never fail."

"This time, you will. You can't get through the barriers, and the ships are designed to sustain the population for generations. You can't starve them out."

"That is true. I, however, will not starve them out. I shall bypass the force field and kill every one of them in their homes."

"That's not possible. You're wasting your time."

"It is my time to waste, is it not? And I think you're forgetting the lessons learned from the planet that felt it too was safe under its magical umbrella. I'm betting you know how close they were to being defeated."

There was no way he could know or duplicate what the Berrillians had. No freaking way.

"You know what, Jon? It occurs to me you wonder how I could know these things and have such confidence. I would hate for you to die unaware of the completeness of your failure. I would not spare you that ultimate feeling of hopelessness before you die." He raised his hands and clapped.

Through the door strode an upright, five-hundred-pound tiger. It was not just any Berrillian; it was Havibibo. The commander of the assault on Azsuram.

"You're dead," I said reflexively.

"Nice to see you again, Jon Ryan," he responded with a snarl.

"But this cannot be the same man. He does not fly in his magical cube," said Varrank sarcastically.

"It is him. His stench has not changed."

"Nor yours," I said with a nod. "Oh, I bet you'd like to know Kelldrek is alive and well. She's in a small cage, but I haven't let her die."

He lunged at me, but two Quelstrums stepped in his path. He skidded to a halt. They scared even Havibibo.

He pointed a massive paw at me. "Soon, Jon Ryan, I will eat your flesh."

Good luck with that, I thought to myself.

"How did you survive?" I asked.

"When I saw your vessel returning to finish us off, I ordered abandon ship. Several escape pods, including mine, made it to warp space before they could be destroyed." He held out his massive arms to say, *and here I stand*.

"So you see, my plan *will* succeed. With the help of my Berrillian friends,

I shall scramble those inside the asteroids until they are dead. I will use gravity waves to destroy their power supplies, and their shields will fall like the tears you are about to shed. Then, the ships will be mine."

"But why. What use do you have for ten thousand worldships? You seem to be living large right here."

He placed a hand on his chest. "I have no use for them. Others, however, do. I plan on selling them to the highest bidder."

"Who would want to buy a worldship? That's crazy."

"Come now. Surely you, a man of the galaxy, knows there are many groups that feel disenfranchised, alienated, or wish to rid themselves of outside influences. They will pay dearly to leave the rest of society in their wake as they sail to their new lives, secure in their asteroids."

"But why not make them yourself? You're going to a lot of trouble."

"It is harder to core an asteroid than you seem to recall, Jon. It is much easier to eject the present occupants than to commit to such a long-term plan."

I had nothing. Varrank was right on all counts. His plan would work. With the Berrillian help, he could breach the worldship fleet. My species was closer to extinction now than it ever was before. And I was powerless. I could kill a handful of meaningless palace guards, Havibibo, and Varrank. But that wouldn't stop whoever the next boss was from committing genocide.

"Ah, I see my tutorial has had its desired effect. You know I will triumph, and you know you have failed. The day has turned out better than I could have hoped. Thank you for that, Jon Ryan." He began to laugh the laugh of the madman he was.

I snapped. I launched the probes into him and slammed him into the ceiling. Crap. I *was* holding an android driven by a remotely controlled AI. I could see the real Varrank through my contact, and he gloated even more.

When the guards seized me, I didn't resist. When they blindfolded me and bound me like a mummy, I didn't struggle. When they tossed me into a small room, I didn't protest. I lay still. All that I was had left me. I didn't want to die. I wanted to have never existed.

Before he closed the door, the robot Varrank said, "I shall leave you here a short while to become as miserable as you possibly can. Though I've found that this process can take days, in your case I will wait but a matter of hours. Then your torture will begin in earnest. Oh, and as you are so proficient at escape, know this. The walls of this cell are meter-thick steel. The there are hundreds of guards outside the door, on the floors above and below you, and in every surrounding room. The door seals like a bank vault, with ten hardened-metal rods that extend a meter each into the frame. The hinges themselves are so redundantly reinforced that a fission explosion would not cause them to fail. I went to considerable trouble designing this space. It was built to be foolproof, even for a fool such as you. I would shake your hand if you escaped from this, but you will not."

I didn't even swear at him as he sealed the door. No snark or clever comebacks. I was done.

EIGHTEEN

I lay on my side motionless for several minutes before I decided to try and sit up. It was difficult. My binding was so tight, it was difficult to bend at the waist. I pushed myself backward a few meters, until I encountered a wall, then shimmied my shoulders so I was almost sitting at ninety degrees. I extended my probes. They cut through the cloth easily. I clumsily yanked off my blindfold. It was pitch black in my cell. I started to unwind the mummy-wrappings. It was slow going. In fifteen minutes, my left arm was free enough to allow me to undo the rest of my cocoon. But so what? I was still locked in a metal coffin, surrounded by guards, and a bunch of Berrillians were close by. I started to say to myself that I had them right where I wanted them. But I trailed off. I was too broken for gallows humor.

I could always release the seals on my fusion-power units. That would blow a big hole where the palace used to be, but that wouldn't accomplish much. Varrank could be anywhere. Crippling his base of operations would delay his horrific plan, but only just. I couldn't stop the successful completion of his scheme, nor could I alert the worldship fleet. I kind of knew going in this was my last adventure. I had to try to save the worldships, but the odds were too long this time. I hated knowing how much we'd struggled as a race, all that we'd accomplished, just to see it all end violently. Humans really didn't deserve such a fate.

I started banging the back of my head against the wall in frustration. Even the iconoclastic, risk-taking mind of Jon Ryan couldn't come up with a solution. I checked in with Al. He didn't have any long-shot plans, rash advice, or impossible interventions to suggest either. He was sad, that much I could tell. I asked him not to let the other two know my situation until after I was … dead? Turned off? Decommissioned? Who the hell knew? Who the hell cared what it was called. I didn't.

Sitting there in the dark, I thought about Sapale and Carl Simpson and Jane Geraty and General Saunders and Offlin and so many others who'd died in my past. I loved them all. That I was about to join them made me feel a little better. That I'd failed my species and my friends more than negated my temporary positive feelings, however.

Almost without noticing, I felt a strange sensation. No sound, vibration, or smell. Just a buzz in the air. I'd never felt such a thing before and had no idea what it was, if it was anything at all. Maybe I was cracking up and that's what people who've lost it felt like. I started banging my head against the wall again, only a little harder.

"That's got to hurt," said a voice in my cell. It was a familiar voice, but I couldn't quite place it. And what the hell was it doing in here? As sure as I couldn't get out, no one could get in. Above all, who'd be crazy enough to break *into* a prison?

"Who's there?" I asked in a hushed tone.

"I might be the boogeyman. Maybe you could, I don't know, turn on a light and see if you should be scared." There was a mirth in the voice completely out of keeping with my grim situation.

I emitted a low-level light beam from my eyes.

No way. No fucking way. I was looking at myself, but not in a mirror. My mind raced. Could it be another incarnation of the evil Stuart Marshall? No. Even if he was reanimated, he'd be unable to penetrate the cell to join me.

"Good," he said, "you got the bindings off. Saves me the trouble. So you ready to go? Or do you want to stay and find out if Varrank is serious about doing you major harm?" He bobbed his head. "I'm thinking he's dead serious, but it's your call."

"Uto? Is that you, Uto?"

"You're such a chump. You know that, don't you? I made that up on the spur of the moment. Figured it'd take you like ten seconds to out me. Now, what, it's two centuries later, and you *still* think that's my name? What a maroon."

Who says *maroon*? Well, I guess I do.

"You can't be here."

"What, should I have asked permission first? I didn't see a No Trespassing sign. You think Varrank would make an exception in our case?"

"Stop it. No, I mean you literally can't be here. There's no way out. Trust me on that. So logically there's no way in."

"Now you're what, Mr. Spock?"

"If I wasn't hurting myself, I'd so punch you out."

He rocked his head sideways rapidly a second. "You want to rumble or leave? I personally don't want to be present when those smelly Quelstrum come to retrieve you. Double the pleasure, double the fun, is not a gift I'd like to give your captor."

"You mean *our* captor?"

"I do not. He caught *your* pansy ass, not *mine*. I'm way too smart for a jerk like that to lay a hand on." He tapped a finger on his chest. "I'm the cavalry."

"Fine. Let's get out of here. But how? What's your plan? I couldn't come up with anything."

"Glad I'm sitting down. That news might have knocked me over."

"Your *plan*?" I said straining my voice.

"Here's the plan. If you escape here, where would you go?" He held out a hand. "Be reasonable. Don't choose Disneyland or Sally Jones's basement."

He really was me. Sally lived next door when I was ten or eleven. We, you know, played in her basement. Okay, I'll just say it. We played doctor in her basement. TMI? Well, sorry.

"After escaping this cell, I'd return to *Shearwater*. I'd be safe and could plan my next move."

Instead of speaking, he gently closed his eyes. He moved his lips silently, as in a prayer or a chant.

Then my eyes exploded with light. We were sitting on the deck of *Shearwater*'s bridge. Two very surprised and confused Beckzel siblings jumped from their chairs. Karnean spilled his coffee on a control panel. He said something akin to *gurulf.*

"Captains plural on the bridge," Al announced blandly.

"What the hell?" yelled Kayla.

"Two of them? Crap," was Karnean's immediate reaction. "One was a lot to handle."

I stood up, the real me. D'oh. I meant the original ... the not really old me. I, the me with Deavoriath command prerogatives, stood up. "Easy. No Problem. I'm fine. We're fine. No problems."

"You said that already," said the other Jon.

"Fine, Jon, there's *no* problem? You return from your suicide mission having cloned yourself rather than dying in a blaze of glory. I assume an explanation is forthcoming," Karnean was no longer shocked, I guess.

"I'm not his clone," said still seated Jon. "I'm hi—"

"His twin brother. So, yes, clone was close to correct," I said speaking very quickly. "Yes. Twin brother," I repeated pointing at him.

"You never mentioned a brother, let alone a twin," said Kayla.

"Long *lost* twin brother. So long lost, I'd put him out of, you know, my mind. Out of sight, out of mind." I smiled for some unclear reason.

"If I'm your twin brother, what's my name?" asked the Jon, then standing and dusting himself off.

"You forgot your twin's name?" Kayla said incredulously.

"Or never knew it?" Karnean said more as an accusation.

"*Davis.* Of course, I know his name." I rapped him on the shoulder and introduced him. "This is my brother, older by eleven minutes, Davis Ryan. Pleased to meet you."

"Isn't that my line?" asked Davis.

Both Beckzels stared incredulously at us.

Can you hear me? I asked in my head.

Of course, I can. Did you think I checked out of this loony bin?

Not you, Al. You, Uto, you.

Is this a knock knock joke? asked Davis. *Knock knock. Who's there? Uto you. Uto you who?*

I'm familiar with the format, I responded to stop him.

I am also, if that's important, added Al.

So, you can hear me? I asked lamely.

No, not a word. Do humans still use the word moron? shot back Davis.

They don't know about the android, live forever thing. I'd like to break it to them gently, at some future date. Is that okay?

"Okay? *Why on earth should I care one way or another? They're your friends, not mine. This is your ship, not mine.*

They're not really my friends. They shanghaied me.

Then it's all right if I hit on the babe?

"No it is not all right if you hit on the b—" I realized I'd switched back to vocal communication.

"Hit on the what, little brother. B ... b... b—" teased Davis

"Basics of my argument." Huh?

"You two weren't arguing. You were standing there, looking at each other in silence." Karnean was so helpful.

"Your eyes were moving a lot," added Kayla. "Are you two telepathic?"

"Telepathic. No," I blustered. "Humans aren't telepathic, silly. It's a game we used to play when we were kids. We'd guess what the other was about to say."

"You were playing a game, and you thought your big brother was about to say *no it's not all right if you hit on the basics of my argument?*" Her cute little mouth dropped open.

"You never were any good at that game, were you, scruffy?" With that, he messed up my hair on his way to sit next to Kayla.

"Scruffy?" said Karnean.

"Long story," I replied.

"And here I was thinking you and I were weird, sis," Karnean said to Kayla.

"Okay, a moment if y'all don't mind," I said trying to sound authoritative. "Al, status report."

"All systems optimal. No messages or traffic from the surface."

"Thank you," I responded tugging at my shirt.

"Since when do you thank me for routine updates?"

"I always thank you some of the time."

I had better shut up.

"Whatever. I'll be in my room if either of you need me," responded Al.

"Maybe if we hold our breath we can swim back to the planet," Karnean said to his sister.

"I'll start practicing and keep you posted," she replied not taking her eyes off us.

I thought she was joking. She looked like she was joking, sort of.

"Davis," I said, again trying to sound in command, "may I speak to you in my cabin?"

"Yes, you may."

I turned to the others. "Official business." I pointed to Davis then toward my quarters. "Nothing big. Mostly personal stuff. He—"

"Please go," Karnean said roughly.

The instant my cabin door closed I blurted out, "What the hell just happened back there?"

"You made a fool of yourself. You convinced your friends you're insane and—"

"*No.* Back on Deerkon. You know I meant on Deerkon."

"I did? All right, I did. But messing with you is kind of fun. I usually don't have a lot of fun, so I seized the opportunity."

"I'm going to seize your throat, if you don't explain what happened."

"You really gotta switch to decaf, bro."

I closed my eyes. "Deerkon?"

"Oh, that. I rescued you. What else would you like to know?"

"Ah, maybe how you knew I needed rescuing, how you knew I was in that cell on Deerkon, and how the hell you pulled that miracle off?"

"It wasn't a miracle. I don't do miracles."

"Me neither. Thanks. We don't do magic either, so how did you do it?"

"Speak for yourself."

I was bethumped. "I am speaking for myself. What are you talking about?"

"No, you said we didn't do magic. Speak for yourself. I don't do miracles, but I *can* do magic."

"If we cannot have a serious conversation, I'm going to walk out that—"

"I'm serious. Deadly serious."

"So you performed magic to get us out of that cell?"

"It was no performance. It was an *act* of magic. Do you have any other possible explanation that can trump my suggestion?"

"You have a transporter beam."

"Like *Star Trek*?"

"So you admit it."

"No. I said, like *Star Trek*. You think I used a 1960s TV science fiction show's imaginary technology to rescue you? You're worse off than I thought."

"Then how. And don't say magic."

"I knew you were in trouble and where you were because I check in with Al periodically."

"You check in with Al? He's my ship's AI."

"He was mine, too. Still is, in the future."

"No. This Al is mine, not yours."

"You'll get used to the time thing. It takes a while."

"Why didn't he tell me you were eavesdropping?"

"Because I wasn't. He knew it was Jon Ryan calling. He's programmed to respond to our queries."

"But he had to know it wasn't me."

He just stared back.

"No, I mean—"

"It takes time. Don't short out on me, okay?"

"Back to the magic. Why are you even saying that?"

"Jon," he said stepping toward me, "look into my eyes. I'm not kidding. I used magic to relocate us here. There was no other solution, even for me."

"So, I'm a wizard in the future?"

"No. A male witch is a warlock. Wizards are completely different. And you're not. I am."

"The human worldship fleet, all of humanity is in mortal peril. I need your help to save them, but now I find out you're delusional. You can per ... do magic? That's insane."

"No. It's hard to imagine, extremely unlikely, but it's not insane."

"But how?"

"That's another story for another time. Right now we need to alert the worldships. Without our help, you're right, they're goners."

"When did you learn of this? Were you working to save them, too?"

"No. The first I heard of it was when you told me just now."

"Then how do you know they're defenseless?"

"*Hello.* Berrillian gravity wave generators. I was at the battle of Azsuram, too. The worldships will be sitting ducks."

"Why did you let them kill Sapale?" There, I said it. It was in the front of my mind since the moment she died in my arms.

He looked at the floor but didn't answer.

"I'm not moving until you tell me. She was my brood's-mate and the love of my otherwise pitiful excuse for a life. Tell me and tell me now."

"I doubt you'd understand. Remember, I loved her, too."

Wait, yeah, he had his Sapale. That made what he did even worse.

"I don't give a shit if I *understand* your reasoning, but I will hear it *now.* If you would have intervened sooner, she'd be alive today."

"And you'd be fat and happy on Azsuram and not here doing your job, your forever job. Defending humanity's right to survive."

Wow, didn't see that coming.

"So you knew if she died—"

"I knew nothing of the sort. I just know a hell of a lot more than you do. I *did* what I had to *do.*"

"So, you live fifteen centuries more than me and that makes you so smart, you can let my mate die? That's offensive."

"Listen, it's like this. I helped you with the membranes because without them, they all died. *All* of them, Jon. I killed the Berrillians when, and only when, it was clear you couldn't. Maybe you would have defeated them without my help. I had to wait and see."

"Why? I don't get why."

"If I helped you, I knew you'd come after me, just as you did."

"And that's worse than Sapale's death?"

"No, just different. I value my privacy. Jon, I'm from the future. I can't allow myself to muddle the time stream to save one single person, whoever she might be."

"But you saved *me* three times."

"We're not a just some person. We're the insurance policy of our species. We always have been and always will be. That's our core mission. I will do whatever it takes to keep them safe."

"What—"

"I failed them *once*, Jon. I will never fail them again." His words were dark and his face was haunted.

"I can only imagine your pain."

He seethed awhile before responding. "No, little brother, you cannot. I watched the Listhelons murder every living human, destroy the worldships in orbit, and then … you know what those horrible creatures did? They ate their flesh, Jon. They *ate* the people I was sworn to keep alive. Then I spent fifteen centuries hating myself, blaming myself, and wishing to *God* I could terminate myself. But I couldn't, Jon. You know why? You know why I couldn't stop, why I couldn't end? Because I had to save the people I didn't save. *That* is my pain, little brother. You will never feel it, so please don't say those words again. No one will ever feel my pain."

He turned away from me. Poor son of a bitch. I had the impulse to go and hug him. I let him be.

"To fully answer your question," he began slowly, "I waited as long as I could to intervene, because I must allow events to progress as they are supposed to. The only exception is when it comes to humankind. They're priority number one. Period."

He was quiet a long while. "If you can live with that set of facts, if you can accept them, then we can work together to save the fleet. If you can't forgive me, I'll understand. I'll take my leave, and you'll never see me again. That's a promise."

"You mean you'll pass the baton to me? I'll be in sole charge of our species?"

He shrugged.

"I turned out to be such a pussy. A big old cry baby who bailed on my own people when the going gets tough." I really put the screws in him intentionally.

He spun on me angrily, only to see me pointing at him as if to say *gotcha*.

Slowly, like an iceberg melting on a cold day he started to giggle. That finally broke into raucous laughter, which I joined in on. Soon, we were hugging each other like the long separated brothers we weren't.

"You are *such* an asshole," he said to me, when we settled down.

"That makes you one, too." I held up one then two digits to be annoying.

"Me, too." He grabbed my fingers and held them gently.

"So, how can we stop the Berrillians?"

"Not easily. This time they'll come in greater numbers. They'll be spread out over a huge distance when they attack the ten thousand worldships."

"Do you even know why the most hostile species in existence would work with a petty crime boss? Eat him, yes. Work in concert with him, no," I asked.

"They're using him for the time being. Soon enough, they'll destroy him and his petty empire. They hate humanoids too much to cooperate for long." He was quiet a moment. "Who knows, maybe the Berrillians want the worldships for themselves and are just playing him to acquire them?" He stared into nothingness a few moments. "I know the Berrillians. They returned in my timeline just like in this one. They wanted two things then and now. To find the Deavoriath, and to rule the galaxy."

"Did they find them?"

"No," he looked over to me. "Neither did I." He held up his hands to show no command prerogatives.

"What happened on Earth, there at the end?" I wasn't sure it was fair to ask him to relive those painful secrets, but I was curious.

"We sent whatever fleet we could muster to meet the Listhelons near Saturn's orbit. They blew past that line of defense like it wasn't there. After that, it was like shooting fish in a barrel." He paused. I think the pun was a gut punch. "Sapale and I stayed on Earth. When their main fleet hit—" He paused again. "When their main force hit, it was a bloody massacre. They landed and did horrible things, then they retreated to space. All they had to do was pin us down and let Jupiter do the heavy lifting in terms of extermination. That's exactly what happened. Billions of humans were forced to watch Jupiter swallow them up."

"How'd you two survive?"

"We didn't." His head dropped. "I did. Sapale didn't."

"Christ, I'm sorry I asked. Look, forget about—"

"Those *Ark* ships didn't really have offensive capabilities. After what little I had was gone, there was nothing we could do. Sure, we could ram one of ten thousand ships. That would've changed nothing. We made a run for it a week before the planetary collision. We made it past the first line of fighters, but one of their cruisers in orbit hit *Ark 1* as we cleared the upper atmosphere. The ship held together, but there was an explosive decompression."

He stopped speaking. I didn't press him. He'd said enough.

"But I escaped. Al and me. No humans survived, but a couple of asshole computers did. I decided I'd do exactly what I ended up doing."

"You couldn't have known you'd succeed."

"I had to try." He sighed. "Anyway, back to the topic of Berrillians. Over the centuries, I battled those big cats repeatedly. They spread like the disease they are and came to rule most of the galaxy."

"And the Deavoriath never raised a finger to stop them?"

"If you didn't have those," he pointed to my hands, "I'd have sworn there was no such thing."

"They're real, but they are very stubborn."

"Apparently so. I was a pain in the big cats's asses, but never much more than that. By the time I returned to find you, they pretty much ruled everything." He shook his head. "Man, can they be ruthless. It's really hard to convey the terror they wrought."

"I can't believe it."

"What?"

"That time travel is possible. All those physicists swore it was impossible, and it turns out it isn't."

"It is."

"It's what?"

"It's impossible."

"But … no. You're going to tell me it was *magic*?"

He nodded in the affirmative.

"But then it's possible. Maybe it just takes magic, but time travel is doable."

He shook his head. "That's not how the universe works, ma boy. Magic is contrary to the forces and laws of nature. Without it you can't time travel, because time travel is impossible."

"I—"

"Give it time, son."

"No, you *don't*. I don't care how old you are, you're not calling me son, pops."

He softly slugged me in the shoulder. "So, what're we going to tell your guests?"

"We're brothers, we're going to help the humans, and they're free to join us or move on down the road."

"Why would they join us? They don't *seem* crazy."

"I was thinking more that one of them would stay. The other can float home for all I care."

"So, you like that Karnean fellow? Hey, to each his own. That's my philosophy." He thumped his chest.

My turn. I slugged him only much harder.

"How are you going to get their ship back if they don't want to go on a quest against unbeatable odds?"

"Can't you," I wiggled my nose with two fingers, "you know, *poof.*"

"No, I can't," he scrunched up his nose, "just go *poof.*"

"Why not?"

"Maybe I'll tell you someday, maybe I won't. Just know it doesn't work that way. It's very hard and the cost is tremendous."

"What cost?"

"Maybe someday. Probably not. Otherwise drop it." He stood and tapped my knee. "Let's do this."

NINETEEN

The first issue was bringing my guests up to speed on the situation, at least as much as I was willing to tell them. They were pirates, after all. Not rumored to be a very trustworthy lot. I explained Varrank's scheme. I told them about the Berrillians. They'd never heard of them. They nodded and asked questions like they were just some other alien species. After I showed them a holo, they understood better what a force of nature the Berrillians were. I glazed over my escape, saying only my brother rescued me. I offered to take them with me or give them a bunch of gold to buy their own ride. Their response was that they would think about it.

The more complex issue was the logistics of location. I was far from home. The worldships were twenty plus light-years away. Azsuram was thirty-five light-years off. *Wrath* was closer, at four light-years, but the Berrillians had FTL speed capabilities. Unless Davis was going to poof us somewhere, figuring out the timing was a headache. Additionally, at the speeds we'd all traveling time dilation had to be accounted for.

The Berrillians could get to the worldships in three years. At maximum speed, I could retrieve *Wrath* in about that same time. But last time I faced those cats, I had *Wrath*, and that wasn't nearly enough. Davis had thumped them soundly, but I didn't know if he had a faster ship, or if he could pull it off again. If he'd used his magic, maybe he couldn't or wouldn't use it on this occasion.

When we were alone again, I asked him straight up. "Can you get us to my vortex or the worldfleet before the Berrillians attack?"

"Yes, I think so."

"Great. Care to expand on that?"

He seemed reluctant. Why?

"My ship is fast, but it uses conventional drives. *Shearwater* is nearly as fast."

Not what I wanted to hear.

"And before you ask, magic is always a last resort. It is never used for convenience or expedience."

Less welcome news.

"I say we retrieve your vortex and go from there."

"But *Wrath* alone couldn't defeat the Berrillians."

"This time you'll have more time to nip at them in warp space."

"Maybe. They might move quicker than we guess, though. We could be too late, again."

"Based on their current tech, I think our estimates are sound. Remember, I know them pretty well. A thousand years from now, they'd be there in a few months, but not this generation."

"Well, I guess that's as good a plan as any. I'd really like to get back in the cube. It makes travel a breeze."

So it was decided. We would slam the pedal to the metal and head to Balmorulam. Davis summoned his ship, and we stowed it on the cargo deck. Nice ship but small. That only left the matter of the passengers.

"So, what'll it be?" I asked. "Pick your poison."

They looked at each other.

"You say you're going to get your faster ship. How fast is it?" Karnean asked.

"Instantaneous travel anywhere."

"That's fast," replied Kayla wide-eyed.

"Well, I'm not big on crewing another man's ship. I'm a captain and would like to keep it that way."

"Fine. I'll give you enough gold to buy two good ships. The shuttle will take you two back to Deerkon. I'll set it to auto-return after you're safely down."

"The one of us," said Kayla.

"Huh?" I said as my heart skipped a whole lotta beats.

"I'm done with that lifestyle. I want to ship with you," said Kayla walking over to me. "If it turns out I regret that decision, you can put me somewhere with your instant ship."

"Yeah, fine," I stammered, "but it'll take, like, three years to pick up my other ship."

She battered her eyelashes. "I'm aware of the physics involved."

"The *biology*, too," grumbled her brother.

"Let's get to it," said Davis very businesslike.

I was happy, to state it mildly, that Kayla was comi … traveling with me. I was as glad to see the last of Karnean. He was too grouchy, and I doubted I'd ever actually allow myself to trust him. So, as soon as the shuttle left *Shearwater*, I sealed the hatch and hit the accelerator. Kayla agreed to see if she could tolerate four-g's for a while, so that's the speed I set. After a few days, she said she was willing to try five-g's. That was overly optimistic of her. She passed out a couple times and had to crawl places, since walking was too difficult for her. So back to four g's it was. Maybe in a few months we'd be going fast enough that I could drop to two or three g's and not lose much time.

I've waxed philosophical about it before. Long space flights are no fun. If it was going to take us three years, there was no way around it. I did have superior distractions on that particular trip however. Getting to know the almost two-thousand-year-old me was unreal. Getting to know Kayla, well, that was, believe it or not, way better.

I respected her space. I knew she was in an awkward position, shipping out for at least a few years with me. We'd become pretty close, but traveling as we were put her in a tough position. Hence, I flirted with her continually, but I let her decide if our relationship went from one level to the next. Kayla, it turned out, was quite the level changer. Show that girl a level and, bam, she graduated up to the next one almost immediately. She got no complaints from me. Within a few months, we'd moved in together. Life was good.

Davis kept to himself most of the time. He took us and our budding romance with a considerable amount of salt. He never gave off the vibe of being an uncomfortable third wheel, and he never acted jealous. He always had an *oh-the-joys-of-youth* look when he saw us together. I guess he'd done it all in his time. Maybe he was done with a lot of things most people took for granted. I tried to draw him out on the subject, but, as with most topics, he kept matters to himself.

Al let it slip that Davis spent a lot of time reviewing the history that his membrane technology made possible. He also liked to study my detailed records of the voyage of *Ark 1*. Was he looking for subtle differences in our journeys? There had to be some, since he hadn't found, or remembered, Oowaoa. I tried to talk to him about it, but he pretended to have no interest.

I did have an interesting conversation with him a year into the trip. I'd been curious about the similarities between so many aliens and humans. I was always afraid to ask a local, because it would have blown my cover. Davis, on the other hand, had a wealth of experience and was safe to consult.

"So, you noticed," he said grinning. "As close as you are getting to Kayla, I'd say it's a good thing you two are so … compatible."

"That's not why I ask. I just can't get over the similarities. It can't be chance alone."

"Probably not, but in this case, there are a lot of unanswered questions."

"So, you don't know for sure?"

"I guess I do. I've run a lot of DNA analyses on a lot of races. There is an inescapable similarity among the DNA of many groups. Can't be chance."

"So what's the hard part to swallow?" I remarked.

"How did the human race spread from planet to planet before they had tools, let alone spaceships?" he asked.

"Any ideas?"

"No. Nothing firm, that is. I've combed historic and archeologic records from hundreds of worlds. I can't find a convincing link."

"Maybe an ancient race brought them as slaves?"

"Possibly, but again, there's no record of that. I would think a highly advanced society would have record of that type of thing, even if it was a very long time ago."

"I'll check with Kymee next time I see him. If anyone knows, it'd be him."

"Who's Kymee?"

"Oh, I guess I never mentioned him, did I? He's the only Deavoriath I actually consider a friend. He's their head scientist. I'll introduce you, if you'd like, when the fighting's done."

He tilted his head back and forth. "Maybe. We'll see."

"What? They're very different from us, but they're all right. They've always been square with me."

"In my time, I've heard a lot about the legendary Deavoriath. I have to tell you, it ranges from bad to much, much worse than bad. They were not a kindly bunch of neighbors."

"I know. I've gone over most of the records *Wrath* carries. They're different now, or at least still trying."

He took a deep breath. "We'll see."

"I tried to get them to help us fight the Berrillians, but they wouldn't. They said coming out of their shell would be worse than anything the Berrillians could do."

"Do you believe that?"

"I don't know. Tough question. I think *they* believe it. I would have liked their help. I'd still like their help."

"Then ask. What can it hurt?"

"Nah. It's only been a few years. For them that's the blink of an eye. They're not ready to act anyway, unless it's on Oowaoa."

"Well then," he said with a wicked smile, "we'll just have to do it all by our lonesome again."

Another conversation we had to have on our long voyage concerned Azsuram. I wanted to know how he destroyed all those ships. I assumed it was magic, but his reticence to use it suggested otherwise.

"How did I destroy the ships?" he asked uncertainly. "You *were* there. I rammed 'em."

"I know you did, but I don't know how it's possible. I've seen your ship. It's too fragile to do the job. You could use a membrane, but then how could you maneuver?" I danced a hand through the air. "You twisted and turned like a cat cashing three mice."

"I turned my control stick and the ship went thataway. That's how the ship's controls work."

"Can't you give me a simple answer for once? There's no way to maneuver that tightly if your ship's in a membrane."

"Ah. I see your hang-up. It's done with gyros."

I pulled my head backward. "Gyroscopes? No way. Attitude control, sure. High speed twists and turns, no way."

"Why not *way?*"

"Because, surfer dude, you'd have to carry gyroscopes bigger than your ship to move that nimbly."

"I'll keep that in mind next time I go on the attack or need to park in a tight space."

"You used your magic, didn't you?"

"Nope. Simple tech. The gyroscopes are sophisticated. But their positioning aboard ship is the key. I'll send you the schematics."

"Okay. I guess. Seems like it has to be more complicated."

"Nope. Membrane, gyroscopes, and skill. Even you might be able to pull it off." He winked, the jerk.

Eighteen months into the trip, I decided to come clean with Kayla. She was romantically involved with a robot, right? It was time to tell her. Maybe she'd jump out the airlock when I finished the tale.

One morning we were lying next to each other just being happy together. "I've been thinking," I said as nonchalantly as I could, which was nervous as all get out, "you probably wonder about me."

"No. Never. Next subject." She was such a pistol.

"Ah, a woman who's not interested in rumors, gossip, and hidden facts."

"That's me."

"He told you, didn't he?"

She put on an overly surprised look and replied, "Me? Who? What?"

"That sneaky son of a bitch."

"Which one? Davis or Al?"

"Davis *or* Al? Which one told you? I'm surrounded be traitors."

"How about this? You tell me what you want to. After that, if the stories are the same, I'll tell you who to hate the most. Deal?"

"Conspirators and turncoats. Yes," I shook her hand, "I'll talk, then you squeal."

"We'll see. If I'm mad enough at you, that option may be off the table."

"No, I meant—"

She giggled as she set her hands on my chest. "I know what you mean, you big oaf. I'm just messing with you."

"I know that."

"And the story begins—"

So I told her. I told her about being an android, my voyages, my age, Sapale, Azsuram, who Davis was, the whole enchilada. I even showed her the probes. Unlike Sapale so many years ago, Kayla didn't ask for a demonstration. Pity. I'd love to snoop in her head just a little. When I was done spilling my guts, I asked her if that was what Davis had told her.

"No. He just said you cheated at cards. The rest is news to me." She held a straight face for three seconds, then nearly snickered to death. Snot came out her nose and everything. She was such a pill. But she was my pill. Kayla was a keeper. I only hoped she thought I was one, too. Love is very costly for us immortals, but Kayla was well worth the pain I was signing myself up for.

By the time we reached Balmorulam a year later, she'd just given birth to our daughter, Gallenda. That was Kayla's grandmother's name. It was unreal. I, of all people, was becoming a normal person for the first time ever. Jane and I had an accidental kid. I was a happy stepfather to Sapale's offspring, but here I was with a beautiful baby girl to match her beautiful mother. I was a *family* man. Davis had so much fun at my expense. He knew how happy I was. Therefore, he kept torturing me.

The three of us went right to *Wrath*. No need to go to the planet itself. Davis and Kayla were duly impressed with *Wrath*. I attached *Shearwater* to her mountings and insisted we get going at once. I needed to go to Azsuram first. It wouldn't be a long stay, but I had to see my family. I wanted to show off my girls, too.

Davis was welcomed warmly once everybody learned he was the person who destroyed the Berrillian fleet. Plus, as he was me, he was family, too. I took Jon to see Toño. I'd alerted both men the other was present. When we entered the lab, Jon was very standoffish, hanging back like he didn't want to be there. I took Kayla to see Kelldrek. I wanted her to see a Berrillian in the flesh. She left Gallenda with Toño, which was a good idea. The poor kid'd have nightmares the rest of her life, if she saw that big cat in the flesh.

We weren't gone five minutes, but when we came back, Jon and Toño were hugging like long-lost brothers.

"God, I missed you, Doc," Jon said.

"I missed you, too."

Wait, how could he miss him? I was here the whole time. Oh, Toño was being the physician and comforting Jon. Okay. I was getting confused.

Kayla took Gallenda from Toño's arms. I don't think he even noticed.

"To know there's still one link to the real past, to my past. You don't know what that means, Doc."

They hugged harder.

"I will always be here and you are always welcome. Once you have dispatched the Berrillians, I insist you return and spend some time here. We must talk."

"I'd love to, Doc. I will."

"Jon, "Toño began matter of factly, "I'm curious. I stand here today, so I know I exist. But you know how my scientific mind is always wondering. In your time line, what becomes of me? Did you and I travel together, after the Earth was lost? I assume I became an android, as politics never change. Did—"

"You died, Doc." Jon stopped a second. "You never made it off Earth." He lowered his head sadly. "At the end, when they were pounding us good, Alexandra, Sean, and you jumped in an Ark ship and made a run for it. You ... you never cleared the atmosphere. I think they hit you with a nuke. Whatever it was didn't leave a trace."

"Oh. Oh, my. Now I'm not so certain I should have asked. I'll probably need to administer Freudian analysis to myself for the next seven years." He sort of giggled, but it didn't sound like too humorous a response.

Next, I had to hook up with the worldship fleet. Yeah, I had to tell them, yet again, that they were in more trouble than they could handle and that their survival would be against all odds.

"Who the *hell* is this Varrank Simzle?" asked Amanda, rubbing her temples.

"Just another bad guy looking to make a profit in a harsh universe. He has a fleet of warships, but he's no real threat. Somehow, he's allied with the Berrillians. It's *them* I'm worried about."

"Tell me about it," she replied harshly.

Then she looked up again at Jon. "And tell me again, you're—?"

"Ms. Walker," said Jon, "you heard Jon explain who I am. I'm here to help."

"So, if I call you Jon," she pointed to me, "what should I call you? And don't—" she added quickly, "don't say not late for dinner, because I'm *not* in the mood."

Davis turned to me. "Wow, she knows us pretty well."

I nodded that I agreed.

"For the time being, keep calling me Davis," he said.

"Why—"

He raised a waving hand, indicating she shouldn't ask.

She accepted his good advice. "So when is doom due?" she asked glumly.

"Three, maybe four months," I replied.

"And do we stand any better a chance this time?"

"It depends—" I started to say.

Davis cut me off. "It depends on a good deal of factors. We're cautiously optimistic."

"That we'll do better, or that we'll be successful?"

He looked at me and pointed to Mandy. "She's sharp."

Her expression suggested one of us had better answer that question, and quickly.

"Mandy," I said, "we'll be fine. It'll be tough, but we'll survive." Now I just needed to believe that myself.

"So, what is our combined plan?" asked Admiral Katashi Matsumoto. He'd been promoted to command all worldship defenses since I last visited.

"I've fought them many times, Admiral. You and I will talk at length after this meeting." Davis and I had agreed on that beforehand. He did know the enemy well. Plus, I figured Katashi might misinterpret Davis's general world-weariness as him being more proper than me.

"Fine. You two go rub your heads together and summon a war genie. Jon and I will stay and chat." Mandy stared at me intently.

Gulp. She already knew about Kayla and Gallenda. This promised to be interesting.

"So, before I go on, congratulations on your wife and baby. Gallenda is her name, I believe?"

"Yes. Cute as a box full of buttons. The best part is she looks mostly like her mom."

"I'm happy for you. Lest you say something suggesting the contrary, I truly am. I know a lot of time has passed. Life happens. I get that."

"Thank you, Mandy. How're you doing?"

"I'm split right down the center on that one. Politically, I've never been better. I get more than my share of pushback and headaches, but things have come together nicely."

"Which leaves only personally."

"Which sucks. No wait, if it did … forget it. Lousy attempt at a bad pun. Personally, you could politely say my love life was on hold."

"Gal like you? Won't last long."

"You know you're the only one whose eyes don't get clawed out for referring to me as a *gal*?"

"I'll take that as a compliment."

She growled softly. "Okay, old friend, it's just you and me alone in a room. Are we dead meat?"

"If I had to pick a winner and place a bet, I wouldn't put that hard earned cash on us."

"I suspected as much. And this Davis/other you guy. Is he okay? Can I trust him?"

"*That* I can guarantee. His commitment to the saving of humanity is more ferocious than a Berrillian mother defending her cubs."

"That's reassuring. In that case, I'll give him lots of responsibility. Will he be with us or with you?"

"Probably here, but no one tells him what to do. We'll have to play it by ear," I replied.

"Fifteen centuries on your own does beget an independent spirit, I imagine. Well, I've got to alert all the governors and then arrange for a summit on *Exeter*. You be around a while?"

"Probably not."

"Dinner? With you and the family, of course."

"We'd love to."

"Then dinner at six, it is."

The next morning I took Kayla to look for Karnean. She wanted to make certain he was okay. They had arranged to communicate through an AI on Pallolo. Sure enough, he'd left notice where he was headed in his new ship. After a couple of jumps, we caught up with *Kayla* mid-flight on some shady mission. For the first time, I saw Karnean happy; the normal happy, not the psycho happy he did way too well. He was thrilled to be an uncle. I think he was even glad to see me. He fell so completely in love with *Wrath*, I wanted to get them a hotel room and a box of condoms. I was glad he was jealous. I know, that speaks poorly for my character, but there you have it. He and I had history.

We stayed with Karnean a couple days catching up, but then it was time to go. I wanted to pick up Toño and join the worldships. We had a meeting with Carlos De La Frontera. Then, unless a better plan presented itself, I'd start hounding the Berrillians in warp space.

"So, the old team is back together," said Carlos as he sat down.

"With an even older new addition," added Toño as he pointed at Davis.

"As one who has lived with his clone, I shall not be disturbed by the double vision of Jon," Carlos responded.

"He's an android. He used to work with his original until the president killed him," I said filling Davis in. From the look on his face, I think I didn't achieve helpful clarity.

"So they don't explode if you let the original and android meet?" Davis asked Toño pointedly.

"In my defense, at the time—"

Davis cut Toño off. "Just messing with you, Doc."

"This is a meeting of the *war* council, gentlemen, not the Rotary Club." That would be the ever-serious Katashi. "I suggest we focus on saving our species and dispense with the fraternal raillery."

"Sound advice," said Davis. I *knew* he'd mesh with Katashi.

"As head of this ad hoc committee," said Katashi, "I will open the floor for discussion. Davis, if you will, please give us your best impression as to what we will face. We can proceed from there."

"Based on what I learned in my timeline, we are witnessing the reemergence of the Berrillian Empire. They started their invasion at roughly this point in time. Assuming history is repeating itself, we're in for a real trial.

"The Berrillians retreated to a far-off sector a few thousand light-years from here after their defeat at the hands of the Deavoriath. They conquered that area, focused on advancing technology, and in multiplying their number impressively. I don't wish to be overly graphic, but the brutal carnivores devastated planet after planet. They presently number in the trillions. Their ships are more numerous than the stars in the sky. They come in waves, each reporting back to the next how to better achieve victory. Each wave is understood to be expendable. All that matters to any of them is that the empire triumph and expand."

"You don't paint a very promising picture," said Katashi.

"I'm certain I understate the case. There is no surrender, negotiation, or quarter with them. *War* and *death* are the same word in their language. In my time, they overran the galaxy and darkness reigned."

"Okay," I said, "on that pleasant note, I'd like to remind everyone that we don't have to dispose of the entire empire just yet, just this next wave that plans on stealing our rides."

"Might it be a smaller group since they're cooperating with Varrank?" asked Carlos.

"Possibly. They're not above a side engagement with a smaller force. The only way to know is to see if there is a reserve force lying in wait further behind the fleet approaching us." Davis was grim. "*Wrath* can take a few stabs at recon, but space is very large. We'll probably not know until they hit us."

"A limited force would be something I expect we could rebuff," said Katashi. Something on the scale of the last incursion would be problematic."

That was putting it mildly.

"I see advantages in both tightening up the fleet's formation and for keeping it spread out," the admiral said. "Your thoughts, gentlemen."

"We don't have enough ships to fend off a concentrated attack, if we're spread to hell and gone," I replied.

"But," said Toño, "a tightly grouped fleet could be heavily targeted."

"Perhaps we should try and circle back to outflank the Berrillians?" asked Carlos. "I doubt they'd expect such an assault."

"Tight, but not too tight. That's my advice," said Davis. "A feint is unlikely to matter. They fight all-out and wouldn't hesitate to fire on their own ships if they chanced to be caught in the crossfire. Plus, these asteroids are crawling snails compared to the Berrillian armada."

"Very well," said Katashi. "I will take your words under advisement. Any last thoughts before we adjourn?"

There were none. There wasn't much to say, when the options were so limited and obvious.

So, I was off to cripple Havibibo's fleet again. I went alone, except for Al, of course, as before. The main difference this time was that I took as many infinity charges as I could hold. They seemed to be the most effective weapons last time. I had one stop to make first. I didn't discuss it with anyone, because I'd only draw criticism. Plus, I didn't need anyone's permission.

I walked into Kymee's work area on a typical, bleak, and colorless day. Ecotourism to Oowaoa was never going to catch on. He wasn't there. I wandered through his quarters, but didn't find him. I guess he could have been shopping or out to dinner. I walked back to *Wrath*.

"Kymee's not in his shop. Do you know where he is?"

"Yes, Form."

Not the Al-verbal-shuffle again. "Where is he?"

"Not far. This is the main vortex landing dock. The maintenance facilities for my kind are a few meters north. He is there."

Cryptic jerk.

I found Kymee. He looked like a grease monkey. He was supine on a roller board under a large metal sheet. It might have been the makings of a vortex. Why he'd be making one was beyond me. Why build the ultimate traveling machine if you refused to leave home?

"Yo, Kymee," I called out.

For under the metal came, "Jon. There you are. I've been expecting you."

Hmm. "Expecting me since I landed or since when?"

"Yes," he said as he slid out and stood.

"You're as bad as me," I chided. We bumped shoulders.

"No. *You're* as bad as *me*." He patted his chest. "I'm the senior member of this duo."

"You are well?" I asked.

"Couldn't be different," he replied.

"I know that social gossip *Wrath* told you I was coming and why."

"He did. Hard to break him of his baser habits. He's always been a chatterbox."

"He's wrong."

"Oh? Don't let him hear that. He might literally explode."

"I didn't come to ask for your help."

"Unexpected. So why are you here?"

"Two things. I want to show you this."

I grabbed my handheld and shot a holo of Kayla holding Gallenda in the air in front of him.

He studied the image with interest and I suspect no little awe. "Is that supposed to make me feel guilty?" he said, narrowing his eyes.

"No, you lunkhead. It's to show you my two girls. They're my pride and joy. Aren't they perfect?"

"Yes they are. I'm pleased you're so happy." Serious again he asked, "And the other matter?"

"I wanted to say goodbye."

"Goodbye, as in, *see you later*, or as in, *never see you again because I'm dead?*"

"You're not making this any easier."

"Was I supposed to? You didn't specifically ask me to, did you?"

"Goodbye, as in, *I love you and I won't be seeing you again.*"

"Is it something I said?" He smiled.

"No. It's because I can't imagine I'll survive. I'm leaving to take potshots at the Berrillians in warp space, but I don't think I'll do much more than piss them off and get my ass killed."

"You can't piss them off, because they're never *not* pissed off. Worst species I ever met."

We chuckled a bit over that.

"I think you'll do just fine," he said resting a hand on my shoulder.

"I will. The issue is, *fine* as defined by whom?"

"By all who witness."

"I'm glad *you're* so confident. I only wish you could give me a transfusion of yours."

"I'll work on that, but I must say, that treatment sounds gross."

"So," I held out my hand to shake, "goodbye, old friend." We shook long and hard. "Oh, and when you see Yibitriander, would you pass along a message to him?"

"Certainly."

I farted. It was loud and extremely wet. "That's the full message. Would you like me to repeat it?"

All three hands flew up. "No, that will not be necessary. I'll recall your sentiments for longer than I care to, without another demonstration."

I turned and started walking away.

He cleared his throat. Never heard one of them do that before. I imagine they had to clear their throats about as much as I did.

"Huh?" I asked turning my head.

"Did you want me to give you your present, or not?"

"Is it my birthday?"

"It is now." He smiled again even bigger.

"Where is it? I don't see a very large box with a ribbon."

"It is not boxable. It is an appropriate size, but it would, err, affect the box unfavorably."

"You got me a stripper in a box? Dude, that's so cool."

"You're not getting warmer. It's a small attachment for *Wrath*."

"Are you sure it's not a stripper in a box?"

"Next time you come, I'll try and arrange for one. I'll decide on the species, however. For now, you'll have to settle for a quantum decoupler."

"Okay, but that's my *second* choice. Just so you know."

"What is, Jon then asked, a quantum decoupler?" said Kymee sternly.

"I know what a QD is. Shucks, everybody does. It takes two quantum thingies and de … you know, decouples them." I put my fists side to side and split them horizontally apart.

"Incorrigible ingrate."

"Okay, what's a QD?"

He rolled his eyes. "It's a device I invented that decouples subatomic particles at a distance. It's based somewhat on that fantastic membrane of yours." He rubbed his chin. "I wish I knew who came up with that. It's beyond brilliant."

"Back to my new QD."

"Yes. What it does is separate quarks in protons. All three to be specific. I'm still working on neutrons. Sorry."

"Kymee, my Ph.D. in physics is from Cal Berkeley, not Oowaoa U, but that's not possible."

"Oh, it's possible. It just takes a lot of energy."

"Yeah, like more energy than there *is*."

"Not really. And they only need to separate a tiny bit and can then fall back together, happy as clams."

I did some back-of-the-envelope calculation. "That would result in—"

Kymee placed two of his palms together and pulled them apart rapidly. "*Boom*."

"No. BIG *BOOM*."

He chuckled. "Yes, I believe you're correct."

"So, if *Wrath* had, say, a QD, and it QDed the leading edge of, oh, I don't know, a Berrillian ship in a warp bubble—"

He placed his palms together and threw them wide apart. "Very large *boom*."

"And, if *Wrath* had one of these, theoretically how accurate would it be?"

"You could QD the tissue of a fly's rectum from a thousand kilometers."

"Kymee. I'm shocked and distressed by your use of vulgar language. I'm only glad Yibitriander isn't here to hear it."

"He'd probably bust a vein in his neck wouldn't he?"

"Can we call him here really quick and find out?"

We laughed.

Two hours later, *Wrath* had a brand new QD installed. I was fully in-serviced as to its use and maintenance. There was no maintenance. Come on, it was Deavoriath tech.

"I'll remind you of what you know. This is an outstanding weapon in space. If a random hydrogen atom is in your firing line, it'll explode. If you tried to fire it in an atmosphere, well, you'll quickly wish you hadn't," explained Kymee.

Made sense.

After we bumped shoulders, I asked the obvious question. "So why the winning edge? Won't you get in trouble?"

"Because I wanted to, and because I don't care. Your people deserve a better fate than that which Varrank Simzle would wish them and Havibobo would supply them. They both deserve to die horribly."

"And One That Is All? Won't they be upset?"

"Screw them."

"Kymee, really. That mouth of yours. I'm thinking of installing a translation filter to guard my purity."

"Seriously, Jon. A bunch of million-year-old prudes sit around contemplating their navels with all three thumbs up their butts. They would let good people die and bad people live because they're so self-obsessed. Screw them. I can do as I please. That has always been our way. If they don't like it, what are they going to do? Fire me? Send me to my room? Hardly. No, I worry less than zero about the common opinion and value more about the individual. I value you," he poked me in the chest. "You have that lovely family to protect. Even a miracle man like you would have trouble doing that from the grave."

I hugged him. No words were needed. We just had a good hug.

TWENTY

Dolirca sat on her bed with her Toes, One and Two. She'd given them their names when she was very young, so they were pretty basic. She never considered changing them. Her imagination didn't run in those directions. They were One and Two, she was Dolirca, and up was up. There wasn't any more to matters in her worldview.

What she did value was order. Order was a good thing. It made life not only livable, but enjoyable. That others valued it less was their failing. She did so hate failing, both in herself and in others. If she had a deficiency, she worked hard and corrected it. She had, for example loved, her stepfather. That was a weakness. He could use her love to manipulate her. If she was malleable and he made her into something she was not, that would result in a failing. So, she worked long and hard, and she stopped loving him. Thus her life was more orderly, more in control. That made it a happier life.

She'd loved her mother, but that wasn't her fault. The laws of nature dictated that one loved one's mother. She was a biological entity and subject to the rules and constraints incumbent upon such inherently fallible units. Fortunately, her mother tended to leave her alone. It was a happy twist that her grandmother was killed while Dolirca was still so young. She, too, was removed from Dolirca's life before any real damage could be inflicted. That saved her the trouble of killing her mother and grandmother, which would have logically been her only choice, once she came of age. Dolirca would have hated to waste so much time and effort at a thing the Berrillians did so economically. To unlearn loving either maternal unit would have proved a challenge. But if such deprogramming had been necessary, she'd have found the requisite resolve and wiped them from her mind.

She brushed One's pelt as they all three sat on her bed. Every night, each of her guards received one hundred strokes from her stiffest brush. Never ninety-nine, never one hundred two. Those options would be ludicrous. Even if their skin started to bleed and they squirmed in pain, one hundred brush strokes was the correct number. Her hair also needed one hundred brush strokes to be orderly.

If she had cared enough about her brood-mate, she'd see to it he received one hundred brush strokes also. He was not worth the expenditure of her time, however. A female needed to have a brood-mate, just as certainly as a male had to have a brood's-mate. To do otherwise would be ludicrous. Nature made demands, and those demands had to be attended to. A few times, she tried to brush his hair properly, but he said it was silly and couldn't they do something else? Perhaps they could have sex or dinner or sit and watch a holo. He was flawed, *deeply* flawed. She doubted she could repair him and was certain she didn't care to expend the energy in any such attempt.

He children were going to be orderly, that much was certain. They were still young and given to laughter and play, but she'd help them grow well, properly. They would forget about their father just as completely as she had forgotten him. Soon, in fact, he would need to have a tragic accident. Yes, that would remove him from the picture. She had his sperm stored. The thought that she or the children needed him to be physically present was ludicrous.

No, she saw the importance of order, and for that gift she was sublimely happy. She would remain orderly herself. Her children would grow to be orderly. Her world would, by her firm yet loving hand, become orderly. No more inefficient discussions in council. No more art projects wasting time and money. No more excess food to make Kaljaxians fat and lazy. Fat lazy people were inherently unhappy. If she didn't help make them happy, what kind of mother to Azsuram would she be? A ludicrous one. That much was certain.

Pivotally, Azsuram could not be a happy world until all the aliens and walking machines were destroyed. Azsuram was a world for Kaljaxians.

Hadn't that been her poor, dear grandmother's law? Diluting her people's purity with the waste of other races was, well, it was ludicrous. No, those pollutants would be expunged so that everyone on Azsuram could be happy.

Happy was good. Soon she would take control and make Azsuram as happy as she was. *Happiness thorough order.* Say, that *was* a nice slogan. A vision of her campaign to purify Azsuram began to gel in her mind. She could see the future. Yes, there it was. She reached out and almost touched it with her fingertips.

"Make Azsuram strong again. Happiness through order," she said aloud. "Those have such a magical ring to them, don't they One and Two?"

One and Two agreed silently. They had not been given permission to speak.

TWENTY-ONE

I had *Wrath* materialize along the straight line drawn between Deerkon and the worldships. He detected the Berrillian ship's location in warp space and we rematerialized a couple million kilometers in front of them.

The Berrillian fleet was much smaller than I'd faced before, only around a thousand ships. That reinforced my notion that this assault on the worldship fleet was a side operation, and not part of a major incursion. Too bad. I would have preferred to kill a lot more of the scum.

They clearly detected my appearance. They spread out significantly. From our earlier encounter, they had to feel pretty confident that most would get past me. What I learned from our last encounter was where Havibibo's flagship was located in the squadron. Yeah, I wanted him to see all his people die before he joined them, the son of a bitch.

So, it was time to test my ultimate weapon. In two centuries, I'd seen my share of foolproof plans blow up in the users face. Hence, I wasn't at all certain I was in the catbird seat. I ordered *Wrath* to target the final vessel in the Berrillian attack formation, said fire, and closed my eyes. I guess I was waiting to hear a *boom*. I know, silly, but I finally peeked one squinted eye at the viewport. There was a blinding ball of fire where the ship had been. *Outstanding*. I danced a little jig alone on the bridge. Professional military behavior? No. We're talking Jon Ryan here, right? Was demonstrating abundant joy at the death of living souls inappropriate? Not if they were Berrillians. Not in my book.

There was no way they could know what happened, that a new weapon was in play. We were light-weeks away from the worldship fleet. I had time. I had *Wrath* maintain our relative position in front of the Berrillians, retreating toward the worldships. They were at superluminal speed, so we couldn't match their pace. We had to leapfrog back through folds of space.

After an hour, I had *Wrath* pick off two trailing ship. The QD worked like a dream. After another hour, I ordered him to take out four rear-positioned ships. As the pattern developed, I was confident they'd start sweating really good. If one knew exactly when one's ship was going to explode, one kind of had to worry, to develop foreboding and angst. Mutiny might cross the crews's minds. There certainly had to be a lot of active discussion among the crews of the ships in back. Awe. Poor kitties. It was so sad. The mean man with the QD was upsetting them.

Before I ordered sixty-four ships fried, *Wrath* spoke up. "Form, why are we toying with these inferiors? Let me kill them all for the glory of Azsuram."

"No. We will kill them all, but I will do it my way, the slow way. I want these cats to suffer."

"Sentimentality has no place in war," he scorned.

"You didn't hold Sapale in your arms after what they did to her. If there were a crueler, more inhumane way to eliminate them, I'd do it."

"I understand vengeance. My name is *Wrath,* after all. But death in war is not a game. We owe it to war to kill them swiftly and completely."

"We what? We awe a debt to *war? Wrath,* you're significantly more insane than I thought. War is, A, not a living being a debt can be owed to, and, B, not deserving of any such consideration if it were. War is the mindless amalgamation of the hate, stupidity, and greed of those incapable of love and compromise. I've seen a lot of things in the universe. I've never seen anything as ugly and as wrong as war. Never speak to me of it in a positive light again. Do you hear me?"

"Yes, Form. We can discuss our differences after the battle."

"Maybe we *can,* but we sure as hell *won't.* You will never change my mind, and I doubt you have one to change. You are a killing machine. That's all you want to be, so it is all you ever will be. When we first met, I was making things up as I went. But now, I *am* a Form, and you *are* my vortex manipulator. This is *my* vortex, not yours. That's how it works. That's how it has always worked. I will not allow you to think you have a say or an opinion in any matter of morals or conscious." I lightened up some. "Maybe over a very long time you can become better, but as of now, you serve me. End of story. Now target those sixty-four ships and continue to withdraw."

"Aye, Form."

His tone was as neutral as I'd ever heard it. If he was pissed off, I could not care less. If his feelings were hurt, all the better.

By the next day, there were only enough enemy ships left that one salvo of QD disturbances would destroy all the ships but one. Throughout my dismemberment of his armada, Havibibo made no course changes or attempts to contact me. I think he long since figured out there was no escape and no defense possible. I knew he'd much rather die than surrender, so why bother doing anything differently?

Finally, there were only two ships heading toward the worldship fleet. Mine and his. He remained at FTL speed. We continued to hop backward to match his pace. I allowed days to pass, waiting to see if he would do anything desperate. I also wanted him to suffer the chance of open rebellion of his crew as long as possible. Finally, I decided it was time to terminate the engagement. Part of me wanted to face Havibibo and wring his life out of his body. Part of me knew that was stupid. If *Wrath* or I was lost, who would protect the humans? Davis could, of course, but he lacked my tools.

In the end, reasonable Jon won out over impulsive Jon. I did hail him however.

"Havibibo, it is your time to die," I said. "I hope the loss of your ships was painful, but I know you well enough to know it wasn't. You're all rage and fury and are incapable of love or understanding. That makes you and your species truly inferior to mine. It is why you failed before with the Deavoriath and why you will fail again. I wanted you to know that before you're vaporized.

"The last thing I want you to know is that your other half, Kelldrek, is still alive. I have held her in a small cage and fed her vegetable mush. She has not seen the sky or breathed fresh air since the day I took her. She will die in that cage. I want you to carry that weight with you into your afterlife, because it is *all* your doing. It is all *your* fault. If you had negotiated, if you had relented, or if you had simply left us alone, she would not suffer as she does. Her endless disgrace is your eternal curse. I fire in one minute."

Thirty seconds later, Havibibo dropped into real space and came to a full halt.

"Is he powering weapons?" I called out to *Wrath*.

"No. He's sitting dead in space. There is hardly any activity aboard his flagship. He's … wait. He's returning your hail."

"Put it on screen."

There sat Havibibo, alone. He was in his captain's chair, one leg lazily draped over an armrest, as he picked absently at his claws. As if it was an afterthought, he looked up at me and spoke. "Jon. Hello, my almost friend. It is good to face you again in mortal combat. You have done well. I am *proud* of you. Congratulations on a victory well earned."

"*Fuck* you," I said flatly. "I mean that sincerely, by the way, with all the trappings the expression carries. Don't patronize me, or worse yet, insult me with your praise. When I require the adulation of pond scum, I'll lift my toilet seat and ask for it. Yours I do not accept."

"But you have won. I am impressed. How should I respond? Wait," he stood up, placed his paws together, and bowed deeply. "Oh mighty human warrior, General Captain Jon Ryan, forgive me for being such a worthless piece of shit. Please know I and my race are bad. You are good and all the universe rightly honors you." He cupped a paw to one ear. "Yes, I hear angels in Heaven singing aloud your praises. Thank *God* the universe has you, Ryan the Mighty."

He sat back down with his other leg dangling. "That better, son of a dresmal?"

"No. In fact, why don't we do this? You *shut* up, and I'll *blow* you up. Hmm?"

"If you wanted me dead, I would long since be. Your species is new to us. I wish to understand what it is you require of me, *other* than to die. What could be so important?"

"Nothing."

"I'm betting there is. You know what? I did receive word that Tantelpro, one of my fiercest warriors, killed a Kaljaxian female shortly before he was slaughtered." He tapped thoughtfully at his ear. "I'm wondering if she was *your* other half. Wouldn't that be ironic? In fact, even if she wasn't, I will hold that thought as you kill me, so I'll die with a *huge* smile. Thank you—"

"Fire."

The screen turned to flickers and pops, then the wide shot showed his flagship erupt into a hot flash.

"Take us to Azsuram."

"By your command, Form"

I arrived back at the worldship fleet two days later. They obviously hadn't known if or when to expect me back, but apparently it was not that soon, by a wide margin. My handheld exploded with incoming calls, and dozens of people rushed to my landing spot. I told everyone the same thing. I'd discuss what happened with everyone, together, once. I said we'd all meet in Mandy's large conference room in two hours. That gave everybody a chance to come, especially the UN folks on *Exeter*. It also gave me a chance to bounce Gallenda on my knee and hold Kayla to my side. I needed that more than I wanted to admit.

I entered the conference room fashionably late. Okay, I owned up to it. I was being dramatic. It felt damn good. There were, even in an immortal lifetime, only a handful of opportunities to be so awesome. I reveled in my spotlight.

"I know you're all anxious to hear my report."

People leaned forward in their seats.

"The Berrillian threat is completely eliminated. I destroyed every ship coming toward the worldship fleet."

A gasp of surprise rose from the crowd. Then a cheers exploded.

"I had much better luck this time than I did when they attacked Azsuram. There were also fewer enemy vessels. In any case, we are all safe for the time being. I also made a concerted attempt to neutralize the danger posed by Varrank Simzle. Toño was happy to learn I would relieve him of a burden he has chafed under at the same time.

"Before returning here, I stopped by Azsuram. I picked up Kelldrek. I told her her mate was officially dead, and that Varrank was responsible for it. I then transported her to Varrank's palace and released her. I provided her with a backpack full of explosives, two captured Berrillian laser rifles, and a detailed map of the compound. I also slipped a nano-transmitter into her ear. Let me show you the video."

Kelldrek leaped to the front entrance and knocked the door open. She rolled to the floor and began shooting. The handful of guards on duty were all dead before they could bring up their weapons. She bounded up a stairway, heading toward Varrank's quarters. A few meters into the hallway, three guards dropped to their knees and opened fire. She kept charging and firing. One, two, three, their chests blew open, and they were thrown backward.

She jumped over the bodies and skidded around a corner. A Quelstrum was running in her direction. He lunged for her neck, but she kicked off the floor in a split second and slammed her fangs into his neck. Her momentum spun her body around him like the arm of a clock, blood spurting out in huge fountains. She pulled him to the floor and released him. The decapitated guard's head rolled to the wall and thudded to a stop.

Kelldrek turned and sprinted on. As she passed an open door, she tossed a grenade in without slowing. The explosion thundered behind her as she continued ahead. She arrived at Varrank's quarters. She shot the door to pieces and flew threw the gaping hole. A handful of guards were waiting and opened fire on her immediately.

The camera jerked a few times, suggesting she was hit. If so, it didn't slow her.

She returned fire and rolled behind a couch. The brief exchange ended when the last guard grabbed his neck and spun to the floor.

She rushed though a series of rooms with blinding speed. Occasionally, she ran into someone and killed them whether they were armed or not. Entering an ornate bedroom, she scanned side to side. No one was there. As she turned to retrace her path, the camera lurched a few more times, and she howled in pain. Two Quelstrums stepped through the door, firing rapidly. She leaped at them, a laser flashing in both paws. Both men jerked backward as they were hit and struggled to remain standing.

She dropped her guns and tore into one of them with tooth and claw. He collapsed to the floor with her face ripping at his, then the other guard lifted her up and threw her against a wall. She spun and attacked him. Standing on two legs, her paw caught his punch. She pulled him to the ground. Her teeth snapped shut on his windpipe. He struggled briefly to pull her jaws open, then died.

Lumbering, causing the camera to swing irregularly, she jogged back to the hallway and headed to the right. An occasional guard would fire on her, and she'd shoot them dead. She seemed to take a few more hits but kept going. Arriving at a metal door labeled ARMORY, she used her laser on the handle and kicked the door open. Reaching into her satchel, she removed and manipulated one of the explosive devices. She stuffed it back into the satchel and threw it into the room.

Muffled screams could be heard from a nearby corridor. She moved toward the voices. Around two corners, she approached the main dining hall. A chaotic stream of ornately dressed guests ran from the room and out an adjacent exit. A man with a white cape sprinted from the door and saw her. He spun and ran the other way. Kelldrek leaped on his back just as he turned to look at her. It was Varrank Simzle.

Just then a deafening explosion sounded. Pieces of ceiling fell to the floor and decorations popped off the walls.

Varrank fell face first on the stone floor. She seized his head in her jaws and began shaking him violently. She looked up quickly. Varrank's head was still in her mouth, blood gushing from his ragged neck. A Quelstrum towered over her. He thrust a massive war hammer downward. The head of the hammer was the size of three fifty-five gallon oil drums.

The camera went dead.

I brought the room lights back up. The audience sat in stunned silence. A couple of people had vomited during the show.

Then someone started tentative applause. Slowly, others joined in. Finally, everyone was clapping.

As the audience quieted, I spoke solemnly. "Secretary Bin Li, President Walker, and I have been talking. We agree that we were fortunate this time. Learning of the threat early enough to end it was nothing but blind luck. For the next several hundred years, as we journey to our new homes, we must be aware that others may try to take what is ours. Plus, we are now known to the greater galaxy. We're not sure that's a good thing, but there's no changing the fact that we are. We must remain ready and vigilant."

I didn't tell anyone about the QD device. It was a hard decision to keep it secret, but I felt it was best that way. I didn't want to encourage more over-dependence on me. Humanity had to live or die by its own merits and by its own actions. I'd learned many times over that I was one screw-up away from being removed from the picture. Since no one else could pilot *Wrath*, it wasn't like anyone had to know about my new weapon.

After the meeting, I sought out Davis. The threat I'd accidentally discovered was gone, but my mission remained. I had to save the man I'd once become.

And wouldn't you know it, Davis was gone. I could be *such* an immature jerk.

Back on *Wrath* I asked when Davis had come to get his ship.

"Twenty minutes ago, Form. He took the ship to a hangar and launched it."

"Are you still tracking him?" My stomach flip-flopped.

"I do not know."

"Explain quickly."

"He left under fusion drive and remained so for ten minutes. Then he sped up abruptly and disappeared from conventional scanners."

"What does that mean? Can you track him or not?"

"Possibly."

"Explain."

"I thought a lot about what he said, about his magic. I came to some conclusions based on a set of reasonable assumptions. He spoke of his magic causing the impossible. Nothing I know of is impossible, just undiscovered or unlikely. Hence, there must be a cause-and-effect basis for any action, even those that cannot occur under the physical laws as we perceive them."

"Ah, *Wrath*, I gotta say you're kind of babbling."

"Why am I not surprised you can't follow a simple line of argument?"

"Well, wrap it up, okay?"

"I'll just say I might be able to locate him by following his trail of impossible outcomes and their consequences."

"There are consequences to impossible things happening?"

There was a short pause. "I'll pretend I didn't hear that, all right?"

"Whatever, bitch. Just go. Take us to him."

Wrath flipped in and out of folded space rapidly. That was fun times for my travel-related nausea. I experienced new heights in yuck. Within twenty minutes, *Wrath* announced he had found Davis's ship. We were next to it in orbit. You'll never guess where we were. Never. Back at PC 1, where I'd met him the very first time. That's where he gave me the membrane technology. We were fifty light-years from the worldship fleet. Yup, he used his magic again.

He was seated in the same small cave he was in the first time. Note to self. I needed to review my use of dramatic effect. I was being Shakespearian to a regrettable extent.

"What took you?" he asked me as he sipped some hot beverage.

"Very clever repartee. I took, what, half an hour to do the impossible?"

"It took me half that time."

"You have experience at it. I'm new at the wizard game."

"Sit, boy," he said pointing to a rock.

"Oh, great. Instant replay of our insulting encounter years ago. My day just gets better and better."

"Coffee?"

"Why the hell not?"

He passed me a mug.

"This is the last time we'll meet."

"You can't know that. I found you twice. I can do it a million times if need be."

"Nope," he said staring into his mug. "After this, I'm gone for good."

"What, you flying into a black hole?"

"Nothing so maudlin, boy. I'm just tired of being found. Where I'm going, nobody's going to follow. That's all."

"Why?" I reached toward him. "Stay with us. We need you." I was quiet a second. "I need you."

"The answers to those questions are because I want it that way, no, no, and no."

"I'm really annoying, we know that, right?"

"So we've been told."

"Jon," I asked, "why leave? Humanity is subject to random threats. You can help."

"You're all they need. Whatever new toy Kymee gave you proves that. It's my time to do something for myself. I want to be free of the burden."

"What about me? I don't get a vacation?"

"Boy, I watched them all die. Then I spent thousands of years trying somehow to save them not knowing if I could. You," he harrumphed, "you get handed the membranes, a cube, and some ultimate weapon on top of it all. You live a charmed life of comparative leisure. You'll be fine."

"Comparative leisure? You call Varrank locking me up with Falzorn *leisurely*? You call battling the Berrillians *leisurely*? Man, you're harsh."

"Yes, I am. A hell of a lot tougher than you. Remember that."

"No, I don't think I will. There I just erased that memory." I stuck my tongue out at me.

"Whatever, you little shit bird."

"Jon, I swear, if you stay, I can help you heal. You need to be with your people, the ones you saved."

"I don't know too much, boyo, but I do know some shit. I know there's no cure for my condition. Do us both a favor and let it go."

"No."

"Just what I need. My knight in shining fucking armor." He rolled his eyes.

"I don't understand why you can't lighten up. Why not try to be happy?"

"I *am* happy. Don't you get it? Does stupid run in your family?"

"I know us," my hands shot back and forth between us. "I know how I'd react to your loss, to *our* loss."

"It wasn't pretty."

"Thank you. So, you agree?"

"No way, my gum-flapping friend. I agreed it wasn't pretty. But you know what? I got over it." He bobbed his head up and down. "Yeah. I picked myself up out of the mud and went on. And you know what? I forgave myself." He chuckled. "Yeah ,we forgave ourselves. Can you believe that?"

"No, not really."

"Well, I did. Now, I have a life, friends, things to do—"

"Magic shows to perform with matinees on Sunday?"

"I'm seriously going to reexamine my sense of humor. I'm *so* lame. Pathetic, actually."

"How do I know I can trust you about being happy, having a life? Why should I believe you?"

He looked in my eyes with ruthless clarity. "Because I wouldn't lie to myself about that. I know how I'd feel, and I wouldn't fib to get rid of myself, unless it was damn well true. That's why."

"You know what? I actually believe you."

"You son of a bitch," he shot back. "I can't believe you're bailing on me so easily. I live under the bus for centuries, and you walk by with no more than a, *hi, how you doing*?"

"No. I walk by because I can see you're fine. Well, as fine as we can be, given our considerable limits."

"Tell me about them."

"Okay, I'm down with the plan. I jump in my cube and that's the end of it. One question."

"No."

"No? How do you—"

"No, I won't tell you where I learned magic. I won't tell you how to do it either. Drop that, too."

"Could *you*?"

He contorted his face. "Probably not. But screw you just the same. You want to learn magic, find it on your own."

"Why?"

"Because you're a sissy."

"What?"

"Because you're a pansy ass."

"Where are you coming from, you senile old machine?"

"Because no man, not even us, should become too powerful. I don't trust myself a whole hell of a lot. I'm sure as hell not trusting you one percent more."

I was silent a moment. "Probably wise."

"Probably? Now you're just being damn insulting." He tossed his remaining coffee to the ground. "I'm outta here."

"Me, too," I said with less conviction.

Jon was halfway to his tiny ship when he stopped. With his back to me he said, "I loved her so much. It hurt then and it hurts now."

"I know. Me, too."

"If I could have her back—" Jon trailed off weakly.

"I know."

"That I can't have her back will forever remain my greatest regret."

"I know. That's why I brought this."

He still stood facing away. I think he was afraid to turn, to know what I possibly offered him. I think he was afraid to care that much. It wasn't easy being the biggest Rock of Gibraltar in the history of large stone objects. Slowly he turned.

I held out a data disk in the air.

"What? This a joke?" he said. "That the one I gave you with the plans for the membranes?"

"Actually, yes. It's the very same disk."

"Why the *hell* would I want the plans for something I gave you?"

"Can't imagine why."

He pointed at the disk. "There's something new on the disk."

"Give the man a cigar. That's the correct answer."

"What?"

"Something I didn't know existed until today. Something Toño gave me just before I came here."

"I may be immortal, but the suspense is killing me."

"Funny guy." I wagged the disk and stood up. "Let's put it in your ship."

He was stiffly reluctant at first, but then he turned and walked slowly toward his vessel. We walked to the bridge. I handed him the disk.

He started to put it in a slot. I grabbed his hand. "This is the one and only copy. There never was another and there never will be another unless you make it."

"Very mysterious," he said with a grunt. He fed the disk in.

After a second there was an electric pop. Then the ship's AI spoke. "Identity confirmed. Override complete."

He looked at the panel, then to me.

"Ask it a question."

"What day is it?" he said staring at me.

"Beats me," was the female voice's response. "I don't know where in Brathos I am. And why in the hell are there two of you standing there looking idiotic? It's not the Stuart Marshall copying thing all over again, is it?"

"Why you," he said lunging toward me. "You gave my AI Sapale's voice. I'll *kill* you."

"It's not just her voice," I said backing up.

He froze mid-attack.

"Wait," Sapale called out, "is that Uto with you?"

"Yeah. Handsome devil, isn't he?" I replied.

"If I wasn't disoriented before, I sure as hell am now," she said.

"I'm totally lost. What is going on?" He was dazed and confused.

"You wouldn't know about Toño telling my Jon he could never make an android out of me," responded Sapale.

"Yes. This copy of Jon never had that conversation," I added.

"He's not a copy of you, brood-mate. He is you."

"What have you done?" he asked.

"Me or him?" Sapale asked.

"Him, I think. No. Yes. Him." It was fun to see him so befuddled.

"Just before the battle on Azsuram, Toño downloaded Sapale's mind into an AI. It was the same as the transfer process to make an android, only he had nowhere else to put her. So—"

"So he shoved me into a computer chip," she finished my thought.

"Why?" he asked.

"Yeah. You specifically told me you'd never do anything like that," I said.

"Because Toño and I knew there'd come a day when only speaking to me would make you do whatever you needed to do. I never wanted to live in an electronic box, but to save you, Jon Ryan, it turns out I'd do anything."

"If it's okay with Sapale, I want you to take her," I said. "You can never have her back like she was—"

"To have you to talk with, to have you back for all time, brood's-mate? That is more blessing than I deserve," he said choking on the words.

"I know," she said. She started to giggle.

"I'll have Al contact you and fill you in on what's happened since … since—" I could *not* finish that sentence.

"Since I what? By Davdiad's veil, I'm not *dead* am I?"

"You … shortly after you and Toño made this download … when the Berrillians attacked—"

"Jon, I'm pulling your chain," she said laughing. "Why would Toño resurrect this recording if I was alive? Hmm? I may be dead, but that doesn't make me suddenly stupid."

"She had you wrapped around her finger more than she did me. Would *not* have thought that possible," he said with a huge smile. "Sapale, if you will come with me, I will be the happiest man in the universe."

"Then it will be my honor," replied Sapale.

"As I was saying, I'll have Al contact you and fill you in on what's happened since you've been gone."

"No, that won't be necessary," she said. "I'll learn the old-fashioned way. We will talk the nights away. My brood-mate will fill in all the gaps."

"Okay. Your call, I guess?" I said uncertainly.

"Jon," he said, "shake my hand and get off my ship."

"Huh? What's the rush?" I asked as he grabbed my hand.

"I need you to leave fast so I won't be here when you change your mind." He dropped my hand like it was a dead fish and began pushing me backward toward the hatch.

"Boys, no fighting. Don't make me crawl out of this box and kick some booty."

"We're not fighting. He's just leaving in a hurry," he responded.

Once I was clear of the hatch, he immediately started sealing it.

"Wait. I need to say goodbye," I protested.

He looked at me, then back at his computer console, then to me. He was torn.

"Make it quick," he said tersely.

"Yeah, right. Because you two only have forever?"

"Faster," he said.

"Sapale. I miss you more than it's possible to miss anyone. I will love you always. Please keep me in your heart if you can."

"I could never forget the man who swept me away. You will be with me always. I couldn't forget you, brood-mate, even if I tried for ten thousand years."

"And as for you, Uto, if you make her sad, I'll hear of it. You don't want me mad at you."

"We shall not meet again. But if I were to hurt her in anyway, I will find you and have you take her back. That is a promise." He saluted me and sealed the hatch. Then, right before my eyes, the ship vanished. Damn that magic of his. What a perfect exit.

I thought *I* was the king of great exits. Wait, I was. Just not me.

EPILOGUE

Deep in a cave of the Mother Tree, Anganctus, King of the Twenty-One Clans, sat on his rough-hewn throne. Anganctus was angry, which is only to say he was angrier than was his usual ill-tempered self. To rule the Faxél was not an easy matter. To command them amiably or kindly would be impossible. But he was asked to tolerate, no, to *accept* failure of inexcusable dimensions. Many would pay dearly. All would suffer. His wrath knew no bounds.

"I sent ten thousand ships, one million warriors. Yet you tell me not one ship, not one *kitten* returned?" He roared loudly. "My most trusted commander Havibibo lived, but he chose to hide from me, to linger in his *sea* of failures. Then, I lose a thousand more ships and crews and then the imp Havibibo escapes me in death. I will not tolerate such insults."

"My lord, wise lord of the Faxél, your anger is just and deserved," said his trembling chamberlain, Lopricious.

"But? You dare suspend in the air before me a *but?*"

"Not a *but*, lord of Mother Tree. An *and.*"

"You defy logic, Lopricious. How can you be so evasive, so sycophantic, yet live?"

"I live by your pleasure, lord."

Anganctus thumped his nose with his tail. "Do you somehow see pleasure in this face, slime?"

"I see, lord, only the face of knowing justice. The very face of—"

"*Silence.*" He stood on all four legs and paced in a tight figure eight. "I see

I shall have to take matters into my own paws. As no one is competent, no one is brave enough, I must destroy the Deavoriath personally."

"Your opinion is as always fact. Your will is our joy—"

Lopricious stopped speaking when Anganctus growled deeply, threateningly.

"... *and*, haste might be incautious. The Faxél can lose much, but not our righteous king."

"So, I would fail as miserably as the rest. Is that your final thought, chamberlain?"

"Never. There is no failure in Anganctus. I would mention, however, the facts as I see them as points of reference only."

Another deep growl followed. Anganctus's tail swept angrily from side to side.

"The Deavoriath of today seem to possess weapons against which we cannot win," whined Lopricious. "They crush and exterminate whatever we send at them. Surely there is honor in, err, *delaying* our next assault pending the development of superior tools and a greater understanding of their wicked devices."

"Another, say, million years?" the predaceous king asked.

Lopricious avoided the trap. "Never, mighty lord. Your wrath must never be asked to wait that long. But vengeance attained is vengeance completed."

"I shall kill you now," howled Anganctus. "The Faxél are beasts of *action*, not old she-cats by the fire." He sat back on the throne. "I see reports of but one vortex. *One* vortex cannot defend an entire sector of the galaxy from the might of the Faxél. Such is not possible."

"When the impossible is observed, lord, one is best advised to stand at a distance and consider it."

"I am not *one*," thundered Anganctus. "I am *king*."

In the belief that it was better to die another day, not that particular one, Lopricious bowed deeply and spoke. "What are your commands, bearer of correctness?"

"I shall lead all of our ships and all of our warriors into battle. Let one Deavoriath vortex attempt to be everywhere at once. Let it dance in troubled spirals trying to stop the unstoppable storm."

"Ah, magisterial lord, that one vortex is *Wrath*," Lopricious dared to remind.

"Even the most cursed ship in Haldrob's hot fires cannot stand against ten million Berrillian warships. Victory will be ours. All the fools who defy me will know only swift, painful, and certain death, and they will know it soon. This I swear. I shall gorge my lust with Deavoriath flesh and shit their remains on the scorched earth of Oowaoa."

To be continued ...

Glossary of Main Characters and Places:

Number in parenthesis is the book the word first appears.

Ablo (2): Led Uhoor to attack Azsuram after Tho died. Female.

Almonerca (2): Daughter of Fashallana, twin of Noresmel. Name means *sees tomorrow*.

Alpha Centauri (1): Fourth planetary target on Jon's long solo voyage on *Ark 1*. Three stars in the system: AC-A, AC-B, and AC-C (aka Proxima Centauri). AC-B has eight planets, three in habitable zone. AC-B 5 was initially named *Jon* by Jon Ryan until he met the falzorn. AC-B 3 is Kaljax. Proxima Centauri (PC) has one planet in habitable zone.

Alvin (1): The ship's AI on *Ark 1*. aka Al.

Amanda Walker (2): Vice president then president, a distant relative of Jane Geraty. Wife of Faith Clinton.

Anganctus (4): King of the Faxél, ruler of Berrill. Mean cat.

Azsuram (2): See also Hodor, Groombridge-1618, and Klonsar. BG 3 was discovered by Seamus O'Leary, the pilot of *Ark 4*.

Balmorulam (4): Planet where Jon was shanghaied by Karnean Beckzel.

Barnard's Star (1): First planetary target of *Ark* 1. BS 2 and 3 are in habitable zone. BS 3 was Ffffuttoe's home, as well as ancient, extinct race called the Emitonians. See BS 2.

Beast Without Eyes (2): The enemy of Gumnolar. The devil for inhabitants of Listhelon.

Bin Li (2): New UN Secretary General after Mary Kahl was killed.

Bob Patrick (2): US senator when Earth was destroyed. One of The Four Horsemen, coconspirator with Stuart Marshall.

Braldone (1): Believed to be the foreseen savior on Kaljax.

Brathos (1): The Kaljaxian version of hell.

Brood-mate (1): On Kaljax, the male partner in a marriage.

Brood's-mate (1): On Kaljax, the female partner in a marriage.

BS 2 (1): The planet Oowaoa, home of the highly advanced Deavoriath race.

Calrf (2): A Kaljaxian stew that Jon particularly dislikes.

Carl Roger (1): Chief of staff to President John Marshall before Earth was destroyed.

Carl Simpson (1): Pilot of *Ark* 3. Discovered Listhelon orbiting Lacaille 9352.

Carlos De La Frontera (2): Brilliant assistant to Toño, became an android to infiltrate Marshall's administration.

Charles Clinton (1): US President during part of Jon's voyage on *Ark 1*.

Chuck Thomas (2): Chairman of the Joint Chiefs of Staff, one of The Four Horsemen, and the first military person downloaded to an android by Stuart Marshall.

Command prerogatives (2): The Deavoriathian tools installed to allow operation of a vortex. Also, used to probe substances. Given to the android Jon Ryan.

Cube (2): See vortex.

Cycle (2): Length of year on Listhelon. Five cycles equal one Earth year.

Cynthia York (1): Lt. General and head of Project Ark when Jon returns from epic voyage.

Davdiad (1): God-figure on Kaljax.

Deavoriath (1): Mighty and ancient race on Oowaoa. Technically, the most advanced civilization in the galaxy. Used to rule many galaxies, then withdrew to improve their minds and characters. Three arms and legs. Currently live forever.

Deerkon (4): Planet where Karnean took Jon to deliver a shipment. Home of Varrank Simzle.

Devon Flannigan (2): Former baker who assassinated Faith Clinton.

Delta-Class vehicles (1): The wondrous new spaceships used in Project Ark. Really fast!

Dolirca (2): Daughter in Fashallana's second set of twins. Took charge of Ffffuttoe's asexual buds. Name means *love all*.

Draldon (2): Son of Sapale. Twin with Vhalisma. Name means *meets the day.*

Enterprise (2): US command worldship.

Epsilon Eridani (1): Fourth target for *Ark 1*. One habitable planet, EE 5. Locally named Cholarazy, the planet is home to several advanced civilizations. The Drell and Foressál are the main rivals. Leaders Boabbor and Gothor are bitter rivals. Humanoids with three digits.

Exeter (2): UN command worldship.

Faith Clinton (2): Descendent of the currently presidential Clintons. First a senator, later the first president elected in space. Assassinated soon after taking office.

Falzorn (1): Nasty predatory snakes of Alpha Centauri-B 5. Their name is a curse word among the inhabitants of neighboring Kaljax.

Farmship (2): Cored out asteroids devoted not to human habitation but to crop and animal production. There are only five, but they allow for sufficient calories and a few luxuries for all worldships.

Fashallana: First daughter of Sapale. Twin to JJ. Name means *blessed one.*

Faxél (3): Name of the fierce giant cat species of Berrill.

Ffffuttoe (1): Gentle natured flat bear-like creature of BS 3. Possesses low-level sentience.

Fontelpo (4): Bridge officer aboard *Desolation.* A native of Kaljax. He was demoted after discussing ship's business with Jon.

Form (2): Title of someone able to be the operator of vortex using their command prerogatives.

Gallenda Ryan (4): Jon's daughter with Kayla Beckzel.

General Saunders (1): Hardscrabble original head of Project Ark.

Groombridge-1618 3 (1): Original human name for the planet GB 3, aka Azsuram.

Gumnolar (1): Deity of the Listhelons. Very demanding.

Habitable zone (1): Zone surrounding a star in which orbiting planets can have liquid water on their surface.

Haldrob (4): Faxél version of hell.

Havibibo (3): Commander of the Berrillian fleet that attacked Azsuram.

Heath Ryan (2): Descendant of original Jon Ryan, entered politics reluctantly.

Indigo (1): Second and final wife of the original Jon Ryan, not the android. They have five children, including their version of Jon Ryan II.

Infinity charges (2): Membrane-based bombs that expand, ripping whatever they're in to shreds.

Jane Geraty (1): TV newswoman who had an affair with newly minted android Jon. Gave birth to Jon Ryan II, her only child.

Jodfderal (2): Son in Fashallana's second set of twins. Name means *strength of ten*.

Jon Junior, JJ (2): Son of Sapale. One of her first set of twins. The apple of Jon Ryan's eye.

Jon Ryan (1): Both the human template and the android who sailed into legend.

Jon III and his wife, Abree (2): Jon's grandson, via the human Jon Ryan.

Katashi Matsumoto (2): Fleet Admiral in command of the UN forces when the Listhelons attacked and later the worldfleet defenses.

Karnean Beckzel (4): Pirate captain of *Desolation*. Shanghaied Jon.

Kashiril (2): From Sapale's second set of twins. Name means *answers the wind*.

Kayla Beckzel (4): Sister to Karnean and first officer of *Desolation*. A real looker.

Kelldrek (3): Second, and hence mate of, Havibibo. Captured by Jon.

Kendell Jackson (2): Major General who became head of Project Ark after DeJesus left. Forced to become an android by Stuart Marshall.

Klonsar (2): The Uhoor name for Azsuram, which they claim as their hunting grounds.

Lilith, Lily (2): Second AI on *Shearwater*. Al no likey!

Listhelon (1): Enemy species from third planet orbiting Lacaille 9352. Aquatic, they have huge, overlapping fang-like teeth, small bumpy head, big, bulging eyes articulated somewhat like a lizard's. Their eyes bobbed around in a nauseating manner. His skin is sleek, with thin scales. They sport gill a split in their thick neck on either side. Maniacally devoted to Gumnolar.

Luhman 16a (1): The second target of *Ark 1*. Eight planets, only one in habit zone, LH 2. Two fighting species are the *Sarcorit* that are the size and shape of glazed donuts and *Jinicgus,* looking like hot dogs. Both are unfriendly be nature.

Manly (2): Jon's pet name for the mind of an unclear nature in the vortex. He refers to himself the vortex manipulator.

Mary Kahl (2): UN Secretary General at the time of the human exodus from Earth.

Matt Duncan (2): Chief of staff for the evil President Stuart Marshall. Became an android that was destroyed. Marshall resurrected him in the body of Marilyn Monroe. Matt no likey that!

Monzos (4): Port city on Deerkon and home base for Varrank Simzle.

Noresmel (2): Fashallana's daughter, twin of Almonerca. Name means *kiss of love.*

Nufe (3): A magical liquor made by the Deavoriath.

Offlin (2): Son of Otollar. Piloted ship that tried to attack Earth and was captured by Jon.

One That Is All (2): The mentally linked Deavoriath community.

Otollar (2): Leader, or Warrior One, of Listhelon. Died when he failed to defeat humans.

Owant (2): Second Warrior to Otollar.

Oowaoa (1): Home world of the Deavoriath.

Pallolo (4): First destination for *Desolation* after shanghaiing Jon.

Phil Anderson (1): TV host, sidekick of Jane Geraty. A moron.

Phillip Szeto (2): Head of CIA under Stuart Marshall.

Piper Ryan (2): Heath Ryan's wife.

Plo (2): First Uhoor to attack Azsuram.

Prime (2): Pet name for the android of Carlos De La Frontera.

Proxima Centauri (1): Last system investigated by Jon at the end of his *Ark 1* mission. PC 1 is where he met Uto.

Quelstrum (4): Planet of origin for some of Varrank's guards. Big, tough guards.

Sam Peterson (2): Chief Justice at the time of Earth's destruction. Member of Stuart Marshall's inner circle, The Four Horsemen.

Sapale (1): Brood's-mate to android Jon Ryan. From Kaljax.

Seamus O'Leary (2): The pilot of *Ark 4*, discovered Azsuram.

Shearwater (2): Jon's second starship, sleek, fast, and bitchin'.

Sherman Collins (1): Secretary of State to President John Marshall when it was discovered Jupiter would destroy the Earth.

Space-time congruity manipulator (1): Hugely helpful force field.

Stuart Marshall (1): Born human on Earth, became president there. Before exodus, he downloaded into an android and became the insane menace of his people.

Tho (2): The head Uhoor, referred to herself as *the mother of the Uhoor.*

Toño DeJesus (1): Chief scientist in both the android and Ark programs. Course of events forced him to reluctantly become an android.

Tralmore (1): Heaven, in the religion of Kaljax.

Uhoor (2): Massive whale-like creatures of immense age. They feed off black holes and propel themselves though space as if it was water.

Uto (1): Alternate time line android Jon Ryan, possibly …

Varrank Simzle (4): Insanely cruel crime boss on Deerkon.

Vhalisma (2): From Sapale's third set twins. Name means *drink love.*

Vortex (2): Deavoriath vessel in cube shape with a mass of two hundred thousand tons. Move instantly anywhere by folding space.

Vortex manipulator (2): Sentient computer-like being in vortex.

Wolf 359 (1): Third target for *Ark 1.* Two small planets WS 3, which was a bad prospect, and WS 4, which was about as bad.

Wolnara (2): Twin in Sapale's second set. Name means *wisdom sees.*

Worldships (1): Cored out asteroids serve as colony ships for the human exodus.

Yibitriander (1): Three legged Deavoriath, past Form of Jon's vortex.

Shameless Self-Promotion
(Try and picture me as the OxiClean spokesperson,
British accent and all.)

Thank you for joining me on the Forever Journey! I hope you're enjoying the ongoing saga. Books 1, 2, and 3, *The Forever Life, The Forever Enemy,* and *The Forever Fight* are available on Amazon now:

The next book in the Forever Series is the *Forever Alliance*. It's most excellent.

There is a sequel to *The Forever Series* now. *Galaxy On Fire* begins with Embers. Once you finish this series be sure to check out the new one. Trust me, it's even better.

The third series in the Ryanverse begins with Return of the Ancient Gods.

Please do leave me a review. They're more precious than gold.

My Website: craigrobertsonblog.wordpress.com

Feel free to email me comments or to discuss any part of the series. contact@craigarobertson.com Also, you can ask to be on my email list. I'll send out infrequent alerts concerning new material or some of the extras I'm planning in the near future.

Facebook? But of course. https://www.facebook.com/craigr1971/

Wow! That's a whole lot of social media. But, I'm so worth it, so bear with me.

Don't be a stranger, well, at least any stranger than you have to be … craig

34496235R00116

Made in the USA
Lexington, KY
24 March 2019